After a while the wooden steps of Staircase Thirteen creaked a little as though someone was ascending. But then the steps creaked sometimes of their own accord when there was no one there at all. When a door opened on the top landing, the noise was considerable. Saffron's voice, indistinct, and his characteristic arrogant laugh could be heard. Tiggie Jones' voice was higher and clearer. She was laughing too, though giggling might be a better word. Tiggie was saying something like: "Oh Saffer, don't, don't be a naughty boy." There was scuffling and more laughing. The door shut.

Then there were footsteps, heavy footsteps, descending.

After that, there was a gasp, a stifled cry or shout, then a heavy protracted crash, as of a body rolling over and over down a staircase. Then there was complete silence.

Bantam offers the finest in classic and modern British murder mysteries
Ask your bookseller for the books you have missed

Agatha Christie

Death on the Nile
A Holiday for Murder
The Mousetrap and Other Plays
The Mysterious Affair at Styles
Poirot Investigates
Postern of Fate
The Secret Adversary
The Seven Dials Mystery
Sleeping Murder

Dorothy Simpson

Last Seen Alive
The Night She Died
Puppet for a Corpse
Six Feet Under
Close Her Eyes
Element of Doubt
Dead on Arrival

Sheila Radley

The Chief Inspector's Daughter
Death in the Morning
Fate Worse Than Death
Who Saw Him Die?

Elizabeth George

A Great Deliverance
coming soon: A Payment in Blood

Colin Dexter

Last Bus to Woodstock
The Riddle of the Third Mile
The Silent World of Nicholas
   Quinn
Service of All the Dead
The Dead of Jericho
The Secret of Annexe 3
Last Seen Wearing

John Greenwood

The Mind of Mr. Mosley
The Missing Mr. Mosley
Mosley by Moonlight
Murder, Mr. Mosley
Mists Over Mosley
What, Me, Mr. Mosley?

Ruth Rendell

A Dark-Adapted Eye
   (writing as Barbara Vine)
A Fatal Inversion
   (writing as Barbara Vine)

Marian Babson

Death in Fashion
Reel Murder
Murder, Murder Little Star
Murder on a Mystery Tour
Murder Sails at Midnight

Christianna Brand

Suddenly at His Residence
Heads You Lose

Dorothy Cannell

The Widows Club
coming soon: Down the Garden
   Path

Michael Dibdin

Ratking

Antonia Fraser

Your Royal Hostage
Oxford Blood
A Splash of Red
Cool Repentence
Jemima Shore's First Case
coming soon: Quiet As A Nun

OXFORD BLOOD

•

Antonia Fraser

BANTAM BOOKS
NEW YORK • TORONTO • LONDON • SYDNEY • AUCKLAND

*This edition contains the complete text
of the original hardcover edition.*
NOT ONE WORD HAS BEEN OMITTED.

OXFORD BLOOD

*A Bantam Book / published by arrangement with
W.W. Norton & Company, Inc.*

PRINTING HISTORY
W.W. Norton edition published 1985
Bantam edition / August 1989

ISBN 0-553-28070-8

Bantam Books are published by Bantam Books, a division of Bantam
Doubleday Dell Publishing Group, Inc. Its trademark, consisting of the
words "Bantam Books" and the portrayal of a rooster, is Registered in
U.S. Patent and Trademark Office and in other countries. Marca
Registrada. Bantam Books, 666 Fifth Avenue, New York, New York
10103.

PRINTED IN THE UNITED STATES OF AMERICA

KR   0 9 8 7 6 5 4 3 2 1

For Diana of the Barn ways
with love

CONTENTS

•

1. A Dying Woman   1
2. Bedside Conference   11
3. Nothing Wrong with Money   21
4. Staircase Thirteen   31
5. Fight Before the Death   41
6. No Long Shadows   50
7. Blood Isn't Everything   59
8. Dress: Gilded Rubbish   68
9. An Envious Society   79
10. Intellectual Advantages   89
11. Who He Is Not   100
12. Love and Hate   110
13. Saffron Ivy   120
14. Tennis Is About Winning   130
15. Drawing Blood   141
16. A Tragedy Must Take Place   151
17. Two Unlucky Lives   162
18. Your Father   174
19. Supper à Deux   185
20. Dancing in the Quad   194
21. Purple for the Rich Man   203

CHAPTER ONE

•

A Dying Woman

"It was kind of you to come at such short notice," said Sister Imelda to Jemima Shore. "We thank you for it." She fixed her large pale blue eyes on Jemima in a long look in which no expression could be detected; nevertheless it was evident that some kind of judgement had been made. "It won't be long now," she added.

"Of course miracles can happen." Sister Imelda gave a brief rather wintery smile as though acknowledging that the words, serious in her case, might be construed in others as some kind of jest. "She might just live out the week. But in fact we don't expect her to last more than another forty-eight hours."

"I'm not that busy—" Jemima Shore spoke deprecatingly. Afterwards she wondered if she had subconsciously expected Sister Imelda to waive aside her disclaimer. After all Jemima Shore was in most normal senses of the word extremely busy. For one thing she was in the midst of planning her next series of programmes and as usual Cy Fredericks, the ebullient Chairman of Megalith Television, was engaged in a campaign to infiltrate some of his own ideas at an early stage.

"So that they will grow up along with the series, my dear Jem. All of us in the melting-pot stage together. You know that I wouldn't dream of disturbing matters later on."

Keeping Cy's ideas, and Cy himself for that matter, out of what he chose to call the melting-pot stage (not a phrase she would have applied to it herself) of her new series, was clearly absolutely imperative. To defeat Cy demanded a good deal of time and energy. But the alternative, Cy's victory, was undoubtedly worse. Particularly in view of the fact that Cy wanted Jemima to follow up her highly successful series about the elderly and poor with a probe into the lives of the youthful and rich, while Jemima wanted to investigate the meaning of middle age. There was quite a difference.

To make matters worse, Jemima's nubile PA—Flowering Cherry, as she was known, the toast of Megalithic House— was in the throes of an unhappy love affair with an older man whose wife approved but whose analyst frowned upon the alliance. While this imbroglio could not be said to impair Cherry's professional efficiency (nor for that matter, Jemima noted, her appetite) it did mean that tears tended to drip over the typewriter, the engagement book and even the matutinal box of Danish pastries with which Cherry was wont to prop up her strength. Weeping Cherry would now be a more appropriate nickname, thought Jemima, torn between affection and irritation. What Cherry needed was distraction; she made a mental note to check the marital (and psychological) status of the men involved in her new series with special reference to Cherry's needs.

On the other hand Jemima Shore Investigator, as she was known through the wide success of her eponymous television series, was in no need of further distraction herself. The last programme of her recently concluded series had been titled HOW DOES THE DAY END? It had culminated in a furious discussion about euthanasia. Jemima Shore (and Weeping Cherry) were still dealing with the correspondence arising out of that one—to say nothing of the prolonged stir in the media. So what with programmes from the past and programmes for the future, it was fair to say that Jemima Shore Investigator was in every sense of the word extremely busy.

While Jemima Shore certainly did not expect Sister Imelda to appreciate the whole of this, she had perhaps anticipated some anodyne remark from the nun in answer to her own self-deprecation; something along the lines that it was always the busiest people who managed to make time.

"I'm not all that busy—"

"No, perhaps not" was what Sister Imelda actually said, quite briskly. "Perhaps you are not really busy at all compared to Nurse Elsie, because she is busy dying. And we are trying to help her die in peace."

"You're quite right," responded Jemima, feeling ashamed of her original impulse and speaking suddenly in a much warmer tone. "It is much more important what is happening to her. And anything I can do to give her peace of mind—"

"Peace of mind. Ah Miss Shore, that can only be given by God." Another gleam of frost from Sister Imelda. The long starched veil she wore was set back upon hair which was visibly white. Her complexion however was quite rosy, set off by the watchful blue eyes which were the dominant feature of her face.

Sister Imelda was the Matron of Pieta House, a Catholic Hospice for the Dying. She was, Jemima knew, a professed Catholic nun as well as a nurse. It was difficult to know whether her clothes corresponded to a nun's habit as modified by the decrees of Vatican Council II, or an actual nurse's uniform. Sister Imelda wore an unfashionably long grey skirt, which left several inches of severe grey stocking visible, ending in heavy grey shoes with straps across the instep. The long, stiff white veil gave the air of a nun, that and the black rosary at Sister Imelda's belt, jostling almost carelessly with her keys. But her starched white apron, decorated with the traditional nurse's safety pins and little watch pinned on the broad smooth unindented breast, belonged entirely to a hospital matron. A large, flat silver brooch with some engraving on it was pinned centrally on her veil; Jemima expected it to be a badge of office. Actually the engraving, rather badly done, was of Michelangelo's statue of the Pieta.

In spite of all this Jemima, who had attended a convent school in youth and was in principle fond of nuns, decided to regard Sister Imelda as a nurse. She was not particularly fond of hospitals and unlike nuns counted no nurses among her friends.

"You appreciate that Nurse Elsie asked for you after she saw one of your programmes on television. You referred to the question of peace of mind for the dying then of course."

"I hope that didn't matter. It is rather a loose phrase." Jemima gave her famous sweet smile, the one that made people watching her on television think what a charming person she must be in private.

"Oh, on television, Miss Shore, I've definitely heard worse." Sister Imelda smiled in her turn. She had very large unnaturally clean-looking white teeth. Perhaps they were false—Jemima remembered from her own convent days that nuns' teeth were always ill-fitting either out of economy or, as was believed among the girls at the time, as a form of penance; but Sister Imelda did not give the impression of one who would easily tolerate inefficiency either in false teeth or anything else.

Sister Imelda stopped smiling suddenly. The teeth vanished from view. There was a very slight pause or even perhaps a hesitation. But when Sister Imelda spoke again she was even brisker than before.

"And then of course there is the question of absolution. You might help her with that too—"

"*Absolution?*" In her capacity as a leading television investigative reporter Jemima had fielded some strange requests from the public in her time. But to provide absolution for a dying woman in a Catholic hospice was certainly the oddest she had yet encountered. "Surely a priest would be more suitable?"

"Oh please, Miss Shore." Sister Imelda raised one hand. Like her teeth, her hands were almost unnaturally clean and white: where were the traditional red signs of washing and scrubbing, common to both nun and nurse? Sister Imelda's hands resembled those of a top-class surgeon, not least because they were notably big hands for a woman. "Nurse Elsie has of course made a full confession. We live next to the Priory here, you know. At any hour of the day or night the Fathers come if they are needed; it's part of what the Hospice is able to offer." Sister Imelda gave another of her tiny significant pauses. "But—absolution is another matter. It's not automatic. I should explain—"

Jemima wondered whether she herself should explain something to Sister Imelda. Having been educated at a Catholic convent (although not herself a Catholic) she was perfectly well aware of the rules governing Catholic confession. Absolution—forgiveness for past sins given by the priest, standing in for God as it were—did not necessarily follow confession; but in all the years when Jemima, half envious, half scornful, wholly in love, had listened to her friends' confidences on the subject, she had never heard of anyone being refused it. Penances could and did vary, of course, in proportion to sins declared. "The five Sorrowful Mysteries of the Rosary! Roseabelle, whatever have you been up to?" That had been a typical half-envious, half-gleeful comment.

But to refuse absolution to a dying woman?

"It can't be long now." By all the rules of the Church, Jemima failed to see how Nurse Elsie Connolly, dying slowly and inexorably here in Pieta House, could possibly have been denied the ultimate forgiveness by a Catholic priest. It made no sense. What crime could poor old Nurse Elsie have committed? No, wait—*anyone* could commit a crime, as experience had certainly taught Jemima Shore. But if Nurse Elsie had committed some sort of a fairly serious crime, why on earth had she not confessed it before? Undoubtedly the good Fathers from the Priory came round regularly to hear confessions, quite apart from the sudden flurry when one of the many failing inhabitants of Pieta House was judged to be on the very brink of death. As Sister Imelda had pointed out, that was one of the important services provided by the Hospice.

Jemima decided that if she was to be of any help in the situation—which was after all why she had postponed an important planning meeting where she intended to worst Cy Fredericks once and for all—she had better come clean with Sister Imelda. Swiftly she explained the facts about her background.

The effect was remarkable. Sister Imelda did not exactly warm to Jemima—it was doubtful from her stance whether she knew how to do so, except perhaps towards the very sick. But she did drop altogether that air of cool superiority which had hitherto distinguished most of her remarks.

Sister Imelda's tiny bare office was furnished solely by a Crucifix, a vast but out-of-date calendar featuring the Pope, and, rather surprisingly, a crudely coloured picture of the Princess of Wales holding her first baby which at first glance Jemima had taken for the Madonna with her child.

Leaning across the ugly wooden desk Sister Imelda spoke urgently to Jemima:

"Oh, thanks be to God"—manifestly she meant it—"a Catholic."

"I'm not." cried Jemima.

"No, no, I realize that. A Catholic education, I was going to say. You understand the problem. You'll help us. I know you will. It's all Father Thomas. A saint you know. A dear good man as well. But ever since he came back from Biafra—such terrible things endured and even worse witnessed. No sense, you know. No sense about this world at any rate."

Jemima Shore had an inkling that where Sister Imelda was concerned this was the ultimate criticism; there was a clear implication too that Father Thomas might well turn out to have no sense about the next world as well. But Jemima made no comment. As a practised interviewer, she recognized the need for silence, an irresistibly interrogative silence.

"Restitution, yes." Sister Imelda's confidences marched on. "Of course that is one of the conditions of confession. To make restitution if one can. Without that, there can in theory be no absolution. The thief for example must give back his ill-gotten gains before he can be absolved. If he is still able to do so. That is the teaching of the Church. But in this case—even supposing it's all true, which I very much doubt—that Father Thomas should land us in this! So many things at stake. The Hospice itself. Our foundation—when you think who's involved." Sister Imelda shot a quick nervous look at the picture of the Princess of Wales, giving Jemima the impression once again, if only fleetingly, that this was some kind of contemporary ikon. Then she visibly reasserted control.

"You'll help us, Miss Shore, I know you will. Help us—

and of course," she added in a less hurried voice which was nevertheless not quite calm, "help Nurse Elsie."

Sister Imelda rose. The smiling image of the Princess fluttered as she did so, in a breeze caused by her starched white veil, her starched long white apron and even perhaps the flap of her long grey skirts. The image of the Pope was made of heavier material and remained static.

"Sister Imelda, could you amplify—" Jemima rose too. But Sister Imelda was by now thoroughly restored to tranquillity, which also meant authority.

"No, Miss Shore, I think it is only fair to let Nurse Elsie tell her own story. I apologize if I have seemed over-emotional." Another glance towards the Princess of Wales, but this time the expression was austere, even condemnatory. "This has been a trying time for the Hospice. But I expect you are used to dealing with that kind of thing on television. Please follow me, Miss Shore."

The first thing which struck Jemima Shore about Nurse Elsie Connolly was the charm, even prettiness, of her appearance. She had expected a skeleton of a woman. Nurse Elsie, with a smooth skin and two long plaits of hair lying down on either side of her pink nightdress, certainly looked an invalid—she was extraordinarily pale for one thing—but she resembled the kind of invalid described in a Victorian novel who may linger for years of interesting if bed-ridden life.

Nurse Elsie was in fact sixty. Jemima learnt this from her very first remark, as though in answer to her unspoken question.

"My sixtieth birthday! Jemima Shore comes to visit me. Now that's a real present." The words, like Nurse Elsie's appearance, were quite girlish. But the voice itself was faint and Jemima perceived that immediately after speaking Nurse Elsie gave a kind of gasp as though the effort itself had nearly extinguished her. Jemima wondered what kind of painkillers she was being given. If faint, she sounded quite lucid.

Jemima produced the small arrangement of strongly perfumed freesias which she had carefully commissioned beforehand at her favourite flower-shop in Notting Hill Gate. A perfectionist where flowers were concerned,

Jemima knew that nothing annoyed busy nurses more than
having to cope with a vast bouquet of ill-assorted blooms
immured within crackling cellophane, demanding the instant production of a vase.

Nurse Elsie smiled with obvious delight. It was almost as
though she had recognized the perfection of the choice as
well as appreciating the nosegay—and perhaps as an ex-
nurse herself she had.

"Like you." Her voice was even fainter. "So pretty."
Nurse Elsie put out her hand and laid it on Jemima's wrist.
It was a claw.

Memento mori, thought Jemima. The skeleton was not
after all so far below this poor woman's skin; and above the
perfume of freesias, mingling with the obvious hygienic
smells of the sick-room, she detected for the first time some
other smell, more lingering, more distressing.

Yet the rest of the scene was pretty, charming, like Nurse
Elsie herself in her pink nightdress, almost cloyingly so.
There were pink blankets, pale pink flowered curtains—a
pattern of hollyhocks and lupins—pale green walls. The
screens which stood around a bed at the far corner of the
room were made of the same ruched material.

There were about six other people present in the ward,
all lying down. One woman—Jemima imagined she was a
woman—with a broad swollen face and very short black
hair, raised her hand. Perhaps she was waving. On the off
chance, Jemima waved back. The hand sank and a look of
puzzlement crossed the broad face.

A large crucifix hung above the door and on the opposite
wall there was a reproduction of Fra Angelico's St. Francis
feeding the birds. A coloured picture showed Pope John
Paul II walking with the Queen in the corridor of Buckingham Palace; both parties faced the camera with smiles of
almost aggressively healthy confidence in contrast to the
sick women below. Some tasteful flowers—a few carnations
and a great deal of greenery chosen almost too obviously to
harmonize with the colour scheme of the room—stood in a
large dull white case on a plinth beneath the crucifixion.
Little bouquets and vases flanked most of the beds, and
most of the women boasted at least two photographs on
their bedside tables.

In spite of this, Jemima was quite unprepared for Nurse Elsie's own array. It might have been a shrine, the resting-place of a saint, there were so many flowers. Some of them were certainly dead, others like Nurse Elsie herself decomposing. But some were like Jemima's own little nosegay, evidently fresh.

The photographs in frames which ranged from plain perspex to silver—quite a few of those—were all of children, very young children, often babies.

The claw scratched at her palm.

Nurse Elsie was smiling at her again.

"My babies," she said.

"*Your* babies—"

"My babies. All of them. I was a midwife, you know. Didn't they tell you?"

"No, I didn't realize. A nurse was all they said."

"A midwife. A state registered midwife. *Later* a nurse. The first month. I used to look after my ladies for the first month. Longer sometimes. Eleven weeks. Those were twins."

Nurse Elsie moved her eyes in the direction of one particular photograph. It was one of those with a silver frame.

"The Fergus twins. You've read about them I expect." Nurse Elsie gave another gasp and closed her eyes. She panted heavily, frighteningly. Jemima wondered if she should ring for help as Sister Imelda had told her she might do in case of need.

Nurse Elsie's lips moved. She was saying something else. "Nor—Nor—Nor—" What was it she was trying to get out?

"Naughty," she managed at last. Her voice strengthened a little. "Naughty. Always in the papers. Little devils. Very *naughty*." Nurse Elsie's eyes closed and there was silence. The dark woman with the broad face waved again and Jemima waved back.

The hold of the claw strengthened.

"Naughty. That's what I wanted to tell you. I've been very naughty, no, *wicked*. I want to put it all right. You've got to help me, Jemima Shore. Just as he says."

"He?" But Jemima knew the answer.

"Father Thomas. He says I've got to put it all right before I die."

"Never mind about Father Thomas," said Jemima gently. "You can tell me anything you like, you know. I won't tell anyone else," she added.

Something like a spasm crossed Nurse Elsie's face.

"No, tell, tell," she whispered urgently. "You've got to tell everyone. Tell a lawyer, anyway. That's what Father Thomas said. You must get me a lawyer. The wrong has got to be put right. Otherwise I shan't get absolution. I shan't die in peace."

"Tell me then," said Jemima, still as gently and quietly as she could.

"And you'll bring me a lawyer?"

"If that's what you really want."

"A lawyer tomorrow—"

"Well, I'll do my best. The day after, maybe." Jemima spoke with the guilty knowledge that it would certainly not be tomorrow, a day already cluttered with a host of highly important meetings and leaving no time for amassing stray lawyers, let alone paying another visit to the Hospice herself.

"It's got to be tomorrow. I'm not going to last very long. I know that. I wouldn't let them give me my medicine this afternoon so I could be clear. It won't be long now."

Nurse Elsie closed her eyes once more. But this time there was no silence. On the contrary she began to speak aloud in a rapid, low but perfectly lucid voice. It was as though she had long rehearsed in her own mind what she had to say.

"When the little baby was born dead," began Nurse Elsie, "the boy, the boy they'd always wanted, I thought my heart would break, my heart as well as theirs. She went into labour early, they couldn't find the doctor. But they got hold of me; I was on another case in London not far away. I did everything, but the baby died. I couldn't tell her. I left it to him. And it was he who said to me, "Nurse Elsie, we have to get her a baby, another baby. I feel so guilty. A proper live healthy baby. Nurse Elsie, would you help us?"

"And that's when it all began. The wickedness."

CHAPTER TWO

•

Bedside Conference

Jemima's next discussion on the subject of Nurse Elsie also centred round a bedside. Only in this case the bed was Jemima's own and it was Jemima herself who was in the bed, or rather lying across it. Unlike Nurse Elsie however, Jemima was not wearing a primly pretty Victorian nightdress but an exotic towelling-robe, honey-coloured like her hair, and beneath that nothing at all. And unlike the ward at Pieta House with its long row of bed-ridden figures, Jemima's bedroom contained only one other occupant.

This was a lawyer called Cass Brinsley. While Jemima lay on the bed in her robe slowly stroking Midnight, her sleek black cat (who responded with a complacent raucous purr), Cass Brinsley sat fully dressed in an armchair beside the bed. One could also say that he was formally as well as fully dressed, since he wore a black jacket, striped dark trousers, a stiff white collar with a spotless white shirt, and a black silk tie with delicate white spots on it. Neither party however, the honey-coloured woman on the bed or the formally dressed man in the armchair, seemed to find anything strange about the contrast.

"What you are saying, darling, is that there was a switch in fact. A deliberate fraud was perpetrated." Jemima noticed with amusement that where professional matters were concerned, Cass Brinsley quickly reverted to the language of the law courts. The contrast between Caspar Brinsley, the precise almost over-deliberate barrister, and Cass, the astonishingly uninhibited lover, never ceased to intrigue her. She eyed his formal clothing so clearly destined for a day in Chambers speculatively and wondered just for a moment what it would be like . . . just once . . . a seduction . . .

Quickly and rather guiltily Jemima Shore reminded herself that Cass Brinsley, seducible under these circumstances or not (probably not), was also not the only one with a busy schedule. Jemima returned with determination to the topic under discussion. At the same time, Midnight, who seemed jealously to have sensed a distraction in her thoughts, gave a mew and Jemima stroked his back too with renewed concentration.

"I'm not saying there was a switch, Cass. She's saying it. Nurse Elsie. By chance the other mother she was looking after was going to give the baby for adoption anyway. I got the impression she was unmarried—a tragic case, Nurse Elsie called it. Anyway it was a cloak-and-dagger delivery. Something that wouldn't happen in these days of easy abortion to say nothing of the Pill. The other baby was also a boy. So she switched babies. She wants me to bring along a lawyer—that's the word she uses by the way, I think it's probably the word used by the batty priest Father Thomas. I suppose in fact it would have to be a solicitor?"

Cass nodded.

"A commissioner of oaths is what you would need. She'd have to make a deposition and it would have to be sworn. A solicitor can act as a commissioner of oaths—so a solicitor would do."

"And then? Where would I go from there?"

"And then, my darling, assuming what you tell me about her health is correct, you would be left with a sworn deposition concerning events which took place over twenty years ago, made by a retired midwife, who was dying of cancer at the time. A woman in great pain and certainly under the influence of a great many drugs, if not literally sedated at the time she spoke to you. Added to which she'll almost certainly die on you the moment the deposition is made, if she lasts that long.

"Jemima," continued Cass in a tender voice, reaching

forward and taking her hand, "stop stroking the insufferably demanding Midnight and listen to me: this is really not one for you. What exactly do you hope to achieve? Especially when you think of the people involved."

"That's exactly what Sister Imelda said—the Matron of the Hospice—the starchy one. 'Think of the people involved.'" Jemima scratched Midnight's furry throat as the cat stretched luxuriously. Cass grabbed her hand again and the cat leapt suddenly and angrily off the bed.

"Darling Jemima, answer the question. What do you hope to achieve? I know you love your cat more than you love me. That has been established." Cass' tone was the sweetly reasonable one that Jemima assumed he used in court for a difficult witness.

"Peace of mind for Nurse Elsie, I suppose," Jemima spoke rather doubtfully.

"'Only God can give peace of mind,'" quoted Cass. "Sister Imelda's line. I rather like it. I shall try it on my clients. Certainly justice being done doesn't always give it."

"You're right to question my motives, Cass," went on Jemima with still more uncertainty. "I certainly don't want to cause great misery to a whole lot of people on account of something private they once did years ago. Jemima the Avenger—absolutely not. If I'm to be honest— it's curiosity as much as anything else. Can her story be true?"

"Jemima Shore Investigator!" pronounced Cass. "I knew it. Your dreadful inquisitiveness." He looked at her and thought how beautiful she always looked after making love; how beautiful in her loosely tied robe, with her famous hair, so much admired on television, now in total disarray and no make-up on her face. What Jemima Shore did not know about the cool and reserved Cass Brinsley was that he sometimes surreptitiously turned on television at night, in the middle of working on a brief, in order to watch Jemima. The sight of the dazzling, poised, intelligent image on the screen combined with the memories of the evenings—nights—they had spent together filled him with a mixture of possessive jealousy and frustrated lust.

Cass judged it wise to keep these feelings a secret from Jemima. Possessiveness in any form he knew to be her bane—as indeed in theory and in practice up to the present time it had been his too.

Two uncommitted people.

Besides, he had a foolish feeling that a great deal of the British nation also felt this way about Jemima Shore's image on television—without the excuse of knowing her, as it were, in the flesh.

That was another point. Cass hated to be one of a crowd. After one of these bouts of secret jealousy he generally solved the problem of the lust if not the jealousy by taking out any one of a number of attractive available girls (Cass disliked pursuing women) and vanishing temporarily from the list of Jemima's admirers. He never knew if she minded—his absences, that is.

Cass, like Jemima, withdrew his attention rather guiltily from these secret thoughts to the matter in hand.

"Tell me, darling, do you believe her story?" It was the witness box again.

"At first sight it's incredible, isn't it? People don't do such things, as Judge Brack said of poor old Hedda G. Listen to what Nurse Elsie suggests happened. That you-know-who, a highly responsible man—he's held every conceivable post in the government from Defence Secretary to the Environment—got this midwife to procure a live baby, a son, in place of his own child that died. And then calmly went ahead and made the substitution, and has lived quite blithely with the situation ever since. As has his wife. And no one has ever suspected. It's incredible."

"So you don't believe her," said Cass, still in his judicial voice, putting the tips of his fingers together.

"Ah, I didn't say that. I haven't been absolutely idle, you know. For one thing I have looked the family up in the peerage—no, you're quite right, Megalith didn't run to such a thing but it does now, since Cherry was quite thrilled to go and purchase one at Hatchard's. It's quite cheered her up—given her all sorts of ideas about her love life."

"Cherry flowers again?" Cass had heard about the untoward intervention of the analyst.

"Exactly. She's heavily into peers now by the way. Her daydreams have gone up several notches in the social register. It's convenient for her that so many of the peers are quite ancient: you know Cherry's perennial yearning for the Substantial Older Man. Even handier, Debrett gives their dates of birth. Also their residences. She's found one Duke of fifty-seven, that's Cherry's ideal age, who's been married four times and is currently divorced, with two residences in the South of France. Her dreams know no bounds. No children too. Where was I?"

"Another noble family. One child."

"One child indeed. Where our noble family is concerned, there was an enormous amount at stake—purely in terms of title, if you like that sort of thing. The title has to go through the male line and the present Marquess has no brothers or sisters. His father and his uncle were both killed in the First World War, uncle very young and thus unmarried. After that you have to go way off to a remote cousin, third cousin, something like that. Brilliant Cherry, by now thoroughly over-excited, went to the British Library and checked on a Debrett of 1959, before this boy was born. Fortunately Debrett makes it easy for you by printing the name of the heir presumptive in capital letters. Otherwise even title-oriented Cherry might have had difficulty in tracking it down. So guess who the heir was in 1959?"

"The traditional New Zealand sheep farmer or Los Angeles taxi driver, who would suddenly have become the Marquess of St. Ives?"

Jemima frowned. "No, not a sheep farmer and not a taxi driver. Very much not. Lord St. Ives' heir was—no, I won't even ask you to guess, because it's so incongruous. Andrew Iverstone!"

"Iverstone!"

"Yes, Iverstone. The family name is Iverstone. Lord St. Ives' full name, according to the industrious Cherry, is Ivo Charles Iverstone, Marquess of, etc."

An unjudicial look of pure surprise crossed Cass' face.

"Andrew Iverstone: that fearful Fascist! I can see you might want to do him out of a title. To say nothing of his yet more dreadful wife. No, wait, that was a remark of pure prejudice, Jemima, forget it. The sheer dreadfulness of Andrew Iverstone is still absolutely no proof that Lord St. Ives carried out a crime to rob him of his inheritance."

All the same Cass thought of the austerely handsome face of the former Foreign Secretary, type-casting for the kind of elegant, detached aristocrat beloved of old-style Hollywood movies, and contrasted it with the florid rabble-rousing image of Andrew Iverstone. On behalf of Lord St. Ives, Cass Brinsley shuddered.

"Shall I go on?"

"Proceed, Jemima Shore Investigator. So—no children for the Marquess and Marchioness of St. Ives—or rather none till this boy. St. Ives must be going on seventy now. So he was fifty-odd when the child was born."

"Correct. But there had been a child, three children in fact, two boys and a girl, all born much earlier, two listed as born and died on the same day, the first lived a little longer. Then this child. Lord St. Ives was fifty at the time and more to the point Lady St. Ives—she's in Debrett too, being the daughter of a lord, very convenient so I could look her up too—she was forty-six. It was definitely the last chance."

"All this for a title? As it happens, I've always admired Lord St. Ives—his stand over Africa for example. If you must have aristocrats, he's always seemed to me a good advertisement for them."

"Nurse Elsie said it was all for her—for his wife. What she called the wickedness. I should tell you that. Very emphatic about it in so far as she had the strength to be emphatic about anything. He loved her, couldn't bear another tragedy. She's very much around, by the way, Lady St. Ives. A good woman. Known to have visited the Hospice, and of course Nurse Elsie herself, quite recently."

Cass whistled.

"So your old bird, inspired by her priest and aided by some friendly neighbourhood solicitor or whatever, provided by her favourite television star Jemima Shore, who just happens to have a tame lawyer handy—" he cocked a quizzical eyebrow at Jemima who with an innocent smile continued to stroke Midnight, returned and now sunk into some distant purrless paradise—"aided by all this, your old bird intends to bring fear and unhappiness into the lives of what is laughingly known as one of our great families. But is in fact a retired highly honourable and distinguished politician, and a lady in her sixties who according to your nurse never knew anything about it in the first place. All this to push the vast wealth and estates of the St. Ives family, including historic Saffron Ivy, in the direction of that rabid racist Andrew Iverstone."

"You're the lawyer, Cass. What *about* justice? Justice *and* peace of mind?" asked Jemima with a smile.

"I'm not a lawyer in this bedroom. Who is to say that in a sense justice hasn't been done? After all if Lord and Lady St. Ives had adopted a child—no, I'm wrong, titles can't go to adopted children. Nor entailed estates for that matter. I imagine Saffron Ivy is entailed, or in some kind of trust on the heir male. That Holbein! Andrew Iverstone to own that Holbein! I digress. What I'm trying to say is this: If Lord and Lady St. Ives had been less grand, less wealthy, they could simply have adopted a baby like any other childless couple. And that is what they have, in effect, done. Twenty years ago. Leave it, Jemima darling, leave it and forget it."

"I can't leave it. Forget it, yes. Leave it, no. You see, I promised. And it was my programme which started it."

"*Your* programme? I thought the priest started it."

"My programme. The one about peace of mind for the elderly and how they should be allowed to die in peace."

Cass groaned. "Oh my God, the ghastly power of television. You mean those few casual words of yours inspired an old nurse who had sat on a secret for twenty years, suddenly to up with it and spout it out to a priest in the confessional."

"I mean just that," said Jemima unhappily. "The penultimate programme in the series was called *Peace of Mind*."

"Peace of mind! What about the mother? What about the boy, for heaven's sake? We haven't even mentioned him. What's his name, for a start? We keep calling him the boy—but he's virtually grown up."

"Saffron is his name, like the house. Lord Saffron, I think, or Viscount Saffron, that's the courtesy title of the heir. Nurse Elsie just refers to him as Saffron."

"A very grand adoption. From bastard to viscount. And imagine a boy brought up to all of that—yes, I know I'm a member of the Labour Party but I've got humanitarian feelings—imagine such a one being suddenly told he's nobody. He must be quite grown-up."

Cass Brinsley stood up and checked his watch.

"My God, look at the time. Jemima darling, you are irresistible. All the same, I absolutely must go." Jemima smiled and rolled gracefully off the bed, abandoning Midnight so that she could throw her towelling arms around Cass.

"Ouch, no fluff. No honey-coloured fluff, if you don't mind. And not too many red-gold hairs either. As I was saying—" Cass picked carefully at his dark sleeve "—you are irresistible. And you are also in a hole, which happens to you but seldom. So what I will do for you is this. I will come down to the Hospice with you on Saturday. Can't possibly manage it till then. I won't take a statement or anything like that—I'm not a solicitor. But I will sort of spread my authority around, persuade that Matron of the foolishness of all this talk, about the law of slander—good point that. See the priest if necessary. It's your peace of mind I'm worried about, by the way, not Nurse Elsie's."

"Angel—and to hell with the honey-coloured fluff."

Jemima launched herself and Cass Brinsley ducked, retreating rapidly.

"Let them know we're coming," he called, "with any luck Nurse Elsie will be dead by Saturday and the whole problem will be solved."

As it happened, Cass Brinsley was right as, in his legal way, he was right about so many things.

Nurse Elsie survived through Wednesday and Thursday; according to Sister Imelda—who spoke in a typically unemotional voice on the telephone—the prospect of Jemima's return with "a legal adviser" had indeed brought about some kind of miracle. Nurse Elsie had rallied.

She was so much recovered that according to Sister Imelda she proposed to receive some visitors on Friday—old friends.

"But she's living for *your* visit," Sister Imelda gave a dry cough. "That's what she says, Miss Shore. You do of course realize that Nurse Elsie remains a dying woman, could in fact die at any time. These little rallies, in our experience, seldom last very long. However, we expect you and—Mr. Brinsley, is it?—on Saturday as arranged. Goodbye, Miss Shore."

Mr. Brinsley and Miss Shore spent Friday night together at Jemima Shore's flat. It seemed convenient that they should set out for the Hospice together. On Saturday morning however, just as Jemima was pulling on the honey-coloured robe, the telephone rang. It was Sister Imelda.

The news she wanted to impart was that Nurse Elsie Connolly had died peacefully if unexpectedly on the previous afternoon. Peacefully, and only unexpectedly in the sense that Nurse Elsie had had a visitor sitting with her at the time.

"Distressing but hardly surprising: she was dead before Father Thomas could be fetched to give her the last rites."

"A visitor?" Jemima knotted the robe around her and listened rather confusedly to the sound of her bath running in the next room, the bath in which she had intended to lie planning their whole course of action at the Hospice.

"The Marchioness of St. Ives was sitting with Nurse Elsie at the time of her death," replied Sister Imelda; Jemima wondered if it was pure imagination on her part that she heard an undercurrent of triumph in the Matron's voice.

"It was so very sweet of her to come all the way from Saffron Ivy when she heard that Nurse Elsie was asking for her. But then Lady St. Ives is such a remarkable selfless person, as we have found here at the Hospice. And she was the very last one to be with her. Nurse Elsie must have been so pleased by that. Lady St. Ives and Nurse Elsie were after all such *very* old friends. Another old friend also came, one of Nurse Elsie's ladies—as she used to call them. But Lady St. Ives was the last.

This time there was no mistaking her tone. Jemima stood by the telephone, still holding the receiver, and wondered if the Matron's normally impassive face was wearing the same expression of cool satisfaction.

"So you see, Miss Shore," concluded Sister Imelda,

"Nurse Elsie did after all die in peace, just as you wished.
You must be glad to know that."

The Matron rang off. But for some time after the noise of
the telephone had been reduced merely to a steady sound
not unlike Midnight's raucous purr, Jemima remained
standing with the white receiver in her hand.

CHAPTER THREE

•

Nothing Wrong with Money

By the end of an agreeable weekend, telephone mostly off the hook, Jemima Shore had come to agree with Cass Brinsley that Nurse Elsie Connolly's death was providential—and natural. Jemima's feeling of unease when Sister Imelda broke the news on the telephone that Saturday morning, she was now prepared to ascribe to her own over-heated imagination, inspired by the atmosphere of the Hospice. The death was providential because it freed Jemima of further responsibility towards the matter.

"Yes, I know you have this famous instinct, darling," Cass said patiently. "But unless you're suggesting that that grim Sister actually went and murdered the poor old nurse—"

"Hastened her death," Jemima put in; but she already sounded doubtful. "Nurse Elsie was dying anyway. No, no, I'm not exactly suggesting that."

"Then was it the boy's mother, the gracious Marchioness of St. Ives no less?"

"No, no, of course not."

"Because according to the nurse's story, and that's all you have to go on, my love, Lady St. Ives didn't know anything about the substitution in the first place. So she didn't even have a motive."

"She could have realized something was wrong later," Jemima countered. "We've agreed that the boy himself must be about twenty now. Twenty years is a long time in which to bring up somebody else's child and suspect nothing. It depends a good deal on what the boy looks like,

21

of course. I never got a chance to ask Nurse Elsie about any of the details. We all know what Lord St. Ives looks like even if we do tend to see him in terms of Marc's cartoons, a series of long thin terribly aristocratic lines, that long straight nose and single narrow line for a mouth. But what about her? I have an image of a typical English lady of a certain type forever meeting her husband at airports with a brave smile."

At which point Cass Brinsley said very firmly, "Enough of this. I'm going to distract you forever with an enormous therapeutic draught of Buck's Fizz. I have in mind filling one of your numerous television awards to the brim: there must be a silver goblet amongst them."

"Unfillable statuettes in the main, I fear." All the same Jemima allowed herself to be distracted.

Under the circumstances it was hardly surprising that by Monday morning Jemima was in a very different frame of mind. She certainly did not expect to hear of the late Nurse Elsie Connolly again, nor of Sister Imelda of Pieta House, still less of the youthful heir Lord Saffron. Besides, Monday morning was to be the occasion of a full-dress confrontation with Cy Fredericks on the subject of their rival concerns—crabbed age, in the case of Jemima Shore, or at any rate the approach of same, and youth "full of pleasance" in the case of Cy Fredericks. The nature of the new series had to be decided shortly, or at least the nature of the first programme.

It never did to have your mind in anyway distracted when confronting Cy, as Jemima knew to her cost; while the information, derived from Cy's secretary via Cherry, that Cy Fredericks was currently pursuing a gilded moppet called Tiggie, filled her with additional dread. Cy Fredericks' romantic attachments were closely monitored by those in the know at Megalithic House, since all too often they provided the vital clue to what otherwise seemed a totally irrational enthusiasm for a particular programme.

If only Cy would stick to Lady Manfred! thought Jemima as she wheeled her little white Mercedes sports car into the Megalithic car park. Cultured, music-loving, above all gracefully *middle-aged*, Lady Manfred demanded no more of Megalith than a generalized support of the opera, of which Jemima for one thoroughly approved. But an attachment for the notorious Tiggie Jones (Tiggie forsooth! could anyone with a name like Tiggie bode well for Megalith?), twenty-three-year-old Tiggie, the darling of the gossip columns according to Cherry, Tiggie of the long legs and roving eyes, according to the photographers, that was definitely bad news. It also helped to explain why Cy was being at once devious and obstinate in his determination to make a programme tentatively entitled—by him—"Golden Lads and Girls." (Had he, Jemima wondered, ever read the actual poem from which the quotation came? The conclusion might come as a surprise to him.)

Cy Fredericks' opening ploy at the meeting was also his valediction.

"You deserve a holiday, Jem, and this, *in effect*, is going to be it." Jemima pondered inwardly on the potential menace contained in those little words "in effect" on the lips of the Chairman of Megalith. Outwardly she merely smiled sweetly, that charming smile which made people watching television think what a nice warm human being she was.

"I'm afraid I don't find the idea of investigating a lot of poor-little-rich kids at university quite my notion of a holiday. It's now the eighteenth of January. How about that programme on the growth of feminism in the West Indies? An interesting subject and an interesting location. I could be ready to leave for preliminary discussions in a week or two. First stop Barbados."

There was a short silence. Cy Fredericks was clearly remembering that he himself had just rented a luxurious villa on that very island and wondered whether Jemima was aware of that fact. (She was: his secretary had told Cherry, who had told Jemima.) Cy solved the problem in his usual galvanic fashion.

"Jem, my dear Jem," he murmured, leaning across the vast desk and grasping, with some difficulty, her hand. "We've been too much out of touch lately. We need to talk, really talk. Miss Lewis!" he suddenly shouted in a voice of great agitation, dropping the hand and gazing rather wildly round him. "Miss Lewis! Are you there?"

There was an acquiescent noise from the outer office.

Although Cy had in fact a perfectly efficient intercom, he never seemed to have the necessary leisure to master it.

"Miss Lewis! When am I next free for lunch?"

Miss Lewis, a neat young woman in a silk shirt, check skirt and well polished brown boots, entered hastily, bearing a leather diary which she deposited in front of her employer. Cy gazed at it for a moment with an expression of outraged disbelief and then, in silence, proceeded to score out a number of entries with great violence. Finally he looked up and beamed at Jemima.

"So! For you, Jemima, I drop everything. We shall have our heart to heart. Exchange of souls. Lunch on February the twenty-eighth."

"I can't wait," said Jemima.

Negotiating the white Mercedes once more out of the Megalith car park that afternoon, Jemima was wearily aware that the chances of her *not* spending a few cold winter weeks in and around Oxford University to say nothing of the other equally unpleasing (to Jemima Shore) haunts of the young and rich, were rapidly diminishing. To console herself, and while away the time in the heavy traffic she put on a tape of *Arabella* and waited for her favourite song beginning: "Aber der Richtige . . ." "The man who's right for me, if there is one for me in all this world." But the thought of the right man coming along put her uncomfortably in mind of Cass Brinsley: did *he* think *she* was the right woman . . . ? Could anyone, even a lawyer, be quite so detached? It was to distract herself from these—essentially unprofitable—thoughts that Jemima jumped out of the car in a traffic block and bought an evening paper.

At the next lights she glanced down at the headlines, particularly glaring this evening, accompanied by a large photograph. The next moment she found herself staring, the car still in gear, her neck still craning down. It took some frantic hootings all round her to tell Jemima Shore that the lights had turned green and that the heavy crocodile of lorries, trucks and cars was supposed to be rattling forward once more up Holland Park Avenue.

The newspaper photograph showed a handsome young man, very young and very handsome: the flash bulb had perhaps exaggerated the dramatic effect of the wide eyes and high cheekbones, the thick hair, apparently black, a lock falling across the forehead. Even so the looks were sufficiently startling to make Jemima suppose for a moment she was gazing at the face of a pop star. And the rather wide mouth and well-formed lips confirmed the impression of a pop star to a generation brought up on the ultimate pop-star looks of Mick Jagger, although this young man was more distinguished, less rouguish-looking than Jumping Jack Flash. His clothes too were more deliberately Byronic: he was wearing something which looked like a white stock above a ruffled shirt. It was not, to Jemima at any rate, a very sympathetic face. Or perhaps the expression of arrogance was, like the contrast in the looks, purely the creation of the flash bulb.

A pop star in trouble. For the young man in question had been photographed leaving some court or other. It was the caption which corrected Jemima's error, and the text beneath it which caused her to stare and stare again at the newspaper.

OXFORD BLOOD SAYS "NO REGRETS"
"GILDED RUBBISH"—MAGISTRATE

Twenty-year-old Viscount Saffron, undergraduate heir of former Foreign Secretary, the Marquess of St. Ives, pictured leaving Oxford magistrates' court yesterday, where he was fined £750 with costs. He was among other students found guilty of causing damage to the Martyrs Hotel, Cornmarket, Oxford, after a student party following an exclusive (£50 a head) Chimney-sweepers' Dinner of the "Oxford Bloods." High-living Lord Saffron, heir to what is estimated to be one of the largest landed fortunes in Britain, told reporters that he had "no regrets" about the damage caused to the hotel, "since he had plenty of money to pay for it." Lord Saffron added with a laugh: "There's nothing wrong with money, so long as you don't earn it."

Jemima, as she sped forward once more amid the hooting cars, felt sick then angry. Oxford Blood indeed! You scarcely needed a knowledge of the latest unemployment figures—which some sardonic newspaperman had in any case thoughtfully placed alongside the lead item concerning Lord Saffron—to be disgusted by such a gratuitous display of upper-class insolence. Jemima felt herself in total sympathy with the remarks of the magistrate who referred feelingly to behavior "unacceptable in supporters of a football club" and all the more disgraceful in someone who had been raised "in such a privileged manner" as Lord Saffron.

The magistrate was also particularly incensed by the fact that Oxford Bloods called their function the Chimney-sweepers' Dinner, thus mocking what had once been a decent profession for a working man; many people, he opined, would regard these young people themselves as mere "gilded rubbish," at the bottom rather than the top of society. And this was the type of delightful young person Cy Fredericks expected her to study in his precious "Golden Lads and Girls" programme. By the time she reached her flat, Jemima had worked herself into a royal rage which even Midnight's soft purring welcome round her ankles hardly assuaged.

She studied the story in the newspaper in detail—nearly a thousand pounds' worth of damage had been caused by the so-called Oxford Bloods at their Chimneysweepers' Dinner (presumably its members, unlike Cy, did know how the "Golden Lads" rhyme ended). Lord Saffron had the pleasure of paying that sum as well as the fine. Glasses and plates had been smashed: well, that, if not edifying, was not so surprising, and various other pieces of minor vandalism carried out; but the principal item consisted of repairs to a marble mantelpiece which had been deliberately attacked by Lord Saffron with a hammer. Hence the fact that the case had been brought against him personally rather than the various other members of the club.

About that damage, young Lord Saffron had been theoretically penitent, or at any rate his lawyer had been so on his behalf. Outside the court however he had positively revelled in the destruction of something he castigated as "artistically beyond redemption and fortunately now beyond repair."

Jemima took a cold bottle of white wine out of the fridge and looked out of her wide uncurtained windows towards her winter balcony. Delicate exterior lighting made it into another room. A large pot of yellow witch hazel was flowering. Daring the cold Jemima pulled back the glass, cut a sprig, and put it in a little vase at her elbow. Soon the delicate sad perfume was stealing into her nostrils.

She would run a bath, allow the Floris Wild Hyacinth oil to challenge the *hamamelis mollis*, sip the wine, listen to Mozart (Clarinet Quintet, guaranteed to soothe and transport) and in complete contrast to that, yes, she would glory in the new Ruth Rendell, hoping it was one of her macabre ones . . . She would forget "Golden Lads and Girls." She would forget the odious and arrogant Lord Saffron. Above all she would forget Cy Fredericks . . .

So that when the telephone rang as though deliberately intending to thwart these plans, Jemima knew, absolutely knew, that it was Cy. White wine to her lips, she allowed the answering machine, a serene robot insensitive to both slight and triumph, to take the call.

"This is Jemima Shore," cooed the recorded voice back into the face of the real Jemima. "I'm afraid I'm not here . . ." The perfect twentieth-century double talk.

She then expected Cy to do one of two things: fling down the receiver with a strangled groan(he quite often did that; after all it was the dreaded technology, something he did not trust as far as he could see it) or simply leave one deeply reproachful word on the machine: "Jem." The implication of this one word was quite clear. "Where are you? I need you."

But it did not happen like that. When the message began, with Jemima's serene recording finished, there was a burst of music, which sounded like reggae, then some giggles. Light not very pleasant giggles. Then the impression of a hand somehow stifling the giggles. After that, silence—the steady silence of the track. Jemima waited, curiously disquieted, for the click-off indicating the end of this non-existent message.

She analysed her disquiet. Her home number was supposed to be a closely guarded secret, at any rate from members of the public who might be expected to express various unwelcome degrees of rage, admiration or even lust, following her programmes. So that such a call was on the face of it slightly surprising. On the other hand the unknown gigglers might have hit upon her number by complete coincidence.

Then Jemima felt her skin prickle. The track was no longer silent. A light androgynous voice had begun to sing softly into the machine: "Golden lads and girls all must," it lilted, "Like chimneysweepers come to dust." There was a pause. A giggle. "You too Jemima Shore," added the voice. "You too." The message was over.

In the interval Jemima's Mozart tape had, unnoticed, come to a stop. So she found herself at last sitting in silence. And the wine in her glass had become warmed by her fingers. Nothing was quite so pleasant as it had been before the telephone rang. It was possible of course to play the tape again and listen to that sinister, silly little message once more, concentrate on the voice, see if she recognized it. But that would be to give the matter too much importance.

Instead, Jemima wrenched her thoughts away from the tape and back to her work. "Golden lads and girls" indeed. As a more relevant piece of masochism, she did re-read the evening paper including that chilling declaration from Lord Saffron: "Nothing wrong with money so long as you don't earn it."

It was then that Jemima took a sudden resolve, spurred on as it were by her mingled indignation towards Lord Saffron and her dislike of the unknown telephonic intruders.

Two could play at that game.

She dialled Cy's private number. He answered with alacrity, which in Jemima's experience meant not so much that he was free but that he was engaged talking on at least two of his other lines, and was picking up the private one purely in order to still its clangour. She had analysed the situation correctly.

"Jem—one moment—Venetia—"(into some other demanding mouthpiece). "Is that you? One moment, Jem, one moment—darling, one moment—No, New York, I hear you, *ne coupez pas, ne coupez pas*. Miss Lewis, where are you?" he suddenly bellowed. "Please take this call from New York."

Miss Lewis' calm voice speaking to Jemima Shore was quite a relief, and once Jemima had made it clear she was neither the switchboard of the Carlyle Hotel in New York, nor that of the Hotel Meurice in Paris, both of which Cy was apparently trying to engage in word play, they were able to have a pleasantly sardonic exchange on the subject of Cy's telephone habits until interrupted by his next bellow:

"Miss Lewis, Miss Lewis, what is the Meurice doing in New York?"

"Mr. Fredericks—"

"Speaking perfect French too," Cy proceeded. "Not a trace of an accent."

All in all, it was sometime before this international cat's cradle was unravelled. Finally Jemima was allowed her own exchange with Cy.

Threatened as she was by New York, Paris, Lady Manfred and some other plaintive little female voice which could be heard bleating occasionally: "Cy, Cykie, Cy," Jemima made her call brief.

"You're right, Cy, right as ever. I think there is a good programme in the "Golden Lads" story—or at any rate something worth investigating further."

"Jem!" explained Cy with ebullience, dropping the receiver, or at least one of the receivers he was holding, with a crash. When normal service was resumed: "I knew you would see it my way."

"The evening paper made me see it your way."

"Oh yes, most exciting." Which told Jemima that Cy had not yet read the evening paper.

"When you do read it, you'll see why I thought I'd start with the Oxford Bloods, as I believe they're called."

"Most exciting, most exciting!" Cy continued to exclaim. This was surely carrying blankness a little too far even for Cy. His next words provided the clue.

"You don't have my memo?"

"Memo? What memo?"

"Miss Lewis, Miss Lewis!" Clearly the bellowing was about to begin. Either to obviate it, or because Miss Lewis had an unspoken alliance with Jemima on the subject of Cy and his lightning projects, Miss Lewis now broke firmly into the conversation.

"I think Mr. Fredericks is referring to the memo concerning Miss Tiggie Jones," she observed in a neutral voice. "Although he has not yet finished dictating it. In fact he has not gone beyond the first paragraph. However I understand Miss Tiggie Jones is to act as a"—delicate pause from Miss Lewis—"a student observer on your new programme."

Complete silence from Jemima Shore.

Into this silence the plaintive female voice of one of Cy's telephoners, which had happily fallen still in the last few minutes, was heard again.

"Golden lads and girls all must," sang the little voice. "Like television come to dust." Something like a giggle followed. "Ooh Cykie, I've been listening to every word."

With an unpleasant feeling Jemima recognized not only the giggle but also the androgynous singer of her anonymous telephone call.

The feeling of unpleasantness was intensified when Cy Fredericks cried out with pleasure:

"Tiggie! Darling, where have you been? I've been trying to reach you on the telephone. We have so much to discuss—"

Then to Jemima, still on her end of the line, as though introducing two people at a party:

"Jemima, I really must introduce you to Miss Tiggie Jones."

CHAPTER FOUR

•

Staircase Thirteen

"That staircase will be the death of someone," said Jemima Shore. She added fiercely as she nursed the ankle: "After our recent encounter I only hope it's young Lord Saffron. Staircase Thirteen, I see. Most appropriate."

"How about Tiggie Jones?" suggested Cherry. "Supposing she ever gets as far as Oxford." Cherry had accompanied Jemima down to Oxford in the latter's white Mercedes. That was because Tiggie Jones, billed to introduce Jemima to *"le tout Oxford"* as Cy Fredericks put it, had failed to show up at Holland Park Mansions on time. Or anything like on time. After waiting an hour, Jemima with difficulty resisted the temptation to make a vengeful call to Cy. Instead she had summoned Cherry from her office.

"Come and hold my hand among the golden ones." Nothing loath, Cherry had arrived with great swiftness, pausing only to exchange a high-necked clinging jersey to something more in keeping with the spirit of youth as she understood it—which meant a T-shirt both clinging *and* revealing. As a result Cherry was now shivering at the bottom of a staircase in Rochester College, Oxford. And Jemima, who had just fallen down the same staircase, was trying to comfort her—"No, go on, Cherry, take my coat, I've got my left-wing fury to keep me warm"—as well as rub her own ankle.

The first steps were made of stone. Dark, vanishing upwards above their heads, the rest of the staircase was made of wood, which creaked from time to time despite the fact that no one was using it. It was difficult to negotiate not only because it was steep and badly lit, but because the distance between the treads was so high. Jemima had stumbled at the top of the last flight and had only broken her fall by clutching the thin wooden rail.

The staircase ended in an arch. It was very cold in the stone interior and slightly dank. The presence of a bathroom to their left and a lavatory to their right was also unaesthetic. A further staircase leading downwards had a cardboard notice reading: "To the washing machine. Do not use after 11 P.M. C.L. Mossbanker." Someone had scrawled: "To hell with that" beneath it. Someone else had added: "And high water." A further hand still had added: "I'm pissed off with late night Lady Macbeths trying to wash it off after getting it off." Jemima had a feeling the dialogue was only just beginning.

It was difficult to believe, in view of all this, that the arch in front of her eyes formed part of a façade rated by some as the finest thing Hawksmoor ever did, outstripping the glory of neighbouring St. John's.

The next excitement was the appearance of a man they assumed to be Professor Mossbanker, from the fact that he emerged from the ground-floor rooms beneath the arch, which bore his name in gold letters.

The professor was blinking and rubbing his eyes. Then he replaced the large thick spectacles, which with their heavy black rims made him appear almost the caricature of the absent-minded academic. Looking at Jemima with some surprise and at Cherry in her T-shirt with disbelief, he asked abruptly what time it was.

Jemima told him.

"How odd!" he exclaimed. "People generally fall down this staircase at night. That and the infernal washing machine leave one no peace. What is the compulsion, I wonder, which makes modern youth want to wash so noisily? And at night." On which note he turned on his heel and retired back into his rooms. The heavy door shut.

"I think he's done that sporting thing." Cherry sounded rather uncertain.

"Sporting thing! I don't call that very sporting. He could at least have given us a glass of dry sherry—"

"No, Saffron just told us. When you slam your door it's called sporting your oak or something. Look, it's got no handle. You can't open it from outside. There's an inner door as well. Saffron had the same set-up."

"Like *The Light of the Word*," commented Jemima, who was an admirer of the Pre-Raphaelites and intended to visit Holman Hunt's celebrated picture in Keble College chapel after lunch, if she could hobble there. At the same time, agreeable memories of other sported oaks in her Cambridge days, doors in men's colleges shut not so much in her face as behind her back on entrance, rather agreeable memories, came back to her.

The sudden arrival of a tiny girl dressed as some kind of clown in a white ruffled pierrot top and very baggy white trousers worn over high-heeled black shoes, distracted them both. The clown figure rolled her huge dark eyes, delineated in black, panda fashion, in Jemima's direction and sucked her finger. Her very short very black hair was topped by a conical hat with a pompom. It was not clear whether this childishness was genuine and thus mildly unfortunate, or assumed and thus extremely irritating.

"Jemima, forgive, forgive," whispered the clown. "You've no idea of the *perils* I encountered on my journey. Oh, if only I had been with you! I know I would have felt so *safe*."

As Tiggie Jones carried on in this vein, rolling her huge eyes the while, Jemima wondered how it was that this diminutive creature, apparently lacking in all intelligence, always managed to put her so neatly at a disadvantage. I mean, how did you cope with the annoyance of being called *safe* by someone you believed to be a mere ten years younger than yourself if that?

"And didn't you just adore him? Isn't he foxy?" Tiggie was murmuring. "Saffer. What a naughty boy. Still we can't *all* be good all the time like you."

"This is unbearable." Jemima Shore pronounced the word quite distinctly. There was a short silence into which Cherry contributed the diplomatic sentence: "Poor Jem's twisted her ankle coming down this lethal staircase. She's in agony."

"Oh poor *darling!*" The next moment—Jemima never quite knew how it happened—Tiggie had somehow produced a long cashmere scarf from about her person, possibly from around her tiny waist, and easing off Jemima's pale leather boot, had most deftly bound up the swelling ankle.

"Now you've got to have a rest." A faint flush of effort touched Tiggie Jones' pearly white cheeks, allowing Jemima to perceive that much of the whiteness was due to liquid white make-up. "And a glass of champagne. For shock. Proffy will simply have to provide."

Before Jemima could stop her, Tiggie had banged boldly upon Professor Mossbanker's heavily shut door—his sported oak. After a few moments, and a few more bangs, the figure of Professor Mossbanker reappeared. Jemima waited for his wrath to fall. To her surprise, the professor's face actually cleared.

"Antigone, it's you," he said with some warmth. "Did Eugenia get back from Washington last night? I've just read the paper she read in Rome in December at the Conference of Classical and Psychological Studies: Neurosis and Anxiety as depicted in fourth-century Greek vases. Excellent, quite excellent."

But the professor, despite an evident affection for his colleague Professor Eugenia Jones, mother of Antigone, still did not have any champagne. "Alas poor Academe, alas poor Academe," he cried. "And especially poor Proffy! Why don't you try our rich young man upstairs? I could do with a glass myself. Make sure it's cold, won't you?"

But the professor, if he had no champagne, did have a very comfortable sofa, from which he hastened to dump a weight of learned periodicals and papers. Then he sat down on it. Jemima, who had imagined the sofa had been cleared for her, then sat on a much less comfortable chair with a certain wry amusement. It was left to Tiggie to fetch the champagne. It did come from upstairs and was borne down by its owner, the occupant of the top room—none other than Viscount Saffron.

So for the second time that day, and after all too short an interval, Jemima found herself gazing into the handsome, sulky, strangely un-English face of that notorious Oxford Blood, putative subject of a Megalith Television programme.

"Is there going to be a party?" enquired Professor Mossbanker, breaking the slightly embarrassed silence. Even Tiggie now seemed to suspect that Jemima's previous encounter with Saffron had been something of a failure and that had she been present—as hired by Megalith—to perform the introduction it might have gone better. The professor alone amongst them displayed a mixture of elation and curiosity, as though he were an anthropologist about to witness strange tribal rites. Jemima thought it surprising that a don, however remote from reality as the professor appeared to be, should not have had his fill of parties, living as he did on the same staircase as Saffron. Or perhaps scientists—it appeared that Proffy was some kind of scientist rather than an anthropologist—were not invited to parties.

But Tiggie Jones cleared that one up. "Proffy loves parties, don't you? He says he got to like parties in the war when he was a spy. Weren't you, Proffy? Apparently parties are awfully important for spying. But *I* think it's because he's got so many children. He finds parties outside the home rather peaceful compared to life inside Chillington Road. He hates the young, of course, having so many children, but he does love champagne!"

"How many children do you have, Professor Moss-banker?" Jemima was relieved to find some conventional subject on which she could make polite conversation with the man obliged by Tiggie to be her host. At which a look of deep suspicion crossed the professor's face.

"Oh, the usual number, the usual large number," he said quite crossly. "I don't know why people always expect me to have that kind of information at my fingertips. You should ask Eugenia if you're really interested."

"Eleanor," put in Tiggie, blinking her panda eyes. Jemima realized she was trying hard not to giggle. "Eugenia is my mother. Eleanor is your wife."

"Eleanor, I thought I said Eleanor. You confused me, Antigone."

"And Proffy, you have eight children."

"Exactly, the usual large number."

"Amid the wonders of Professor Mossbanker's philopro-geniture, one question remains," remarked Saffron in his

habitually languid manner. "Am I going to open this
champagne here or am I going to carry Jemima Shore
heroically back up the staircase to my rooms? A terrifyingly
macho thought, but I might impress you, Jemima, and then
we could re-create it for television. It would do wonders for
my image, a little tarnished at the moment: you know, the
monkey lord, *Greystoke* and all that, so sweet."

Jemima smiled coldly. She had the feeling she looked
much as the professor had a few moments ago when asked
the exact number of his children.

The next thing she knew, Saffron had whisked her up in
his arms and was carrying her quite fast back up the steep
staircase. He was surprisingly muscular: Jemima, slim as
she was, was tall. Saffron's languid manner and pale
complexion were something of a delusion. Besides, there
had been some sporting equipment about in his rooms,
otherwise more noted for the smell of expensive Rigaud
candles and the sight of empty champagne bottles. Jemima
had noticed a cricket bat in a corner (was it quite the
season, this icy spring?), a tennis racket and a couple of
squash rackets.

"I boxed for my school," murmured Saffron in her ear. "I
always thought it would come in useful."

Back in his rooms, Jemima sat down on another sofa—a
more elegant one this time, covered in a dark green velvet
with a lot of patchwork cushions—and gazed up at him. Yes
he could have been a boxer, once you got over the illusion
of effeminacy, or perhaps decadence was a better word.
Saffron's shoulders were not particularly broad but he was
tall and wasn't that nose slightly flattened out? It was
certainly not the perfect aristocratic shape of her imagination.

Then from her new position on the sofa, she saw
something she had missed on her previous visit. Standing
on the table beside her was a framed photograph, a family
group. The background was a large country house, late
Elizabethan—Saffron Ivy itself. The figure of Lord St. Ives,
so familiar from the newspapers, was easy to recognize, and
the woman next to him with her hand on the head of a large
dog was presumably his wife. But what attracted Jemima's
attention was the figure at the end of the row, a figure

dressed in nurse's uniform; allowing for the time lapse and the harrowing conditions under which she had visited her at the Hospice, she was almost sure that she was gazing once more at the features of Nurse Elsie Connolly.

"Oh, that," said Saffron carelessly, "that's my parents' Silver Wedding. I was four at the time—the happy afterthought. *Very* happy, at least for them. Look, there's my cousin Andrew Iverstone—you know, the famous Fascist beast, looking sick as mud at my mere existence. Sixteen years later he still hasn't forgiven me for being a boy. And Cousin Daphne."

"Who's the other boy holding your hand? He looks a little older."

Saffron sounded even more cheerful. "Oh that's my cousin, Jack Iverstone, Cousin Andrew's son. He would be looking forward to getting the lot if it wasn't for me. He's at Oxford too, as a matter of fact. In his last year."

"And does he hate your guts as well?"

"Christ, no. Jack doesn't hate anyone's guts. He's a member of the SDP and it doesn't go with gut-hating. Pure reaction against Cousin Andrew of course. With parents like that, *you* would be a member of the SDP."

Jemima forbore to say that she had indeed flirted with the possibility not so many years ago, before returning to her traditional Labour stance—and without Jack Iverstone's excuse. Instead she asked: "And the woman at the end of the row, the nurse?"

There was a tiny pause, so brief that Jemima even wondered afterwards whether she had imagined it.

"Oh, that was someone, an old retainer if you like, she used to be around a lot in my childhood; my mother was quite ill after I was born, quite depressed I believe, despite the Super-Happy event; something to do with her age I dare say."

"And is she still around? The nurse. I mean, we could interview her," Jemima improvised. "Part of your privileged background. A live-in nurse at the age of twenty."

"Privileged! Nurse Elsie . . . You have to be joking."

Saffron had abandoned his usual languid tone for a kind of bitter briskness, "No, as a matter of fact, she's dead. Died the other day. Of cancer. I went to see her. It was horrible.

Very upsetting. My mother forced me to go and see her. The trouble with my mother, she's a saint, and she expects everyone to do likewise. Only its no trouble to her, and a great deal of trouble to the rest of us. In short I wish I hadn't gone, for any number of reasons, and if Ma hadn't bullied me I would have got out of it altogether because Nurse Elsie died suddenly the day after I visited her.

"As if there weren't enough members of my family crowding about her anyway," he went on. "Nurse Elsie produced my cousins as well as gorgeous me; in fact her invaluable attentions were about the only thing Cousin Daphne Iverstone and my mother had in common, and they both competed in being sentimental about her. So if Cousin Daphne went, Ma had to go, and if Jack and Fanny went to say the final goodbye, I had to go. What rubbish. Nothing to do with death."

In spite of all her good resolutions, Jemima found herself feeling both excited and apprehensive. For the first time that day, young Lord Saffron had genuinely engaged her attention. She was determined not to let the opportunity drop, determined not to return to the tedious (to her) subject of his luxurious Oxford life-style. She was wondering how to frame her next question when she heard hurried footsteps on the stairs. Expecting either Tiggie or perhaps Cherry mounting a rescue operation, Jemima saw instead a tall, thin young man whose appearance was so essentially English that you could have mounted his photograph as a travel poster. With curly brown hair, rather small blue eyes, a longish nose and high healthy colour, the stranger had the air of an eighteenth-century gentleman, except for his clothes which were distinctly modern—jeans and a baggy brown jersey over a check shirt. He also had a pile of books under his arm.

"At the champagne already, I see, Saffer—" Then the stranger noticed Jemima and paused.

"Miss Jemima Shore," said Saffron in a silky voice. "May I introduce my cousin Jack Iverstone? He probably wants me to subscribe to something thoroughly decent. In which case I shall refuse. He also comes fresh from a lecture by the look of him which always has a deplorable effect on the temper."

"Oh don't be so affected, Saffer," said a girl's clear voice from the doorway. "As if you'd ever been *near* a lecture. Good afternoon, Miss Shore, I'm a great admirer of your work, particularly that programme *The Pill—For or Against*? It certainly needed saying. Why should we all drop dead for the sake of some international chemists? Now listen Saffer, you've got to come and have lunch with us. Oh, I'm Saffer's cousin, Fanny Iverstone, by the way, Miss Shore. You see, Saffer, Mummy's come down to talk to Jack about his wicked political views—or wicked according to her and Daddy. We thought you would distract her—"

"Certainly *not!*" exclaimed Saffron. "This is going too far, even for you, Fanny. You out-boss Mrs. Thatcher sometimes, besides not being nearly so pretty. *I* am having lunch with Jemima Shore. She's going to do wonders for my image on television."

Fanny Iverstone turned her eyes—clear blue like her brother's—on Jemima Shore. In other ways too, she was like a girlish version of Jack Iverstone, Jemima thought, with her fresh complexion plus a few freckles, paler pink cheeks, and shoulder-length curly brown hair tied at the back with a bow. Her expression, however, was not particularly girlish.

"Miss Shore!" cried Fanny. "Now why don't *you* have lunch with all of us? We're having lunch at *La Lycée*, in any case wonderful material for your programme—anybody who can afford the Lycée mid-week has to be a golden lad or laddess."

Jemima noted that Fanny Iverstone knew all about her programme. She was coming to the conclusion that everybody in Oxford knew everything they cared to know about anything they cared to know about. Which left a good deal unknown.

"Which college are you at, Fanny?" she asked politely. Although not suitable for the "Golden Lads" programme—there was something far too sensible about Fanny, even her clothes were quite sensible—her remark about Jemima's previous series had struck an agreeable chord. Maybe when Jemima had researched the "Golden Lads" sufficiently, and assured Cy it would not make an interesting programme, she could return to Oxford and make something of this new intelligent generation of women undergraduates, the post-Brideshead types, living in colleges in equal numbers and on equal terms with the men. Fanny Iverstone would be most suitable material for that.

"Good heavens, I'm not *at* Oxford," exclaimed Fanny cheerfully, shattering this dream. "At the school Mummy sent me to, they raised a cheer if you got a couple of O-levels, let alone A-levels. No, I'm doing shorthand typing at Mrs. Bone's."

"All the same Fanny *is* at Oxford," commented Jack. "Wherever Fanny *is*, she's *at*."

"I'm looking after my little brother!" Jemima thought Fanny was probably not being ironic. "And my little cousin too," she went on in the same fond voice, "except that's impossible."

Then Fanny returned to a more bracing tone.

"Come on, Jemima—may I call you that? I've seen you so often on the telly. Do come to lunch. Mummy's not nearly as terrible as the Press make out. And then she simply adores Saffer here; it's her dreadful snobbishness I fear, the future head of the family and all that. *She* doesn't object to his wicked ways one bit. Unlike us."

And yet Saffron was convinced that Daphne Iverstone's husband Andrew hated him, thought Jemima, if not on the surface at least deep down. Had hated him since birth. Did Daphne Iverstone really not resent Saffron's late appearance in the family tree? Out of curiosity about the Iverstone family rather than some finer professional instinct towards the programme, Jemima accepted the invitation to, lunch. At all events it would be a relief to leave Staircase Thirteen, with its slightly sinister atmosphere, for the peace of a comfortable restaurant.

CHAPTER FIVE

•

Fight Before the Death

In the course of lunch Jemima decided that Fanny Iverstone was wrong. Mrs. Andrew Iverstone was worse, really much worse than the Press made out. What made her worse was not the nature of her neo-racialist politics, which seemed to have been fairly accurately reported, but the odious whimsicality with which she presented them. There were references to "horrid freezing old England" and the "sweet negroes, why do they want to come here and get pneumonia, the poor darlings? I wish someone would give *me* a lot of lovely money to go to Jamaica."

"Blacks, Mummy." Jack Iverstone looked at his plate as he spoke. "Blacks, Mummy, not negroes."

"I know, darling, I know. And I know you have lots of lovely friends like that. That marvellous cricketer. But that's different. You can't compare someone who looks divine in white flannels, someone at *Oxford*, with some illiterate monkey straight off—"

She's going to say it, thought Jemima, she's going to say, straight off the trees. I don't believe it. In 1985, in so-called civilized society. Then Fanny Iverstone saved the day as Jemima suspected she had done on more than one occasion.

"Oh come on, Mummy," she said brightly. "You know how you loved going to India and staying with that Maharajah. Didn't you and Daddy go tiger-hunting on your honeymoon?" This certainly had the effect of stopping Mrs. Iverstone in her tracks and changing her tone from one of persistent whimsicality to that of nostalgia, even tenderness.

"Ah but Sonny Mekwar was different, quite different. A thousand years of breeding went into that man. You knew it immediately you saw him play polo for example. Such an aristocrat. Some of those Maharajahs go back almost as far as the Iverstones, you know."

"Crooks and robbers. Successful crooks." Jack spoke as before, looking at his plate.

"What was that, my love?" Jemima thought she detected a sharper note beneath Mrs. Iverstone's honeyed sweetness.

"I was referring to the early history of the Iverstone family. I thought you were too. The first Iverstones were robber barons who managed to terrorize their neighbours in East Anglia sufficiently to acquire large amounts of land . . ."

Throughout this conversation, Saffron had remained quite silent, occasionally eyeing Tiggie Jones. The latter had insisted on joining the lunch party in her usual imperious fashion on the grounds that she had been sent down to Oxford by Megalith in order to accompany Jemima Shore, and could not desert her.

"I'm your *chaperone*, Jemima," Tiggie had said with a roll of her eyes. "I can't let Saffer just abduct you and not protest." That however was not the full extent of her interference with the lunch arrangements. When Tiggie discovered that the party would be at least two men short, she promptly roped in Professor Mossbanker. He was now having an earnest conversation with Cherry about classical ethics in the television world, a subject on which Cherry was enchanted to give her views, having unaccountably never been asked before. To Jemima's expert eye, the professor was very promising Cherry-material, being sufficiently advanced in years, and certainly substantial, if you counted an Oxford professorship; which Jemima guessed Cherry, distracted from the Dukes, now would. The father of eight children was certainly substantial, in some sense of the word.

Then Tiggie had routed out Saffron's neighbour at the top of the staircase, a dark-haired young man, not unlike

Saffron himself in build and type, if less handsome, whose name no one (except presumably Saffron) seemed to know. At least the unknown had a large appetite. Jemima asked his name and, between mouthfuls, the unknown said something that sounded like "Bim." After that she let him get on with his food.

But the unknown's appetite prompted Jemima to wonder: who was paying the bill for this large lunch party at Oxford's most expensive restaurant? If the answer was Megalith Television, then the idea of paying for Daphne Iverstone's lunch stuck in her gullet. On the other hand it seemed unfair—at least by normal standards—to make Daphne Iverstone pay a huge bill for what had originally been a family lunch party, whatever her political views.

The question was suddenly solved.

In the middle of the conversation, Saffron stood up. He did so before the unknown "Bim" had finished his double ice-cream (Professor Mossbanker, the other sweet-eater, had eaten very fast, so fast in fact that his spoon had on occasion been seen to skim an extra scoop of ice-cream off his neighbour's plate).

"All this talk of ancestors is so terribly exhausting, it reminds me that I simply must go and have a sleep before my tutorial at five. No better preparation, don't you think? A fresh mind and all that."

"No essay again, Saffer?" But Jack Iverstone sounded indulgent as well as reproachful.

"My dear Jack! You know I've been in London for days. . . . My magic moment in court left me with an urgent need to recover. Then I had to go home to pacify Pa and Ma. Adieu, one and all. Oh and by the way, Cousin Daphne, don't worry about the bill. I've signed it. Nobility obliges."

Lord Saffron sauntered off. Jemima watched his retreating back. Reluctantly, she had to admit that he had a certain style. To her annoyance, however, she still had not the faintest inkling whether Daphne Iverstone loathed or adored the boy who had dispossessed the claims of her own husband—and son—to inherit Saffron Ivy. To that extent, the lunch had been a failure, since Daphne Iverstone had been too busy discoursing on race to address Saffron, and he had been too busy gazing at Tiggie Jones. So much for her famous detective instinct. This meditation was interrupted by a very loud clear voice somewhere at the front of the restaurant.

"There goes Saffer, the biggest shit in Oxford," said the voice.

Lord Saffron's steps did not falter.

"There goes Saffer the Shit," repeated the voice. "Come on, aren't you going to break up this restaurant too? And then pay up with Daddy's money?"

Jemima now focussed on a table at the front of the restaurant, to be compared with their own in size, except that all those sitting at it were apparently young. There was no Daphne Iverstone figure, let alone a Professor Mossbanker. The most noticeable figure—because of his remarkable colouring—was a young man with a shock of violently red hair, and an accompanying pallor which was almost morbid. He reminded Jemima, still in her pre-Raphaelite mood, of the dying poet Thomas Chatterton in Wallis's portrait. Oddly enough, the girl next to him was also red-haired, but the colour more russet, the pallor less pronounced. The man next to her was also striking, not so much through his colouring but because he was exceptionally big; the huge shoulders and thick short neck of a rugger player, or at least that was the impression he gave.

"Rufus Pember," Fanny Iverstone spoke with something like a groan, "and that frightful heavy of his, Big Nigel Copley. Worst of all, Little Miss Muffet Pember is along as well. *Now* what's going to happen?"

Afterwards Jemima found it difficult to remember exactly what did happen, or rather the order in which it happened. Did Saffron turn and hit Rufus Pember first? Or was the whole fight set off by Tiggie Jones, who scurried to the distant table, surprisingly fast on her tottering high heels, and slapped Rufus Pember in the face? At all events, both blows were certainly struck, followed by other blows, as Big Nigel Copley lurched and blundered to his feet, revealing his breadth to be fully matched by his height. And at some point the innocent Bim got involved, cheered on by Tiggie but receiving quite a lot of punishment at the hands of Big Nigel as a result.

Jemima found herself watching the faces of the group at her table. Daphne Iverstone's prim little face—she had incongruously rosebud looks, a rosebud faded and dried up with the years but still recognizable for what it was—looked ardent, excited. As Saffron felled Rufus Pember, who fell with a crash on a nearby table, sending glass and forks flying, Daphne Iverstone gave a kind of sigh. She certainly did not hate Saffron even if her husband did. This looked more like the adoration to which her daughter Fanny referred.

Fanny herself had an air of weary tolerance as though she had witnessed plenty of such incidents among undergraduates in expensive Oxford restaurants (as no doubt she had). Cherry screamed and clutched Professor Mossbanker's hand, a situation he accepted with equanimity, patting the little hand briefly before pouring on with his conversation. His own participation in the proceedings was limited to the expression "tribal rites" which he repeated several times with evident satisfaction, before returning to his dissertation on wartime parties at the Dorchester, on their importance in bringing to an end all proper Anglo-American understanding.

Only Jack Iverstone looked absolutely horrified at what was happening. After a minute he jumped up, crying something like: "Why *will* he do it?" and then "For Christ's sake, Saffer." So saying he rushed over to the fray, which was being watched helplessly by two young French waiters, definitely too slight to deal with the burly figures of the contestants. Tiggie herself had by this time retired to the sidelines, or rather the lap of one of the other lunchers not involved in the fracas—one could only assume he was a previous acquaintance as Tiggie seemed much at home in her situation, sucking her finger and cheering on Saffron. Saffron himself, in spite of the blows landed on Rufus Pember, was beginning to get very much the worst of it at the hands of the huge Copley, while Bim remained prone on the floor.

"It's disgusting!" said a woman in a brown velvet hat very loudly at the table next to Jemima's. "Why doesn't someone do something? We haven't come here to watch a fight."

"They should all be sent into the Army," remarked her companion, a middle-aged man, grimly. "These young fellows need a good sergeant-major to take the stuffing out of them. When National Service ended—criminal, I said so at the time—" Jemima stopped listening, but not before the woman in the brown velvet hat had contributed something about the waste of taxpayers' money.

It was Jack Iverstone in fact who ended the fight, ended it just as the proprietor—a very small and very angry Frenchman—announced his intention of sending for the police. With admirable courage, Jack pushed his way between the contestants and put his hand on his cousin's chest.

"You bloody fool, Saffer. Do you want to be sent down?"

Saffron stared back, dishevelled, panting, and said nothing.

"Do you want to make the headlines in the *Post* every day?" went on Jack.

"Come on then, man," said Saffron after a minute, in an approximation of his usual languid manner, inhibited by breathlessness, "let's leave this unholy mess. Oh yes, yes, I'll pay—" thrown in the direction of the proprietor "—Viscount Saffron, Rochester College."

Staggering slightly, but with his shoulders squared, Saffron headed for the stairs as though the mess of wine and glass and food he left behind him simply did not exist. Jack Iverstone hesitated, looked round where his party still sat, stunned, at their table, and then went after Saffron.

"See you later, Saffer!" called out the man named Bim suddenly from the floor.

"See you in Hell!" shouted a voice from the rival table. Was it Rufus Pember or the enormous Nigel Copley? Or one of the others at the table who, to do them credit, had not joined in the affray. "We'll get you, you—" a stream of obscenities followed. "And when we get you, Saffer, there won't be anything to help you, not Daddy's money, not *The Tatler*, nor the Queen."

"Aren't they terrible?" Daphne Iverstone's voice cut sweetly across the invective, like some light soprano joining a bass ensemble. "I don't think people like that should be allowed to eat in good restaurants, do you, Miss Shore?

Poor darling Saffer. He's led a very sheltered life, you know, with such elderly parents, wonderful people of course, but so old when he was born. He was terribly protected. I did try to warn Gwendolen. I wonder if he was quite *ready* for Oxford."

There was a sublimity about Mrs. Iverstone's blindness to her young cousin's failings—well, almost a sublimity. No question but that she adored him. No question also but that there were a great many other people presently within Oxford who did not.

The lunch party—what there was left of it—dispersed. Jemima came upon Jack Iverstone unlocking his bicycle from a nearby railing as she left the restaurant. Saffron had vanished.

"Are you going back to Rochester?" she asked.

"No, to the Bodleian," he answered rather shortly. Then as if to apologize for a temporary lapse in courtesy, he added with a smile: "The Bodleian is a wonderful cure for bad temper." Then: "So what did you think of Rochester, Miss Shore?"

"It's a beautiful college. Architecturally."

"Oh quite. I'm at St. Lucy's myself." And Jack Iverstone rode away on his bicycle.

That night anyone within Rochester gazing at Hawksmoor's exquisite façade would have seen one patch of darkness among the lighted archways: Staircase Thirteen alone was not illuminated by an overhead light inside the arch. The impression given by this dark gap might have been mysterious and even slightly sinister. Unless a watcher reflected that a missing light bulb, far from being an abnormal phenomenon in the archway of an Oxford college, was in fact nothing out of the ordinary, given the relative durability of light bulbs and the lack of housekeeperly attention to detail in such surroundings.

It was silent on Staircase Thirteen. Visitors were not admitted to Rochester after 11:30 P.M. (although no check was made as to whether all the many visitors freely admitted throughout the day had actually left). Rochester's own undergraduates and dons were of course at liberty to move freely about the college, its two main quadrangles and the newly built library all night if they so pleased. The library, a recent gift of a rich Turk, reposed beyond the Hawksmoor quadrangle, all glass and steel, looking like some vast beached ship or ark which had sailed into classical Oxford on some vast flood tide, and been deposited there unable to float away again. There were still lights burning in the library.

After a while the wooden steps of Staircase Thirteen creaked a little as though someone was ascending. But then the steps creaked sometimes of their own accord when there was no one there at all. When a door opened on the top landing, the noise was considerable. Saffron's voice, indistinct, and his characteristic arrogant laugh could be heard. Tiggie Jones' voice was higher and clearer. She was laughing too, though giggling might be a better word. Tiggie was saying something like: "Oh Saffer, don't, don't be a naughty boy." There was scuffling and more laughing. The door shut.

Then there were footsteps, heavy footsteps, descending.

After that, there was a gasp, a stifled cry or shout, then a heavy protracted crash, as of a body rolling over and over down a staircase. Then there was complete silence.

Nothing happened at all. No door opened on the various landings. Professor Mossbanker's door remained shut, which was just as well for something which looked horribly inert and lifeless lay right across it, and it was doubtful that the professor could have managed to open it in any case.

After about five minutes the creakings resumed. Someone was coming very carefully and softly indeed down the stairs. There was a noise as of a body being dragged down the stairs to the basement.

A few minutes later the deep cyclical hum of a washing machine was heard from the depths of the building, the noise loud and sepulchral in the night silence.

The washing machine continued to revolve ardently, but its noise could not of course wake the dead man lying beside it. It was not until sometime later that Professor Mossbanker, in the absence of lights, stumbled down to the basement. In the darkness of the launderette the light of the machine glowed at him. He stood staring at it for quite a long time, as if not quite comprehending what he saw.

Then he bent over the dark shape at his feet, much as the prowler had done earlier.

Professor Mossbanker gave a deep sigh, or something more like a sob than a sigh.

CHAPTER SIX

•

No Long Shadows

The police came to the conclusion that Bevis Ian Marcus (known to his friends as Bim) had died as a result of a late night fall down a steep staircase in Rochester College.

The nickname "Bim" was not actually used by anyone at the inquest. It would have doubtless seemed too cosy, too intimate for such a grim occasion as an inquest on a twenty-year-old undergraduate who had broken his neck following some kind of party. Those who gave evidence included Miss Antigone Rose Jones, twenty-three, of Launceston Place, SW, Saffron Ivo Charles Iverstone, commonly known as Viscount Saffron, twenty, of Rochester College, and Professor Claud Lionel Mossbanker, of Chillington Road, North Oxford. Sundry other undergraduates, female as well as male, who had seen Bevis Ian Marcus on the last evening of his life gave evidence. These undergraduates rather self-consciously also referred to him as Bevis, since that was what the coroner called him. One of the girls, who was at Rochester, sobbed a bit, thinking how Bim had hated the name, virtually denying its existence, pretending his real name was something like Brian, and how he would have hated the coroner announcing it like that, so persistently, for all the world to hear.

But then the girl, Magdalen Mary Irina Poliakoff, twenty, (known to her friends as Magda), was already tremulous with guilt over the death of Bim. It was her belief that if she had not rejected Bim's invitation to the cinema on the grounds that she had an essay to write, he, Bim, would not have fallen down the fatal Staircase Thirteen.

Magda Poliakoff needed little prompting to share this feeling of guilt with the coroner.

"But in any case you thought he was drunk?" asked the coroner, a doctor with a cynical view of the drinking habits of undergraduates. "Quite apart from the question of your work, Miss Poliakoff, the real reason he turned you off, as you have just put it, the deceased that is, was because he had been drinking. Drinking, in your opinion, all day."

"Since lunch," and Magda Poliakoff shot a defiant look at Saffer and Tiggie Jones sitting on the opposite side of the small court room. "She—whoever she is—forced him to go to lunch, actually put her arm round his neck, pulled him away. I mean I was just sitting there when it happened. And then of course—well, you know what *he's* like—" She transferred her trembling but still venomous gaze to Saffron! "Er—*Bevis* wasn't like that. Like them. He was jolly poor. And he worked jolly hard. Most of the time, anyway. If only he hadn't been on the same staircase as *Lord* Saffron. People like him shouldn't be allowed places at university when there are plenty of other people—"

"Now Miss Poliakoff," said the doctor firmly but kindly. "We are here to establish the truth about Bevis Marcus' death, if we can, not to discuss the merits or otherwise of the admissions policy of the University." He paused and then went on: "Can I take it then, Miss Poliakoff, that by 7 P.M., Mr. Marcus was in your opinion too drunk to know what he was doing?"

It was the question of the bruises as Jemima reported to Cass Brinsley later that day, sitting in their favourite local restaurant, Monsieur Thompson's, in the dell at the end of Kensington Park Road.

"Certainly he died of a broken neck caused by a fall. The medical evidence is quite clear on that point. But what caused the fall? Was there a fight? At the top of the staircase causing the fall. But of course Bim had had some kind of punch-up, totally drunk, earlier in the day. The police are satisfied it was an accident. A tragic—but not atypical—undergraduate accident, they called it. No second fight."

"Saffron denied it strongly," Cass pointed out. "And Miss Tiggie Jones—my God, what a sexy-looking girl! Are those eyelashes real?—Miss Tiggie backed him up. They finished drinking, because they finished the last bottle of champagne, no less, and Bim stumbled away—Saffer's words—to his own room—as they supposed. Shall I ever meet her, do you suppose?"

"I very much doubt it." Jemima sounded cold. "Since I hope not to meet her again myself. And I doubt whether Tiggie Jones features a great deal in Lincoln's Inn Fields, wandering about on her own, singing a happy song."

"Ah well. The point is, does that mean she's a liar as well?"

"To be fair, not necessarily," said Jemima who saw herself as someone who always did try to be fair. "It was all very mysterious as well as tragic. But the coroner was sufficiently satisfied to go for accidental death."

"As you know, Professor Mossbanker, or Proffy, as your beguiling friend Miss Tiggie calls him, found the body in the middle of the night, having been aroused by the noise of what he called the infernal washing machine. Apparently he's always carrying on about the noise it made if used late at night. A few minutes later—he was very clear about it—Saffer accompanied by Tiggie came *down* the staircase. Of course she shouldn't have been in the college so late, but under the circumstances the professor wasn't going to complain. In any case, everybody at Oxford seems to turn a blind eye to that kind of thing these days, officially that is. Their story was that Tiggie wanted to go to the loo on the ground floor and Saffer was escorting her."

"A likely story?" queried Cass.

"Not altogether unlikely, given the lack of bathrooms and loos in the former all-male colleges at Oxford. I've never seen such squalor. That's one advantage we had in all-women's colleges, bathrooms; but I digress. Not an altogether unlikely story. Look at it like this. If Saffron had really had a fight with the unfortunate Bim, thrown him or caused him to fall down the staircase, I can't believe he would have waited till he heard Proffy emerge, and then come down the stairs plus Miss T. He would either have tried to help straightaway, the decent reaction, or kept well clear of the proceedings altogether."

"Then there's the whole question of Miss Tiggie and the fight, isn't there?" pursued Cass, pouring Sancerre purposefully into his own glass, and after a gentle reminder into Jemima's too. (As Cass normally had excellent manners, Jemima privately put this aberration down to distracting thoughts of Tiggie Jones.) "I may be prejudiced in her favour by her eyelashes," went on Cass, unaware of these cross reflections, "but supposing Bim did fall or was pushed down the staircase in Saffer's presence, would Tiggie really have let him calmly return to his own room, leaving Bim in a crumpled heap at the bottom, right at the bottom, in the launderette?"

"I'm not so prejudiced that I can't agree to that," Jemima was sipping away happily at her refilled glass. "She'd have swooped down on him like some dreadful little bat and given him some terrifyingly predatory form of First Aid. However that's not the real mystery. The real mystery to me is why Bim Marcus set the washing machine in motion. The police think he was badly concussed. Crawled there, set it in motion and then died. It's still odd. But concussion—and alcohol—does odd things to you."

"Interested in this investigation, darling?" Cass was only half teasing. When Jemima's unofficial criminal investigations took over from her official sociological ones for Megalith, she was apt to have even less time for Cass for a month or two: Cass Brinsley, finding himself for some reason put in mind of the big black eyes and long black eyelashes of Tiggie Jones, thought he would like to have notice of an extended period of absence on Jemima's part. To give such notice was not exactly in their (unspoken) contract of a liberated relationship; any more than Cass had given Jemima notice of finding Flora Hereford, the new pupil in his Chambers, astonishingly attractive.

Jemima however had somehow suspected it and reacted by having a devil-may-care affair with a handsome cameraman at Megalith. Well, she was not called Jemima Shore Investigator for nothing. Sometimes Cass even wondered whether some more permanent arrangement might give him yet more joy, much less heartache. In what should such an arrangement consist? There was one obvious kind of arrangement. . . . Cass, wryly certain that such a thought had never crossed Jemima's own mind, put it resolutely from his own.

"I'm interested in the investigation, yes," Jemima, blithely unaware, cut across his thoughts. "The nurse's story grabbed me from the start, as you know. I'm not talking about exposure here, of course: Saffron's secret is safe with me, if it is his secret. But I can't rid myself of a feeling—my famous instinct rears its head here—that it's not altogether a coincidence that Bim Marcus died on Saffron's staircase, as a result of a quite unforeseen association with Saffron. They weren't even friends. Tiggie pushed Bim into the party. The police won't buy it— evidence not instinct is what we are after, my dear, as Detective Chief Inspector Gary Harwood of the Oxford CID informed me—but I'm privately wondering whether the right man actually fell down that winding staircase. Let's just suppose someone thought *Saffron* was lurching down to his room, and instead got the wretched Bim in the darkness—the two men were quite alike in an odd way, the same height and build—then we have to think of anyone who would wish Saffron ill. Quite a few in Oxford no doubt, though murder is perhaps going a bit far. What is more, if Saffron is or rather was the target, *that* brings us back to Nurse Elsie's death bed revelation," concluded Jemima triumphantly.

"I follow your argument about Bim and Saffron on the stairs. You mean, no one could have expected Bim to be up at that time? But I still don't get the Nurse Elsie connection."

"Don't you *see*, darling? I know you think I'm obsessed with Nurse Elsie—instinct again, and you feel about my instinct roughly as does Detective Chief Inspector Harwood—"

"Not all your instincts," interposed Cass mildly.

Jemima paid no attention but swept enthusiastically on. "Don't you see that Nurse Elsie revealed Saffron to be a kind of changeling, the happy accident, whose appearance, late in his parents' life, did horrible Andrew Iverstone and horrible Daphne Iverstone out of their inheritance? And by implication, that nice fellow Jack, I have to admit. That's a lot of enemies. Saffron is not married, has no children; if he died on that staircase, Andrew, and in the course of time Jack, would still inherit Saffron Ivy."

"That's true whether Saffron is a changeling or not," pointed out Cass.

Jemima sighed.

"I know. I have to say that I still don't get the connection. I just think there *is* a connection between Nurse Elsie and the Rochester College death. For one thing, there were so many of the Iverstone family at the Hospice those last days—quite out of the blue. Saffron himself revealed that he'd been there, and Daphne Iverstone, she was there too. From what Sister Imelda said, I think she came on the last day of all. She referred to another old friend, 'One of Nurse Elsie's ladies,' and that could have been Daphne. Then there were the Iverstone brother and sister."

"So what is the next step, Jemima Shore Investigator?"

"Oh, to forget it all," responded Jemima. "What else?"

Jemima Shore, while she was as good as her word for the rest of the evening and night, found herself rapidly reminded of Rochester College at Megalith Television the next morning. This was because she received a letter. The envelope was fairly undistinguished other than that it bore the crest of Rochester College, Oxford; this revealed the foundation to be something vaguely episcopal and not, as Jemima had romantically supposed, connected to the poet Rochester. The quality of the envelope was thin and white. The writing paper within was, on the other hand, nothing if not distinguished.

To begin with, the paper was so thick as to give the momentary illusion of parchment, and its very thickness brought a glow in the tint of the ivory. Then there were great curly black swirls in the address, which was so heavily engraved that the letters positively stood out from the paper. Luckily the address itself could afford to be inscribed in this lavish fashion since it scarcely constituted a space problem. The address read simply: SAFFRON IVY. There was no mention of a neighbouring town, not even a county, let alone anything as common as a postal code (or telephone number).

Jemima read on with interest. That very morning a conference had taken place at Megalith in which she had utterly failed to shift Cy Fredericks from his profound conviction that, as he put it, "these Golden Kids are Big

Bucks, and I don't mean our expenses, I mean our sales. Have you seen the Brideshead figures? We can make Brideshead look like peanuts. They were just a bunch of actors. We've got the real thing." So discussions about the "Golden Lads and Girls" programme meandered on; no scheduling as yet, apart from a general feeling that summer was the time to get to grips with that kind of thing. "Girls in long dresses, nothing punk. And those long boats," murmured Cy, lowering his voice for once, as if in deference to the scene he was summoning before their eyes. "Punts," suggested someone helpfully. "Nothing punk," repeated Cy with a wild glare in the direction of the speaker before continuing: "Long shadows across the July grass. No long shadows across their future, these are Golden Kids— remember, Miss Lewis, make a note of that line—*no long shadows—*"

"Long dresses, long boats, long shadows, I mean, *no* long shadows," murmured Guthrie Carlyle, Jemima's old friend and potential director of this epic. "Will it be a long programme to match?"

"What's that, Guthrie?" asked Cy Fredericks sharply. One could never count on Cy's total absorption in his own flow of words, reflected Jemima, especially if there was any hint of disloyalty in the room. Cy had uncanny hearing for disloyal echoes. "The programme, like all Megalith programmes, will be exactly the right length," he swept on, "not a minute more or less. And I mean *artistic length.*" He looked round as if to ask Miss Lewis to inscribe that thought too on her tablets, but by now more exciting matters called, and Miss Lewis had vanished to sort out a flurry of messages from New York.

The main result of the conference was to rechristen the programme "Golden Kids." This was to avoid the possible charge of sexism implicit in Shakespeare's line, which by placing the word "Lads" before "Girls" might be held to suggest that the "Girls" were mere appendages to the "Lads." Guthrie had in fact floated this suggestion as a joke, but finding it enthusiastically endorsed by Cy (who was always desperate to avoid sexism, if only he could put his finger on what it was) Guthrie quickly took the opportunity to atone for his previous levity by proposing it in earnest.

"How about 'Oxford Bloods'?" suggested Jemima at one point, "or even 'Bloody Oxford'."

"Jem," said Cy reproachfully, "I had expected better from you. This is not a bloody programme."

So "Golden Kids" it was. Everyone felt a good deal of progress had been made, and as Cy had to leave for Rome—or as he absent-mindedly described it, New York, until Miss Lewis coughed and corrected him—the meeting broke up.

Jemima was left wondering whether she should have pointed out that the Oxford academic term ended in June. In July, the long shadows in Oxford would be falling on innumerable tourists, while the Golden Kids played elsewhere, departing in long aeroplanes for the long shores of the Mediterranean, the Far East and the United States.

She now gazed at the short note beneath the ornate Saffron Ivy address and thought that under the circumstances a polite invitation from Lord Saffron to lunch in Oxford was not unwelcome.

"Ooh, watch it Jemima," was Cherry's reaction. "Supposing he sports that oak thing once you're up there."

"I shall of course ask him to keep his oak thing to himself," replied Jemima sweetly. "In any case I intend to direct operations from a suite at the Martyrs Hotel. Could you be an angel and book it for me? A nice large suite, so that Lord Saffron and others can keep their distance. Megalith owes me a nice large suite for working on 'Golden Kids.' And get onto that man, what's his name, that don who went on television the other night calling for more compulsory admissions from comprehensive schools in arts subjects—what *was* his name? Barber or something similar. He's got this campaign called COMPCAMP. I'm not going to let 'Golden Kids' get by without a suitable class struggle."

Jemima was reminded of these bold words a few days later when she found herself sitting with Saffron at lunch in what was in fact a very small and unfashionable restaurant off the Broad.

"For some reason my name is mud in most Oxford restaurants," explained Saffron plaintively; he also fluttered his eyelashes in a flirtatious way which, whether joking or not, for a moment reminded Jemima of Tiggie Jones. "And as you know the Martyrs have banned me for my lifetime, or their lifetime, whichever shall be longer. I feel the Lycée won't give me the big hand in future. Luckily when I came here before, I had the wit to book myself in as Colonel Gadaffi and they haven't twigged yet, beyond thinking I'm rather young for a military man. Alas, I can't even set foot in your lovely suite, I fear. I could shin up those pillars, I suppose, and lope in through your balcony. You have *got* a balcony? Looking on the Broad—looking *at* the Martyrs Memorial, oh that's the best one. What a relief. Anyway so far as I am concerned, life at Oxford is just one class struggle."

Jemima, in spite of herself, had to laugh. But Saffron merely pressed her hand.

"No, I do so understand what Marx meant. The class struggle! When will it ever end? I ask myself. Only the other day Tiggie and I and a few others took ourselves off to the Highgate cemetery to visit the dear fellow's grave. Vodka and Blinis were judged appropriate, though as Poppy Delaware pointed out, who is a Marxist, albeit a Catholic one, something German like beer and bratwurst would really have been more appropriate. Ah, Marx! What a prophet. It's seldom a day I don't think about him, as one tries bravely to keep one's head *above* beer and bratwurst, with due respect to Poppy."

Saffron, presumably with this admirable objective in view, had ordered champagne on arrival, what he described to an unsurprised waitress in smock and jeans as the Colonel's special. Now he poured it yet again (he was, Jemima noticed, an attentive host; perhaps all the Oxford Bloods were, since they were used to playing the role to each other; or perhaps Saffron had been trained to it since childhood by his parents).

"As if I didn't have enough to contend with, what with the class struggle and beer," Saffron continued in the same genial voice, "on top of it all, somebody round here is trying to kill me."

CHAPTER SEVEN

•

Blood Isn't Everything

"Look, Jemima, I'm going to hire you. That's the point. What are your rates? You're going to find out who's trying to kill me. It would also be quite nice in an off-beat kind of way to know why. Who would want to kill poor little me?" Again Saffron's look of mock innocence reminded Jemima of Tiggie Jones. She did not mention that fact to Cass Brinsley, to whom she related the conversation later that day by telephone. I don't want to inflame him further, thought Jemima sternly. In any case, what Jemima did relate was quite enough for Cass to be getting on with.

"And you let him?" gasped Cass incredulously. "You let him hire you? As his own personal private investigator. May one enquire the price?"

"You may," answered Jemima. "We've struck a bargain. If I discover what's going on, he's going to give a huge donation to the Radical Women's Settlement for Single Drop-Outs. If I fail, he gets to take me to Ascot."

"Why the Radical Women's Settlement? That's the one you filmed in January, I take it."

"To be honest, I thought it was the cause he would most dislike," replied Jemima. "Originally I considered CND, but unfortunately he actually supports it, although for all the wrong reasons. He told me the noise of the American bombers from the aerodrome near Saffron Ivy disturbs the sweetness of his slumbers. Of course, it's a good thing he supports it," Jemima added hastily. "But you see what I mean about it being annoying."

"Quite," said Cass who was a multilateralist.

"The real point, darling, is that I am not properly enthusiastic about 'Golden Kids'—even if *my* reasons are all the wrong ones," went on Jemima. "All the reccying I'm doing, interviews with absolutely everyone in Oxford including dons from Professor Mossbanker whom I adore to Kerry Barber whom I'm hoping to adore because he's so worthy, it's all now a cover. So naturally I feel much better about it."

Although Jemima had worked out for herself that the killer—accidental or otherwise—of Bim Marcus had probably been aiming at Saffron, she was taken aback to find that Saffron himself had made the same calculations and come to the same conclusion. An intelligent and quick-witted Saffron was not quite what she had expected to find. Still less had she anticipated finding him sympathetic. Yet away from his friends, the newspapers, away from his *public*, one might almost have said that sympathetic was what Saffron was. The poses were dropped. And the story he unfolded was in itself sufficiently startling and upsetting to deserve some sympathy in its own right.

"Someone's trying to kill me," he repeated. "At first I couldn't take it in. The brakes failed on my car. Yes, I know I'm not the world's safest driver, but I do look after the car, and if I don't Wyndham does—he's the old chauffeur at Saffron Ivy. It was Wyndham who finally convinced me that something very odd had been done to the car; he put it down to Oxford undergraduates of course. All the same: 'You could have been deceased, my lord' he pronounced with great solemnity, Wyndham having the bearing of a bishop rather than a chauffeur. There were one or two other odd incidents too, but of course I was getting pretty jumpy about everything. Then Bim was killed."

"When did all this start?" asked Jemima. "I take it you don't count the fight in the restaurant. The man with the red hair and the appropriate name of Rufus, plus his enormous friend. *That* wasn't an attempt on your life?"

"Rufus Pember and Big Negel Copley." Saffron laughed in a brief return to his airy manner. "Oh yes, they would like to kill me all right. I must write to the Vice-Chancellor about it. Where did it start? A girl, I believe. Muffet

Pember, to wit, but this is not sex and violence. This is *serious*."

It all began, Saffron told her, on the terrible day he went to see Nurse Elsie at the Hospice.

"If only Ma hadn't made me go—but as I told you, she made such a point of it. Said Nurse Elsie was asking for me specially—you bet she was—wouldn't die happy unless I went. Then that ghastly place. No, I know it's a wonderful place and all that. But Nurse Elsie, her hand like a claw clutching mine—that was what was ghastly. Like a skeleton from the past. Isn't it odd? I'd always hated it even more when she came to look after me sometimes when Nan was on holiday. And she used to bring Jack and Fanny to stay sometimes. She *looked* at me so oddly, I swear she did. Hugging me when we were alone. Telling me I was her own special little boy. Touching me all the time when we were alone. Nan hugged me of course, but there was something creepy about the way Elsie did it. I knew it was wrong. Children always know things like that, don't they, even if they don't know *why*.

"And now here she was, this terrifying skeleton— hanging on to me—and telling me—she was a lunatic—she was telling me—of all things—" Saffron was sounding increasingly incoherent, even hysterical. All the same, Jemima was astonished when he leant forward and without bothering to push aside the glasses or the champagne bottle, now three quarters empty, simply buried his face in his hands. The large green bottle rocked to and fro twice and then fell heavily over. The remains of the drink began to bubble out and flow goldenly across the table.

Jemima saw that Saffron was crying.

When he finally looked up, however, his expression was quite steady. "Such a relief to tell someone," said Saffron after a while. He took Jemima's hand and pressed it.

"You haven't told me anything yet." Jemima spoke gently; after all she knew—who better?—exactly what he was going to say. What she had not known till this minute was the fearful strength of Nurse Elsie's dying obsession—if that was what it was. It had never occurred to Jemima, famous instinct for once at fault, that Nurse Elsie, as the days passed and death came nearer, with no lawyer arriving, might have passed on her story to anyone else. Yet she *should* have known it of course: when Sister Imelda referred to Nurse Elsie's "peace of mind" at the end, Jemima *should* have realized that Father Thomas had granted absolution—which supposed some form of revelation to someone. To how many others did Nurse Elsie tell her story, was the unspoken question in Jemima's mind, even before Saffron told of his own interview with the dying woman.

"Why me?" was what Jemima said when Saffron had finished relating Nurse Elsie's story. Then she received her second surprise. Saffron spoke flatly, as though all his emotion had for the time being been drained away.

"Because you knew already. That's true, isn't it? You were going to bring a lawyer. Expose the whole thing. Aristocratic fake. Phoney lord. Those were going to be the headlines on television."

"For heaven's sake," exclaimed Jemima, "who on earth told you that? It is true I was going to bring a lawyer— " She stopped. What had she intended exactly? Oh wise Cass! she thought, why didn't I listen to you before I got involved in all of this? Too late now to step back. "That was to bring comfort to a dying woman," she went on carefully. "The priest wouldn't give her absolution unless she made restitution, as it's called. Making a statement to a lawyer— he wasn't a solicitor by the way, so he wasn't a commissioner of oaths, just a barrister friend of mine—that was a kind of well-meant sop."

Something else struck Jemima. "Phoney lord, aristocratic fake. Those were never Nurse Elsie's words. Who else have you discussed this with—your parents—" she paused delicately. After all, one of the main points of Nurse Elsie's story was that Lord St. Ives had proposed the deception; he might have been motivated by a desire to spare his wife pain, but the consequence would be to deprive Andrew Iverstone—or more likely his only son Jack—of his inheritance.

"It's not true. Don't you understand?" Saffron said this very fiercely. "It's not true! Of course I haven't told Pa. As for Ma, it would kill her. She's in a pretty dickey state anyway." Now it was Saffron's turn to pause. "As a matter of fact I did tell Tiggie. Not the truth, of course. Just that you were trying to rake up some scandal about me. Spill dirt all over me. And *she* put the point about television. She's into that kind of thing. After all, she screws Cy Fredericks, doesn't she? Or maybe she doesn't. With Tiggie, who knows? She said she'd fix it."

"Fix me?"

Saffron gave her his disarming smile. "Fix the programme if you like. Get Megalith so involved with me, your original Oxford Blood, that they wouldn't even want to expose me—not that there's anything to expose," he added quickly.

"Ah." One thing which Jemima had tucked away in the corner of her mind as not-to-be-forgotten and one-day-to-be-investigated was the reason for Tiggie Jones' hostile "anonymous" telephone call. As for Cy Fredericks—to adapt the words of Saffron, who cared if he was screwing Tiggie or not—but in either case she understood the passionate advocacy of the "Golden Kids" programme which had infuriated her; clearly Tiggie was putting pressure upon him.

"So how does it all fit in? The murder attempts—if that's what they were—and Nurse Elsie's story. In view of what she said, why should anyone want to *kill* you—" Jemima stopped rather awkwardly, then decided that she might as well be frank. "Wouldn't it be better for an interested party"—that was a delicate phrase— "to *expose* you?" That was somehow less delicate, but Jemima ploughed on: "Expose you as not being your father's real son?"

"Don't you see, that's for you to find out. All I know is that there have been these attempts. The car; that night when poor Bim died. And they all began when that horrible old woman died."

"In short," Jemima ended up telling Cass Brinsley, in a voice which she hoped was as disarming as that of Tiggie Jones, or Saffron himself, "in short, I've agreed to go to the Chimneysweepers' Dinner at the beginning of next term as his guest. I'll pretend to be researching the programme. But actually I'll be there as a kind of protection. In case someone has another go."

"Will you be wearing a gun?" enquired Cass. It was his

turn to sound cold. He began to appreciate the irritation Jemima had felt at his interest in Tiggie Jones (although that was of course totally platonic, mere sociological interest in one so young, so bizarre—and admittedly so pretty). Was it possible that Jemima fancied the odious Saffron? "Phoney lord"—yes indeed.

Reflecting later on this conversation with Jemima, Cass angrily hoped that Saffron would turn out to be the son of a butcher and then quickly corrected himself, realizing that this was a concept highly insulting to butchers. The trouble with Jemima was that she was so convinced that her head ruled her heart, that she never seemed to notice her extreme vulnerability to any rash suggestion on the part of the aforesaid heart, added to which, what was all this heart nonsense anyway? Saffron was an extremely handsome as well as extremely arrogant young man, and when had Jemima ever been averse to a handsome man, young or old?

Absolutely resolved to put all these thoughts away from him, Cass Brinsley reached for his telephone book and looked for the number of Flora, that pupil in his Chambers about whom Jemima had been so surprisingly suspicious. He then wondered idly what Tiggie Jones' telephone number might be and whether Cherry could be persuaded to disgorge it. . . . When Jemima returned to London, he would try to dissuade her from further involvement with Saffron, involvement beyond the call of professional duty to the programme. Nothing personal. Merely his concern for Jemima's own best interests.

But it turned out that Jemima's own concern for her best interests did not exactly tally with that of Cass. During the academic holidays, Cy Fredericks' appetite for the "Golden Kids" programme was further sharpened by various exciting encounters with Tiggie Jones (faithfully reported to Cherry by Miss Lewis, who ran a nice line in quiet bitchery behind her agreeable Sloane Ranger exterior). And the beginning of May found Jemima once more installed in her suite at the Martyrs Hotel. What was more, she was preening himself in the mirror, preparatory to attending the Chimneysweepers' Dinner on the arm of Lord Saffron.

"Preening" was the word because she was not going to

wear a gun to dinner, she was going to wear a new Jean Muir outfit consisting of wide flowing crepe culottes, a silk blouse, and a crepe jacket cut like a very grand cardigan. Jemima was now trying the effects of a scarf against the soft grape-coloured folds of the blouse. She was sufficiently distracted not to notice a large packet on her desk until it was almost time to sally forth.

Inside the packet was a book and a note. Jemima frowned. The title was not immediately seductive to one about to cut a swathe (in a new Jean Muir dress) among the notorious Oxford Bloods. She read the note first.

Study it, Jemima Shore Investigator. I actually went as a blood donor over Easter at Saffron Ivy because Ma is the local President or whatever, so my good blue blood was in demand, to prove giving blood is harmless in spite of AIDS. The Prince of Wales had just given *his* even bluer blood, and I was out to please poor old Ma. After recent events. I do have my nice side, you know. Except my blood wasn't blue exactly, it was AB like a reader of *The Times*. Which, according to the uniformed vampire who took it, is a fairly rare group. At least she made me feel my blood was socially useful even if I wasn't. Something else the vampire said made me ask Ma what her group was, and she said: "O, I think, darling, same as Pa's." "Oh no, Lady St. Ives" says the vampire importantly, that's not possible . . ." which set me thinking. Of course blood isn't everything, I hear you say. Or isn't it?

The paper was the familiar crackling parchment headed by the curly words "Saffron Ivy." There was a similarly curling S as a signature. A scribbled PS read, "Why don't you come to the above noble pile? If you and I both survive the Chimneysweepers. You could say it would be for the sake of the programme."

The title of the book (which had the book-plate of the Rochester College library) was *Medical Jurisprudence and Toxicology*. A marker had been put in a chapter entitled "Blood Grouping." Page 349 contained a simple table, so simple in fact that even Jemima Shore, who had been woefully or perhaps wilfully stupid at science at school, could not fail to understand it. The table, entitled "Derivation of Offspring After Landsteiner," illustrated a subsection called "Blood grouping in cases of disputed paternity." There were three headings in the table: "Groups of Parents," "Groups of Children" and "Exclusion Cases." Under "Groups of Parents" Jemima traced down to O. The only possible blood group of children whose parents' own blood groups were both O, was given as O. The blood groups A, B and AB were specifically excluded from possibility.

That seemed clear enough, rather horribly clear in fact. In case it wasn't, there was a further Note appended: "A and B agglutinogens cannot appear in the offspring unless present in the blood of one or both parents. This is common to the theories of von Dungern and Hirszfeld, and of Bernstein." So if the table was correct—Jemima glanced at the date of the book—and if she had understood the table aright and if matters concerning blood groupings were really quite so simple, and above all if Lady St. Ives had got it right about her own and her husband's blood group, then Saffron could not be his parents' natural child, because the A and B agglutinogen, whatever that was, could not be present in the offspring of two O group parents. According to Landsteiner, von Dungern, Hirszfeld, old uncle Bernstein and all. The date of *Medical Jurisprudence and Toxicology* was 1950 and its author was one Glaister.

How odd, how truly ironic, if Saffron's blood, to which he paid such store, proved in the end to be a fatal liability!

Was it that simple? Could it be that simple? A good deal seemed to rest on the evidence of Lady St. Ives, speaking off the cuff at some function which was only vaguely official; after all she could have easily been mistaken about her husband's blood group if not her own. Jemima remembered a recent case of a baby's disputed paternity which had been settled by blood tests taken from the two possible fathers; but details of the process had not been given. What was an agglutinogen anyway and could a blood test lie? Questions like this made a bizarre contrast to the evening ahead of her when the only blood likely to be under consideration was the aristocratic blood of the participants. At least she hoped it was.

And that blood was not actually going to flow. At least she hoped it wasn't.

CHAPTER EIGHT

•

Dress: Gilded Rubbish

Jemima's first reaction to the sight of the assembled rout of the Oxford Bloods at the Chimneysweepers' Dinner was that for once the newspapers had not exaggerated. The theme of the evening, Saffron had informed her, was to be taken from the magistrate's remarks at the end of the Martyrs case in which he himself had featured so prominently. "Gilded rubbish" were the words used by the magistrate, and "Dress: Gilded rubbish" was printed at the bottom of the Chimneysweepers' ornate invitation. Jemima herself could not have thought of a more exact description of the medley of peacocks which confronted her. It was as though a Beckett play was being enacted by a set of Firbank characters.

The club, for obvious reasons no longer welcome at the Martyrs, had taken refuge in a slightly down-at-heel restaurant on the edge of the river called The Punting Heaven, which was presumably prepared to overlook the Oxford Bloods' fearsome reputation for the sake of pecuniary reward. Now these sparkling tramps—was that Tiggie Jones emerging from a scanty parcel of newspaper sprayed with glitter dust?—congregated on the small lawn in front of the restaurant. Some of the Bloods were sprawled on the grass and champagne bottles already rolled among the gilded dustbins with which the path to the river was artistically lined.

Had the Bloods actually arrived in the enormous dust-cart, suitably gilded and hung with other golden dustbins,

which jostled with Jemima's white car at the edge of the
lawn? Or was it perhaps for display purposes only? Was it
indeed a genuine municipal object, decorated for the
evening, or somebody's bizarre creation? Jemima touched
it. Papier mâché and paint: characteristically superficial
glamour. The structure began to sway perilously even to
her light touch, and she backed away lest this *oeuvre* come
to dust even before the Chimneysweepers' Dinner had
begun. Along its flank was painted the insouciant motto:
"Gold is all that glitters"—another characteristic touch.

At the side of the river a series of punts were chained
together. Although it was only the beginning of May, it had
been a sunny afternoon, the temperature quite hot once
one got out of the wind, and Jemima had noticed a number
of boats being poled enthusiastically up the Cherwell, amid
the pollarded trees whose outlines were being rapidly
blurred with green. She imagined that these chains were
strong enough to withstand any attempts of similarly enthusiastic Bloods to take to the river after dinner. Jemima
trailed her fingers in the river. The water was icy.

Afterwards, in view of what happened, Jemima came to
look back on the comparative serenity of the early evening
with a kind of awed nostalgia and her own part in it later
with something like amazement. Did she really sit with
Proffy on the bank of the river under a full moon riding high
across the water meadows discussing whether the rich were
happy, with a goblet of pink champagne in her hand? (To
hell with the new Jean Muir dress.) While all around them,
stretched out in the deep shadows left by the moon's
pathway, the bodies tumbled and caressed like nymphs and
shepherds in a Poussin landscape. Most of their fragile
sparkling clothing had in any case been crumpled or torn
away, so that classical garlands or brief wisps of trailing
material were all that some of them were wearing. Occasional laughter from that direction, the creaking of the
chained punts and a splash—a bottle? a glass?—indicated
that the boats, if captive, were still being put to some use.

At this point Jemima decided that champagne was responsible for a good many of the excesses in her life, but
this was one of the oddest. It was true that she had decided
politely not to tumble or be tumbled with the rest of the

nymphs: although one particular undergraduate rather reminded her of Cass and there was always of course Saffron. . . . Cass' ridiculous jealousy on that subject had, to be honest, been rather counter-productive. She also received several invitations, rather, she thought, as one might be invited to dance. But since she had reached her thirties without participating in an orgy (unless you counted certain scenes in a jacuzzi on the West Coast of America which she didn't) it seemed a bad plan to start a new way of life in the purlieus of Oxford University. Deep as the riverside shadows might be, Jemima had a feeling that the harsh light of the *Evening Post*'s gossips column, to say nothing of *Jolly Joke*'s vicious searchlight, would somehow manage to penetrate them. On the other hand she had to admit that the decision was a cerebral one.

It was extremely tempting to go with the exotic hedonism of the evening—fortunately the presence of Proffy and the particular subject which they were discussing kept her attention more or less concentrated on the conversation to the exclusion of thoughts about the shadows, beyond brief amused reflections that Cy's cameras should really be present for such an occasion. Oh well, she had no doubt that the Oxford Bloods would re-create the scene, if asked, with enthusiasm when summer came. If this was their style in early May, what on earth would June bring forth? The aggressive heat of The Punting Heaven had driven her out of doors; no doubt similar scenes were being enacted inside amid the wreckage of the flower-decked tables. The gold music of *Rheingold* being played very loudly indoors ("*Rheingold! Rheingold!* Tumty ta-ta") covered other sounds.

"We always play Wagner at Chimneysweepers' bashes," explained Saffron, "because it's so cheerful. Besides, it covers up the noise of breaking glass a treat. Do you suppose that was why old Wags wrote it?"

The presence of Proffy, and indeed of various other more senior guests, was a surprise to Jemima, until she realized wryly that their participation—and indeed her own—was intended to rehabilitate the Oxford Bloods' somewhat tarnished image. (That impulse had however evidently exhausted their plans for reform.) There was, for example, an older woman present, rather handsome, with greying dark hair worn in a bun, and a beaky, almost Roman, nose. Her gold lamé dress, judging from its cut, might have been newly acquired for the occasion, since it was in the height of the current fashion; on the other hand it was the sort of dress that a woman like this might have had in her wardrobe, regardless of fashion, for the last twenty years. The same could be said for her prominent necklace of large amber and jet beads. Although she appeared to be rather silent compared to the rest of the company, Jemima had the impression of a strong personality; one of those people whose presence at any particular gathering marks it, without one being able to define exactly why.

The multiparous Mrs. Mossbanker? It turned out that the handsome woman was in fact that mysterious Professor Eugenia Jones, mother of Antigone, alias Tiggie—she who had been last heard of returning from the States. Curiously enough, Proffy had addressed her consistently as Eleanor, which if Jemima remembered rightly was actually his wife's name.

Studying Eugenia Jones, one could see where Tiggie's looks came from, if not her particular sense of style. She was also quite short, like her daughter, although her flowing golden robe gave her an air of dignity. Who was Jones, Jemima wondered, and what was his profession? She would have to ask her friend Jamie Grand, currently visiting professor at a new college founded by a shy millionaire apparently entirely for Jamie's delectation since it provided vast funds for lavish dons' dining, but none for the sordid everyday needs of undergraduates. Jamie combined a fierce insistence on the highest standards of academic criticism and study with an endearing propensity to gossip, an activity which he pursued with exactly the same informed seriousness, expecting others to do so too.

Thinking of Jamie and the tabs he kept on society—with both big and small S—Jemima was at least not surprised by his presence among the older guests. A little blonde girl, of the sort of which Jamie appeared to have an endless supply, hung on his arm. A large gold fez crowned the countenance whose veriest frown could cause a shudder in the literary world (to quote *Time* Magazine—and Jamie often did).

"Who's Jones?" blurted out Jemima without preamble. At exactly the same moment Jamie said: "Do you know Serena of Christ Church?" He swept on: "Isn't it enjoyable hearing that? I'm old fashioned enough to adore it. These days I only go out with girls from the best men's colleges, or rather the former men's colleges that were formerly the best. Rachel of Magdalen, Allegra of Trinity, I don't know anyone at Balliol yet unfortunately." He turned to Serena of Christ Church.

"Do you know anyone at Balliol, my dear? Blonde of course. About your height and weight."

"I don't want to distract you but I was wondering about Jones, Eugenia's husband. Tiggie's father," broke in Jemima before Serena of Christ Church could answer.

"Ah, that Jones. The ideal husband. In the sense that he was never there when she was wanted. Or so Eugenia once told me, in not quite so many witty words. He vanished before my day. No, I can't tell you anything about Jones. I've sometimes suspected Eugenia of inventing him. She's certainly been totally happy ever since in a so-called unhappy personal situation, as you are doubtless aware. Eugenia is one of those women who thrives on personal unhappiness. It leaves her plenty of time for work—after all, think how successful she is. And then Eleanor has all the domestic responsibilities. Which are considerable where Proffy is concerned, to say nothing of the butter mountain of children."

So, when Jemima was swept away from the heat of The Punting Heaven to the moonlight of the river bank, she was for the first time aware that she was on the arm of the lover—the long-term lover according to Jamie—of Professor Eugenia Jones; as well as the abstracted husband of Eleanor, and still more abstracted father of innumerable Mossbanker children. By now she was curious enough about Eugenia Jones to make a mental resolve to interview her for the programme—difficult to see how she could be fitted into "Golden Kids," other than as the mother of Tiggie Jones, which might not be the most tactful approach, but Jemima would think of something. Eugenia Jones herself had vanished discreetly after dinner before Jemima could have more than the briefest exchange with her.

Nevertheless, her impression of a strong personality had been confirmed. Although their conversation in recollection was not particularly scintillating, at the time Eugenia Jones managed to invest slightly commonplace remarks with something of her own dignity.

One of Jemima's personal preoccupations, based on her own past, was with long-term, extra-marital relationships, particularly from the woman's point of view—the other woman's point of view, that is, when the man was married and she was not. A serious programme on the subject would have been impossible so long as her painful long-drawn-out relationship with Tom Amyas MP prospered—if that was the right word, which on the whole it was not. And now? She still did not imagine that Professor Eugenia Jones would welcome an overture based on such a premise. All the same, the connection between her own success and that time early in her career at Megalith, when she fought down jealous thoughts of Tom's domestic routine with hard work, was not to be denied. Had she ever quite forgotten the pain of the moment when Tom was obliged to break it to her that Carrie, his wife, was pregnant? And yet Professor Jones had presumably had to endure that kind of scene with extraordinary regularity in view of the amazing fertility of Mrs. Mossbanker. Maybe Jamie was right, and it had allowed Eugenia Jones to get on with her own work uncluttered with domesticity.

Compared to Professor Eugenia Jones, Fanny Iverstone was not such a surprising guest. (And maybe Eugenia Jones was only here to have a glimpse of Proffy? However improbable the thought, Jemima knew from personal experience that nothing of that nature was ever totally improbable where the so-called "other woman" was concerned.) Fanny was after all a young girl living in Oxford, and a not unattractive one, even if she was not quite in the same dazzling class as two ravishing girls introduced to Jemima merely as Tessa and Nessa. In the old days such girls would have been marked down as arriving from London; nowadays all the prettiest were probably at the University.

Saffron was rather uncharacteristically vague about who had invited Fanny, to the extent that Jemima was led to expect he had actually done so himself at some earlier date, before seizing the opportunity to bring Jemima as well. It had to be said that the style of "Gilded Rubbish" did not suit Fanny's looks and perhaps it was for that reason, or perhaps she was generally discomforted by the company, but in any case Jemima found Fanny much less ebullient than on the famous occasion of the Lycée lunch. Tiggie Jones was exactly the sort of girl who shone at a party like this, and there was Tiggie—shining. Shining also was Poppy Delaware, a girl so like Tiggie (except for the colour of her hair, which was partially blue and partially orange) that Jemima wondered if they might not be sisters until she realized that the effect of the glittering tattiness of the costumes as well as the short-cropped hair-cuts of both sexes was to make everyone young look rather alike.

All this made it very easy to recognize another surprising guest, Daphne Iverstone, and wait—*could it be*? yes it was: Andrew Iverstone MP, Mr. Rabblerouse himself. With his broad build and heavy shoulders, his pink face and fast-receding light curly hair, Jemima disgustedly thought that Andrew Iverstone resembled nothing so much as a big white porker; certainly his looks, arguably representing some kind of Anglo-Saxon stereotype, constituted no kind of advertisement for the sort of racial purity he was fond of advocating. And yet it was always said that he possessed the kind of charm which made the unwary overlook the precise import of his views until it was too late, and some kind of implicit approval had been given. Jemima however had never met him and did not wish to do so now.

Only Jack of the Iverstone family was missing. But then the Chimneysweepers' Dinner was scarcely his form. He was after all in no sense an Oxford Blood.

"Not one's bright idea, I assure you." Saffron spoke in her ear. "I can't bear him, the old Rabblerouse. Some other bright spirit invited him and Cousin Daphne. Almost as tactless as Bernardo Valliera inviting Muffet Pember." Saffron pointed to where a man, looking vaguely South American, was clothed in bonds of tinsel wound round the rather small base of a leopard-skin jock strap; he had his arm round a girl in a gold mask and high-heeled gold boots, with a skimpy leopard-skin bikini in between. From her russet-coloured hair which was left free, Jemima recognized Muffet Pember, sister of the aggressive Rufus.

There was, Jemima had realized from the first, a certain amount of fairly discreet drug-taking going on. Discreet in the sense that no one had actually offered her some of the various little substances being shared around: cocaine presumably—another expensive taste like champagne. There appeared to be an unwritten law by which the "adults" such as the Iverstones, Eugenia Jones and Proffy were ignored in this connection, and they themselves in turn ignored it. Bernardo Valliera, on the other hand, whether he thought his South American blood granted him some immunity, was not being particularly discreet in whatever it was he was pressing upon Muffet Pember.

Saffron however seemed quite indifferent to that aspect of the situation and Jemima had to admit that she never actually saw him involved in it; as far as she could make out, champagne—and a great deal of it—was enough for him.

"At least Muffet is pretty enough outside as you can observe for yourself," he went on, "if all venom inside. But Cousin Andrew is so terribly unaesthetic, isn't he? I wish he would wear Muffet's mask, which incidentally I take to be disguise from brother Rufus' righteous fury if he finds out she's come to the dinner. So likely Bernardo won't tell everyone in Oxford. As for Cousin Andrew's celebrated views, give me the West Indians any day. There's a fantastic black girl at New College—unfortunately her radical prejudices make her reject all my advances. Looking at Cousin Andrew makes one realize all over again that blood isn't everything."

It was the only allusion he made to the note and the book on her dressing-table.

The presence of Andrew Iverstone had the effect of making Jemima concentrate more than she would perhaps have done otherwise on Professor Mossbanker's ramblings on the subject of wealth and happiness. She still hoped to avoid the social burden of an introduction to the MP but it was not quite so easy. Andrew Iverstone had not maintained a prominent position in public life over a number of years by undue sensitivity on social occasion where liberals were concerned. Particularly when they had access to the media. His invitations to "a civilized lunch" issued the day after a journalist had criticized him savagely in public were notorious: somehow the journalist was never quite so savage about Andrew Iverstone again.

"Of course I can't bear the fellow's views, perfectly ghastly but you have to admit he's not afraid to meet his critics. Never mind, the lunch was delicious—gulls' eggs! and a fantastic claret later—all the same I gave him a frightful bashing"—Jemima had heard this speech on more than one occasion. The lunch guest never seemed to notice that Andrew Iverstone's public utterances, unlike their own, remained quite unaltered by the frightful bashing he had received.

Now Jemima found herself receiving the treatment.

"Miss Shore, I would never have expected to find *you* at an evening entitled 'Gilded Rubbish.'" Even in his dinner jacket—no fancy dress risked—Andrew Iverstone gave the impression of lifting an imaginary hat to Jemima.

"But darling, I told you, Jemima is really absolutely one of us."

Daphne Iverstone, prettily dressed in spotted powder blue and white chiffon, twittered from somewhere near her husband's elbow. Andrew Iverstone ignored her.

"It's providential. I was so interested in that programme of yours about Asian women and the dramatic conflict between our culture and theirs. You might be surprised to learn how many Asians regard me as a kind of father confessor. They really do want to return to their own culture." Andrew Iverstone twinkled his little eyes and his fair eyelashes, short but very thick, fluttered. "I thought we might discuss the matter over a civilized lunch."

"How truly kind. Actually my programme was about the assimilation of Asian women, bearing in mind their traditional values. I think you must have another programme in mind. I should hate to have lunch, especially a civilized lunch, under false pretences."

It was helpful that throughout this exchange Proffy had not ceased philosophizing on the subject of Dives and Lazarus. Jemima turned back to him with relief. Proffy was capable of drinking from an empty glass without noticing; he could also cheerfully eat off an empty plate while taking, as well as dipping his spoon into his neighbour's pudding as he had done at La Lycée. None of this diminished the rapidity of his conversation. Jemima did not notice what happened to the elder Iverstones as the more orgiastic aspects of the evening began to develop. But as she sat herself gracefully down on the river bank alone, Proffy suddenly appeared from nowhere. He picked up the conversation concerning wealth again as though it had never been interrupted.

"Dives—a very happy and contented man!" he exclaimed several times, pumping the night air with his hand. "Whereas Lazarus undoubtedly needed the services of a psychiatrist, supposing he could have afforded one. People don't understand that it's most agreeable wearing purple and fine linen, particularly if you have a beggar at your gate to eat up your crumbs. Purple for the rich man: oh yes, indeed. When Saffron succeeds to that Elizabethan gem, perhaps I shall try to persuade him to allow me to come and live at his gate as the token beggar to ensure him happiness, yes, yes—but what about the children?" he paused, then rattled on. "Not perhaps with all the children. I don't think Eleanor would like it either. Lazarus has no family in the Bible. But I shall be there, with my official sores for his dogs to lick. I wonder what *kind* of dogs they have at Saffron Ivy? Rather large dogs I daresay. No, on second thoughts, I think I will persuade Eugenia to bring the children, at any rate during the holidays, they're fond of dogs I expect, children are so sentimental about animals, and they can take some of the burden of being licked off me. Take them for walks and that sort of thing!"

"Didn't the story of Dives and Lazarus end rather badly?" enquired Jemima, "for Dives, that is. Didn't Dives find himself in Hell, looking up at Lazarus in Abraham's bosom?"

"My dear girl," cried Proffy. "Surely you don't believe everything you read in the Bible. A highly corrupt text. I assure you Dives was immensely happy until the day of his death, when he was promptly received into Abraham's bosom as a reward for his kindness to Lazarus."

"Money, like blood, isn't everything—" began Jemima. She was stopped by the sound of a loud splash or perhaps two splashes, coming from the river. There was the sound of wood crashing on wood and some kind of splintering, as it might be two boats colliding. From the noise of it, a fight was taking place.

There were shouts. Jemima distinctly heard the word "Pember" and then: "Look out—Christ, what *have* you done?"

Then a girl's hysterical voice cried out: "It's Saffer. He's covered in blood. I think he's dead."

CHAPTER NINE

•

An Envious Society

The screaming girl was Fanny Iverstone. As she ran out of the shadows, Jemima saw dark patches on her gaudy dress: patches of blood, black in the moonlight. At that point, as if on some ghostly cue, the moon went behind a thick black cloud and for a moment the only light came from the coloured dancing globes of The Punting Heaven, still streaming across the lawn as the noise of the *Liebestod*, which had succeeded *Rheingold* (ancient Flagstadt? modern Linda Esther Gray?), bellowed out.

"They've got him, they've got him," she was crying. "Proffy, *do* something."

The continuing sense of chaos was made worse by the fact that the grandeur of the music, the glorious voice of Flagstadt (yes), went on soaring above it all. When someone at last saw fit to switch off the home-made Wagnerian tape, special to the occasion, the babble of cries and voice left behind sounded quite puny in the silence.

Fanny went on sobbing hysterically as Benardo Valliera—recognizable by his leopard-skin—and another man called something like Luggsby ran towards the river. Proffy, who had stood quite still and for once silent through all this as though in a state of shock, eventually put his arm round her. The emergence of the revellers from the grass and a couple from the most distant punt, both male it appeared, together with a powerful searchlight turned onto the scene from the boats, meant that the evening had lost all its classical Poussinesque magic. A comparison to Stan-

79

ley Spencer was more appropriate. Several of the girls were shivering. Everyone was suddenly aware that it had become very cold.

It seemed an extraordinarily long time before the ambulance arrived. Before that, Saffron's motionless blood-stained body was borne out of the bushes at the edge of the bank where he had been found lying by four of his friends, using the door of the boathouse as a kind of bier. As the searchlight fell on his face travelled across his body, still partly clad in its gold finery, the Wagnerian comparison to Siegfried was irresistible; would his arm suddenly rise and would he sing of the past before dying?

Who was his Brunnhilde? Fanny Iverstone? But she hardly looked the part; not romantic enough. Tiggie Jones in a way-out modern version? Or perhaps Muffet Pember who, mask abandoned, was sitting distraught on the grass, quite alone, dishevelled red hair round her shoulders. She looked infinitely pathetic in her leopard-skin bikini; nobody had thought to put a coat round her shoulders. Jemima, who wanted to do something to help and was frustrated by her inability to think of anything practical, went and covered her with her cardigan.

Muffet looked up. Her first words reminded Jemima that Muffet's correct role in *Götterdammerung*, if she was to pursue the comparison, was that of Gutrune, bride of Siegfried and sister of Siegfried's slayer Hagen.

"Everyone thinks it's my fault," she sobbed. "But I didn't tell Rufus I was coming here. I'm not such a bloody idiot, am I?" Muffet gazed rather angrily at her. It occurred to Jemima that Muffet, apart from her unusual Pre-Raphaelite colouring, was not really all that pretty: her brown eyes were quite small; her neat little nose was quite sharp and snipey. When one looked at her closely Muffet Pember looked more shrewd than naive. Perhaps she was not so pathetic after all. Jemima remembered Saffron's words: "all venom inside."

"Do you mean that it was your *brother* who attacked Saffron?" asked Jemima sharply. Beyond the fact that Saffron had been assaulted with a boat hook and had a large gash on the back of his head, Jemima had not managed to gather many details of the attack. Despite the great loss of blood—the AB group blood—from the scalp wound he was however very much alive and his pulse was strong.

"No, of course it wasn't," said Muffet, sounding even more indignant and less woebegone. "It was just an awful coincidence. Rufus and Nigel and their friends came up the river in a couple of canoes to—well, I don't know exactly what they came to do"—slightly coy tone—"and before they could do anything, before they even landed, Fanny found Saffer all covered with blood. I know it sounds rather odd," Muffet finished lamely. "But it was just an awful coincidence. I mean, why should Rufus use a boat hook?"

"Why indeed?" asked Jemima rather grimly. Muffet seemed to imply that other methods of assault—the fight in the restaurant for example—were lawful. At this point they were joined by Fanny Iverstone, hysterics now remarkably vanished and a coat—Proffy's? No, too smart—flung over her stained dress. Under the circumstances Jemima admired her control, as she had admired her breezily bossy character on the occasion of their first meeting. It took some strength of character to be smoking a cigarette by the river, when you had discovered the blood-stained body of your cousin a very short time before. Even if Fanny's hand was shaking, her conversation made sense. Nor did she seek to blame Rufus Pember.

"*Somebody* must have had it in for him," said Fanny. "But not necessarily Rufus. He was just lying there. And then I heard the splashes. The trouble is, you know what Saffer's like. People absolutely loathe him. All that money. And then he never tries to hide it, when most people here are so poor. Lots of people hate Saffer who've never even met him. I'd hate him myself, I expect, if I'd never *met* him."

"Well you don't hate him, do you? Not exactly." Muffet still sounded sulky. Nor was she apparently grateful for Fanny's defence of her brother. Altogether, not a very appealing little character, thought Jemima.

The next day Jemima related this conversation on the telephone, along with all the other lurid details of the evening, to Cass in London. Considering Cass' doleful prophecies about Jemima's presence at the Chimney-sweepers' Dinner, he was remarkably tolerant towards her

revelations, showing more interest in the possible identity
of Saffron's attacker than in Jemima's own experiences
during the evening. The jealous cracks about Saffron were
also missing.

It was not until later, when she was walking with her
usual aesthetic satisfaction down the long curve of the High
Street on her way to visit that well-known moralist Kerry
Barber at St. Lucy's, that this absence of jealousy struck
Jemima as significant. A sense of fairness in Cass—one of
his marked characteristics as curiosity was hers—meant
that he generally abandoned any questions concerning her
private life when his own would not bear examination. So
Jemima, ineluctably, began to wonder who . . . All at
once the elegance of the curved street, paraded graciously
down towards Magdalen Bridge like an Edwardian beauty
at the races, failed to move her. Ignoring for once the
classical façade of the Queen's College, she felt like Emma
during the Box Hill expedition: "less happy than she had
expected."

Jemima put her mind resolutely forward to the prospect
of her encounter with Kerry Barber at St. Lucy's. The bells
of evensong were sounding as she passed St. Mary's, the
University church, and soon other bells began to chime in.
Jemima did not imagine that the groups of the young—all
undergraduates? at any rate all young—lounging and scur-
rying along the pavement were on their way to evensong.
Nevertheless, for all the evening sunshine now casting its
romantic stagey shadows on pillar and alley, there was
something uncomfortable at the heart of the idyll. At any
rate to Jemima's fancy; another kind of disquiet replaced
the vague dissatisfaction about Cass' absent affections.

An open car, small and red and noisy, passed her: the
driver and the male passengers were wearing white. A girl
in the front seat, wearing pale blue, waved: it was Fanny
Iverstone. Jemima waved back. Fanny at least had perfectly
recovered from the events of the previous night, even if
Saffron was lying in the Radcliffe Infirmary, eight stitches in
his scalp, but otherwise not as badly injured as that glimpse
of him white-faced on his bier had seemed to indicate.

It was this sight of Fanny which jolted Jemima towards
the source of her own disquiet: at least about Oxford. It was

all very well for Cy Fredericks, as chairman of a commercial television company, to talk enthusiastically about "a post-Brideshead situation," followed by his famous pronouncement: "these Golden Kids mean Big Bucks." But the various attempts on Saffron's life (for so she certainly regarded them) cast rather a different light on the social situation at Oxford University, "post-Brideshead" or otherwise.

Some person or some people hated Saffron enough to wish him dead, or at best very severely injured. Leaving aside the mysterious business of Bim Marcus' fall, an attack with a boat hook was not to be put in the same category as some form of undergraduate jape on the river. The kind of jape for example that Rufus Pember and Nigel Copley had stoutly sworn they intended to carry out that night, only to be thwarted by some previous more murderous intrusion.

"Saffer is a shit" had pronounced a huge and dripping Nigel Copley: Saffron's claim to this noun was evidently received wisdom in the Copley/Pember set. Big Nigel had been hauled with some difficulty out of the river where he had attempted to hide beneath his own overturned canoe, following the discovery of Saffron's body. "But we wanted to abduct him, you know, not to kill him."

"*Abduct* him?" Jemima heard one of the dinner guests exclaim, possibly Bernardo Valliera, because he added: "This is not South America, my friend."

"Duck him, he said. *Duck* him," Rufus Pember, equally wet but somehow more composed, interrupted. "Duck him. A good old-fashioned British custom." He glared at Valliera. In Jemima's view, not every red-haired person justified the reputation of their kind for aggression; Rufus Pember however, for all his physical resemblance to the dying Chatterton, certainly did.

For the time being Jemima suspended judgement on the involvement of Messrs. Pember and Copley in the attack on Saffron. (Although she certainly did not believe a mere ducking had been intended: who would take canoes late at night, travel a mile upstream, merely to administer a ducking? It made no sense. So to Rufus Pember's aggressive quality, she added a capacity for quick thinking: Copley's admission had been neatly turned.)

But now as she reached Holywell, and the long secure wall of Magdalen, she considered Fanny's words anew: "Lots of people loathe Saffer who've never even *met* him." Was that uncomfortable thing at the heart of the idyll simple human envy? In an age of grants, declining, and unemployment, rising, it was easy to see how some undergraduates might actively envy Saffron for his advantages. Not only the media found themselves in "a post-Brideshead situation." Many students came up to Oxford, envisaging themselves enjoying their own mini-Brideshead existence for a year or two, before setting down to a more serious way of life. Oxford was a place of great expectations. What happened when those expectations were disappointed? Great envy? Even, perhaps, great hatred? For that matter what price the classless society based on merit which many might hope to find at a university if nowhere else in Britain? The cars, parties, dinners of the young and rich ensured them not only a sour spotlight within the university, but the rather more appreciative attention of the media in the world outside. Jemima reflected that Cy Fredericks' enthusiasm for Golden Kids was really quite typical: you could not imagine him mounting a whole programme on the lifestyle of comprehensive-school students once at Oxford, with due respect to the views of Dr. Kerry Barber whom she was about to visit.

Jemima's conversation with Proffy came back to her. Who was to say what Lazarus actually *felt* about Dives, as he ate up the crumbs from the rich man's table? And maybe being forbidden to give Dives a glass of water afterwards, an instruction from Abraham, was one of the pleasurable experiences of his (after) life.

As Jemima reached the porter's lodge of St. Lucy's College, she was thinking that money—and blood—had a lot to answer for. Blood! That unlucky word again. Better to concentrate on money.

"Money and where it comes from, money and where it goes to," Kerry Barber was saying a few minutes later as he lay back in an ugly modern chair which was ill-suited to the large panelled room in St. Lucy's famous Pond Quad; he was airing long rather good legs clad in a pair of crumpled white shorts. Dr. Barber had evidently just taken part in some active game although it was difficult to make out exactly what, since the single thing his room had in common with Saffer's was the amount of sporting equipment littered about. "Did you see my piece on the redistribution of Britain's wealth as reflected or rather *not* reflected in the average income of an undergraduate's parents? 'Grants should Get up and Go.' Shocking, quite shocking."

Kerry Barber jumped up and poured Jemima another large sherry. It was of excellent quality; very dry and if you liked sherry, delicious. Jemima felt it would be ungracious to say that she actually hated sherry, when Barber was such a generous host. Furthermore, he clearly did not drink himself, but took occasional swigs at a china mug bearing a symbol of international goodwill; goodness knew what it contained.

All in all, he was really a very decent man. It was only under gentle pressure from Jemima—the trained interviewer—that he revealed he had spent the afternoon playing squash with paraplegics; further discreet questioning, centred on the mysterious china mug, elicited the fact that he gave the money he would otherwise have spent on drink to the Third World.

"It's a decision Mickey—my wife—and I took years ago and you'd be surprised how it mounts up." He smiled rather sweetly. "You see we both enjoyed a drink before—and we try not to cheat by pretending to drink less as the years go by. If anything, as Mickey pointed out, we might be drinking *more*. So many of our friends are drinking more these days. We notice it at our own parties, where of course we try to keep the drink flowing as much as possible. Mickey seriously questions whether the price of three glasses of wine each is enough to put in the box at the end of an evening. Judging from our married friends, at least one of us would be an alcoholic by now—if we drank that is. But which is it to be?" He smiled. "Statistics suggest Mickey but as she has the lower income that doesn't seem quite fair."

Jemima, self-consciously clutching her own second sherry, looked nervously round the room. Was there a box—the box—visible? She thought she saw something which looked like a collecting box near the door and made a mental resolve to donate handsomely to it (the price of a half bottle of champagne at least) on departure. In the meantime, as Kerry Barber was much the most decent person she had met in Oxford, with the possible exception of Jack Iverstone (Proffy with his views on Dives deserved the epithet of engaging rather than decent) Jemima looked forward to his confrontation with the so-called Golden Kids on the programme. What would the Oxford Bloods make of his policy concerning drink and the Third World? Why, their donations if made along the same lines would keep several African states going for months. . . .

She wondered if any of them had crossed Kerry Barber's path. The answer, under the circumstances, was slightly surprising.

"Lord Saffron, as I suppose we must call him, although the sooner that sort of thing goes the better. Yes. He came to me for economics his first year." Jemima realized rather guiltily that it had never even occurred to her to enquire what subject Saffron was reading; or was it an indictment of his own deliberately frivolous approach to the University?

"He's rather bright, you know," went on Kerry Barber, still more surprisingly. "Good mind. Much brighter for example than his cousin Jack of our college. A good man, but almost frighteningly conventional in his thinking. To make up for that dreadful father, I suppose. Hours in libraries and very few minutes of original thought."

"What's he reading—Jack?" enquired Jemima.

"Oh history of course," replied Kerry Barber in what for him passed for a malicious remark.

Jemima grappled with the unexpected phenomenon of Saffron being naturally intelligent.

"You don't mean he actually did any work?" she asked incredulously.

"Good heavens, no! And it's perfectly disgraceful that he hasn't been sent down. A prime example of the sort of thing COMPCAMP would put an end to. Coming from a comprehensive school, he would of course—" And Dr. Barber launched into his favourite subject. To Jemima's general satisfaction, however—for was he not now saying exactly what she wanted him to say on the "Golden Kids" programme? Provided she could somehow get it past the eagle eye of Cy Fredericks. Cy had a tiresome habit of returning to Megalithic House after weeks of absence in some luxurious haunt, as though by instinct, just as a programme-maker was trying to slip a fast one past him at the editing stage.

All the same, she judged it right to leave after about twenty minutes of elucidation on the aims of COMPCAMP. She did so as gracefully as possible, pausing at the door of the room to deposit a five-pound note in the collecting box.

"For my two delicious sherries."

"Good heavens, you could have had many more for that!" exclaimed Barber generously. "Are you sure you don't want to come back? I feel I've only just scratched the surface of our discussion. COMPCAMP is such an important issue." He sighed as though Jemima was perhaps not the only television interviewer to back away through his door, leaving the depths of his campaign unprobed. "Ah well, another time. But I must say I envy you having the forum of television for your views."

"We'll share it," promised Jemima, generous in her turn, vowing inwardly to defeat Cy even if it meant bribing Miss Lewis to muck up his return flight arrangements for the first time in her life.

Jemima wandered back into Pond Quad still thinking about envy. She gazed rather distractedly into the large round stone-built "pond" itself, with its statue of St. Lucy, Virgin and Martyr, in the centre. As a result of undergraduate binges St. Lucy sometimes had to endure further forms of martyrdom. She was currently wearing a large painted notice on her bosom: "St. Lucy votes SDP." Below someone had written: "I know. That's why they killed her." How old were the golden carp in the pond supposed to be? Old enough not to want to go on television programmes, whatever the motive. Old enough not to envy any of the hurrying undergraduates who thronged the quad.

One of the undergraduates stopped and smiled at Jemima.

"Are you going to feature the fish in your programme? They *are* golden."

It was Jack Iverstone. He was carrying a pile of books, as

on their first acquaintance in Saffron's rooms, and Jemima was reminded of Kerry Barber's judgement: "hours in libraries and very few minutes of original thought." She decided to put it down to the natural disdain of the economist for the historian.

"I've just been to see Saffer," he went on. "I must say he has the strength of ten. Enormous gash in his head and he's asking me to smuggle in some champagne for a celebration."

"A celebration?" queried Jemima incredulously. "What on earth can he have to celebrate beyond being holed up in the Radcliffe?"

Jack Iverstone continued to look at her with his easy charming smile. But there was now something quizzical about the smile which she did not quite understand.

"You know Saffer," he said after a pause. "He celebrates the oddest things. Why don't you ask him yourself?"

CHAPTER TEN

•

Intellectual Advantages

It was Jemima's intention to visit Saffron as soon as she got her interview with Proffy out of the way: she thought it would be good to be able to contrast the Mossbanker way of life with that of the heroically abstinent Barbers, for she somehow doubted whether Proffy and his clever wife Eleanor had a collection box in their North Oxford house—that is, if Proffy's appetite for food and drink at the Lycée restaurant and The Punting Heaven were anything to go by.

She still wondered at the nature of Saffron's celebration and the meaning of Jack Iverstone's quizzical glance as she collected her car from the Martyrs car park and drove up St. Giles, leaving Rochester College, Saffron's theoretical residence, on her right (and the Radcliffe Infirmary, his actual dwelling on her left). Arrival at the Mossbankers' house, however, drove these thoughts out of her mind. Chillington Road was a pretty tree-lined backwater, part of a network of similar roads off the Banbury Road. Thus the exterior of the Mossbankers' house, despite the ugliness of its late-Victorian architecture, was agreeably tranquil, soft-ened as its façade was by blossom, the door masked by a weeping tree. The interior on the other hand was the reverse of tranquil. In fact Jemima's first reaction was to decide that marriage between consenting Oxford intellec-tuals should probably be banned for the future (unless sworn to be childless).

To begin with, the combined force of Mossbanker chil-

dren was in itself daunting. Were there only eight of them?
Alternatively were these tow-headed infants and occasional
tow-headed adolescents really all Mossbankers? So many of
them seemed to be the same age. Jemima had not thought
to enquire from the Professor whether the Mossbanker
Eight included twins or even triplets: but then what made
her think he would have known the answer to such an
essentially domestic question? As Tiggie had expressed it
on their first meeting, he liked *having* a lot of children (the
children themselves he rather disliked).

However, it was not so much the sheer mass of Mossbankers which persuaded her that intellectuals should not
be allowed to marry each other. Nor did she necessarily
ascribe the untidiness-beyond-parody of the North Oxford
house, books and potties competing for attention, frequently doing an exciting balancing act in the same pile, to
the presence of an intellectual mother. After all, take the
case of Jemima's fiercely clever friend, Dr. Marigold Milton, whose students were notoriously terrified into an
appreciation of English literature which lasted them for the
rest of their lives no matter how they tried to get rid of it.
Marigold Milton had as a matter of fact given birth to four
children, making a point of reading Proust between pangs
of labour (she was a quick reader), yet her house was so
exactly polished that even the students wiped their feet
reverently on entering it, before having their essays merrily
pulled to pieces.

No, it was apparently the fatal combination of both
Mossbankers which made life in Chillington Road such an
ordeal: Jemima knew that Eleanor Mossbanker had as
Proffy's pupil gained her own First in something or other
before leaving scholarship for parturition in a dedicated
way. For the effect of this union of intellects was, as Jemima
quickly discovered, to make the Chillington Road house a
kind of debating chamber concerning the education, past,
present and to come, of the numerous Mossbanker offspring, into which any unwary newcomer was immediately
plunged.

Proffy let her into the house, trampling on a small bicycle
as he did so (admittedly the alternative would have been to
hurdle it). He guided Jemima towards the sitting room,

negotiating various physical hazards—a carry-cot, another bicycle and two satchels—in the same ruthless manner.

"Eleanor is just giving him—" he looked closer "—I mean *her*, an intelligence test to see whether the last report from the local comprehensive has anything to be said for it at all. Can any child of ours, can any child, really not be able to read at the age of eight?"

"Ten, Proffy, actually," said a sulky voice emanating from one of the tow-heads. Jemima got the impression that Proffy's boasted dislike of the young might actually be reciprocated.

"Exactly!" cried the Professor with the triumphant air of one who had just proved a point. But the dark Egyptian head bent over the blonde child was surely that of Eugenia Jones. While Eleanor Mossbanker had to be the fair Saxonesque beauty, heavy but not unbecomingly so, some years younger than Eugenia, with a baby in a sling round her neck (which also contained a couple of books). Not for the first time the professor had mixed up their names.

It was Eleanor Mossbanker who proceeded to give Jemima a warm but hasty welcome. The welcome was hasty because she wasted no time in scrabbling in the sling for one of the books, the baby giving a single regal shriek at this interruption to its dignity.

"There, what did I tell you?" she demanded, as though continuing some previous conversation, although as far as Jemima was aware, they had never met before. "Isn't that a ridiculously unimaginative poetry book for a child of seven? At that age I was reading Yeats, or at any rate—"

"For God's sake, Eleanor!" shouted Proffy quite angrily—and for once there was no doubt who he was addressing. "You *chose* that school."

"You did, Mum, honestly," said one of the tow-heads, looking up with a mild expression from a rather noisy television set for a moment or two. "Proffy chose St. Albert's and then it was your turn and you chose Mandells."

"But I've never even been there," countered Eleanor Mossbanker heatedly, poking the offending poetry book back alongside the regal baby and adjusting the sling.

"Of course you've never been there," contributed another tow-head, also flat out on the floor in front of the

television. "That's because you've always been to St. Albert's by mistake, thinking that was the school you chose."
Then he turned the sound up on the television. No wonder
Proffy went to parties to get away and drink champagne,
thought Jemima.

"Could you all be a bit quieter while we're watching
telly?" the first tow-head threw over his shoulder.

"Sigi and Lucas are taking part in a controlled television
experiment to see if watching television six hours a day
interferes with their enjoyment of reading the classics,"
explained the Professor. This left Jemima wondering wearily how on earth she was going to detach him sufficiently
from the fascinating topic of his offspring's mental development in order to discuss her own television programme.
Champagne might once again be the answer.

One of the further ironies of the Mossbanker household
was that compared to the ancient splendour of, for example,
Rochester College, it gave the impression of great penury
as well as discomfort. No wonder Proffy had fantasized at
the Chimneysweepers' Dinner about a house at Dives'
gate. Jemima did not imagine eight children left a great
deal to live on out of a don's salary, particularly one who
enjoyed champagne.

In the event the question of the programme did not arise.
For at that moment the figure of Tiggie Jones, clad in very
small pink shorts covered in butterflies, darted into the
room through the French windows. Some iridescent butterflies gleamed in her dark hair. She posed for a moment,
head on one side, pinky-purple lips pursed, as though
considering the order of kisses, before laying her long
lashes against Jemima's cheek, then Proffy's, then Eleanor's, finally her mother's. The Mossbanker children she
ignored, much as they ignored her.

"I've just come from seeing Saffer," she pronounced.
"Such foxy news." There was a pause. "We're going to get
married," she said. "Don't you envy me?" continued Tiggie,
with her pretty little cat's smile, addressing no one in
particular. "I'm going to be Lady Saffron. And I'm going to
be terribly, terribly rich."

There was a sharp intake of breath somewhere in the
room.

"No—"

"Stop it, Eleanor," said the professor.

But it was Eugenia Jones, still half crouched beside an infant Mossbanker, who now gazed in evident horror at her daughter.

"Antigone, you can't be serious! This is one of your jokes. Proffy, *do* something!"

It was odd, thought Jemima, how women were constantly asking Proffy to *do* something—as Fanny Iverstone had urged him to *do* something after the discovery of Saffron's body at The Punting Heaven—and yet here was a man whose detachment from awkward reality was sufficiently marked for him to regularly and unabashedly mix up the Christian names of his wife and his mistress. Engaging as Proffy was in conversation, Jemima suspected that there was something quite sweetly selfish at the heart of his lifestyle, for all the physical impression he gave of heavy patriarchal reliability.

Perhaps it was the perpetual hope of discovering this phantasmagoric reliability which had kept Eugenia Jones in thrall to him for so long. Weakness or selfishness in a man was often a most successful grappling-hook . . . why else had Eugenia Jones remained devoted to Proffy throughout so many years, including the years when he married his brilliant pupil Eleanor and procreated all those tow-headed children; the children to whom Eugenia was now administering intelligence tests?

"I think your mother means something like: you're throwing yourself away." Proffy spoke in that slightly irritable tone which Jemima noticed he tended to adopt when obliged to form part of a conversation as opposed to holding forth in more light-hearted monologue. "Considering all your intellectual advantages," he added, "that kind of line of attack."

Was he being serious? Intellectual advantages! Tiggie Jones, the toast of the gossip columns (which would be lost without her if she married, or again perhaps not), Tiggie, the happily idiotic Golden Kid, Miss Tiggie who was or was not screwing Cy Fredericks, in the words of Saffron himself—Jemima was interrupted in these reflections by Eugenia Jones.

"Antigone, have you no shame?" The fierce voice was worthy of Dr. Marigold Milton herself, ringing the editor of *Literature* to complain about a misprint in her review. "You got a very good Second, but touches of Alpha there in certain papers, admittedly in English—"

"Your mother means that you would have got a First if you had done any work at all. And now you're throwing yourself away on a very rich man, two years or so your junior, so that you will eventually endure the unspeakable fate of being Marchioness of St. Ives, mistress of Saffron Ivy. I think that's what your mother means."

"Oh Mum!" cried Tiggie in a tone of sheer exasperation. It was the first time Jemima had heard her speak without any affectation. She even sounded quite fond of her mother. But then Jemima was seeing Tiggie through new eyes in more ways than one. A good Second in English. For a moment, thinking of the constructed personality Tiggie now displayed, hedonism not to say sheer silliness and irresponsibility strictly to the fore, Jemima found herself agreeing with Eugenia that Tiggie was doing something called wasting her opportunities. Then she pulled herself up. Wasn't Tiggie actually using her so-called intellectual advantages to get exactly what she wanted? A rich husband. Purple and fine linen for the rest of her life. Or at least until they divorced—and then a good lawyer would probably see to it that the supply of purple did not diminish for Saffron's ex-wife.

The exasperation, and the naturalness, passed quickly from Tiggie. "Saffer and I are going to settle down. We're going to be old folks. Isn't that sweet?" And she did a little pirouette, setting all the gauzy butterflies in her short dark hair a-quiver. "We're going to have lots and lots of children just like you, Proffy. Mum, don't be cross. You'll *love* the library at Saffron Ivy. You can live in it if you like. You can have a wendy house in the library. A sort of hut. Think how adorable."

"I know the library at Saffron Ivy," was all Eugenia Jones vouchsafed by way or reply.

"Oh really," said Tiggie incuriously, "I didn't know you'd ever been there. *I've* been there."

"There was a life on earth before you were born, Antigone," said Proffy.

Eugenia Jones herself did not speak again but turned back to the Mossbanker child on the floor, who had by now joined the ranks of the television viewers and was highly indignant at being recalled to an intelligence test (the upbringing of the young Mossbankers, thought Jemima, unlike that of Tiggie Jones, was full of intellectual disadvantages). But Jemima saw that Eugenia Jones' eyes were full of tears.

Even more astonishing, Jemima surprised on Proffy's own face a look of absolute despair. The look was purely momentary, transforming Proffy's normally benign if eccentric countenance into something really rather tragic as if a mask had been applied. Then he relaxed, blinked and patted Eugenia on the shoulder. The whole incident had not lasted more than a few seconds.

It was not time to press Proffy on the subject of Golden Kids. Jemima departed as rapidly as possible, unnoticed by the majority of the Mossbanker family, feeling that a visit to the putative bridegroom was now indicated. As to the motive behind his unlikely engagement, as Jack Iverstone had suggested with that quizzical gleam in his eye, "Why don't you ask him yourself?"

Her first sight of Saffron however had the immediate effect of driving his engagement from her mind. She thought instead of his blood. That was because Saffron, although propped up on high pillows, and smiling at her quite strongly, was demonstrably still wired or tubed or taped up to some form of blood transfusion.

"AB blood like readers of *The Times*." Jemima remembered all over again the note sent to her at the Martyrs on the eve of the dinner, which circumstances had not yet allowed her time to discuss with Saffron, let alone investigate its contents for herself. Was now the time to discuss it when blood—presumably AB, the fairly rare group—was so obviously being replenished in his veins? On the other hand, perhaps Saffron still felt too weak to discuss a subject which was potentially so painful. While Jemima hesitated, she heard the sharp sound of a crackling uniform behind her, and she was accosted by a woman's voice speaking with great command and indignation in a strong Scottish accent. Jemima swung round. This was clearly a very senior type of nurse. She was also black.

"Ye may be his relative or ye may not—I'm thinking this laddie has an unco' lot of relatives all of them gairrls— " she pronounced the word with relish—"only one visitor at a time, relative or no relative; and that in visiting hours." The nurse stopped. She stared at Jemima Shore. Then she beamed. There was no other word for it.

"Jemima! We met in Glasgow when I was doing my training. Do you ken that? Young black nurses, a whole lot of us. Suella May Mackintosh, that's me. What was the series called now? 'New Scottish World.' Something like that."

Jemima beamed back. "New Scottish World" had been a very early series, and an embarrassing memory as it had pleased neither new nor old Scottish worlds, due to her handling the subject of colour with insufficient directness from which she had learned a valuable lesson. At least it lived on in the memory of Suella May Mackintosh, now a formidable hospital Sister. In a matter of minutes she had secured the privilege of a short uninterrupted interview with Saffron.

The patient himself regarded these negotiations with a sardonic air. "And you think I'm privileged, Jemima Shore," was what he said eventually. "Would you like some champagne? Faithful Cousin Jack brought it. I bought it and he brought it."

Why not, thought Jemima, if only to expunge the taste of Kerry Barber's exquisite sherry. She had never got as far as a drink at the Mossbankers', and in any case Ribena had been the only visible liquid refreshment.

"I hear I have to congratulate you," she said as she sipped a glass of vintage Bollinger (just as well the rich Saffron had paid for it and not the poor-but-honest Jack) out of a plastic hospital toothglass. "Tiggie told me, in the process of telling her mother."

"I'm going to settle down." Was it her imagination or did Saffron sound slightly defiant, compared to Tiggie who had sounded plainly ecstatic at the thought of her purple future? Jemima also noticed that Saffron did not even bother to enquire how his prospective mother-in-law had taken the news. Furthermore: "We're going to settle down"—that was Tiggie's version. "I'm going to settle down"—that was Saffron's.

"This last attack decided it," said Saffron.

Jemima leant forward impulsively and squeezed the hand free of the tubes, lying docilely on the light hospital blanket. "I'm sorry, Saffer, I wasn't much of a protector, was I?"

"Not much you could do against a bloody boat hook, was there?"

"So you remember? In which case—"

"Oh Christ no—" wearily "—the police asked me all that till our darling Scots Sister drove them away. They're after Pember and Copley of course, except they can't prove it. She's great, isn't she, our Sister? Took particular pleasure in turfing out dreadful Cousin Andrew by the way, who insisted on dropping by out of hours in the hopes of finding me moribund, and thus transforming him at one sweep into being The Heir. I'm sure Sister Mackintosh recognized him. Spoke in her broadest Scots accent, and when Cousin Daphne had the cheek to ask her what island she came from, replied: 'Glasgow, madam, and what island might you be coming from yourself?'"

His vitality flagged: "No, I remember nothing. Nothing at all. Dinner, the end of dinner. Cousin Andrew's ghastly speech: ghastly but I have to admit quite witty. Conversation with Cousin Daphne, who definitely was not witty: unless you think the suggestion that Jack is sowing his wild oats in the SDP is in itself a form of wit. She sometimes hints after a drink or two that I might do worse than marry Fanny thus keeping everything in the family; I've put paid to that one at least. Fanny is a good girl, but I would rather marry Mrs. Thatcher. Dancing to the *Liebestod* in a carefree way, possibly with Tiggie, possibly with Fanny, or was it Poppy? I can't even remember that. Then nothing more. Not even going down to the river. Or with whom. Apparently it's quite usual with a blow on the head. I may remember later."

Jemima thought again of *Gotterdämmerung*. Would some woodbird's song suddenly awake this Siegfried to a full memory of what had gone before? In which case would he recall the actual identity of the person who had made the murderous attack on him with a boat hook?

"And Tiggie? Your marriage—are you very much in love?" As she spoke, Jemima realized the question sounded perfectly pathetic.

"Rather an adorable idea, don't you think?" Saffron had become frivolous again although his eyelids with their long black lashes had begun to quiver as though with exhaustion. "We get on, you know. We think alike. We want the same kind of life. As to love, I'm not sure I'm into love. But then nor is Tiggie. So that's all right. We'll probably live at Saffron Ivy when I've finished here. If they let me finish. And have children. That's the whole point. I don't want to be an aged parent like Ma and Pa."

"Saffron—" Jemima paused. If he was putting the whole strange matter of the blood groups behind him, who was she to raise it? And yet it was Saffron who had sent her the book on medical jurisprudence. Was this decision to marry and settle down a bold declaration that he was the one true heir to the St. Ives title, no matter what a crazy midwife might mutter?

"But there is one other thing, Jemima." Saffron smiled engagingly. "I thought you might find out who I am. If I'm not who I think I am, if you get my meaning. Very secretly. Just between you and me. Check out that odd blood group thing. You're still my sleuth, remember.

"I can't handle it," he went on. "No, not the violence exactly. Not knowing who I am is worse. It was after the—the dread revelation of Nurse E., that I bashed up that foul mantelpiece in the Martyrs. I had to take it out of someone, or something."

"An innocent victim?" queried Jemima.

"You should have seen it," said Saffron sternly. "That mantelpiece was definitely not innocent. Look, you're coming to Saffron Ivy. We'll have a big engagement weekend, ask everyone, including Tiggie's mother and Proffy as her escort. He's insisting on coming: he loves high life. Then you might do some sleuthing there. All the same I'm quite sure I am *me*. That's why I'm going to marry Tiggie and have as many children as the Mossbankers."

At least Tiggie and Saffron were united in their aim, thought Jemima: a Mossbanker-size family. But she ought to refuse to have anything more to do with Saffron and his identity. Why not let the matter rest? Get on with the programme and treat Saffron purely as a Golden Kid . . . Yes, she definitely ought to do that. It was absolutely against her better judgement that five minutes after leaving Saffron, she found herself seeking out Sister Suella May Mackintosh.

"Sister," began Jemima Shore Investigator. "Now that I've happily bumped into you again after all these years, I wonder if you can help me over something to do with a new programme. It's a little matter of blood groups: how would I get certain information? Just quite privately, you understand."

CHAPTER ELEVEN

•

Who He Is Not

For one whose life had been spent in a world of blood, or at any rate test tubes thereof, Professor Mavis Ho looked remarkably fresh and trim. In the tiny over-heated office off the main buildings of the Kensington Hospital into which she escorted Jemima there were flowering plants. Professor Ho herself wore a flowered dress and white court shoes with a slight platform sole: with her white handbag, square, clean and authoritative on her desk, she bore a certain resemblance to a member of the Royal family, a resemblance encouraged by her pleasantly gracious smile; except since she was Chinese, perhaps Professor Ho should be compared to an Empress Dowager rather than a Queen Mother.

"It may sound a strange mission," concluded Jemima, as she drew to the end of her story: a carefully edited version of events. She supplied no proper names, nicknaming Saffron Moses for good Biblical reasons; she merely related the theory of the baby swap and the facts of the blood groups. Then she explained how "Moses," now twenty, had stumbled on the old story by chance, with obviously distressing consequences. "It may sound strange, but as Moses-in-the-twentieth-century-bulrushes put it to me, he does want to find out who he is."

Professor Ho considered for a moment, neatly coiffed head on one side. How calm she was, what a sense she projected of internal serenity, sitting in her little hot beehive with its uncomfortably glaring plate-glass window;

beneath them the various denizens of the Kensington—a
teaching hospital—scurried about, much as the undergraduates had scurried in Oxford. Except that the hospital
surroundings, built in an amalgam of styles at an amalgam
of dates, ranged from the dreary-but-functional to the
plainly-temporary-but-long-standing. Here were no colon-
nades, no Hawksmoor façades, no green quadrangles, no
ancient somnolent carp, above all no dreaming spires or
at least only one, above the Victorian arch of the most
antique part of the building. All the same Jemima thought
that Professor Ho was far closer to the image of the
sage dispensing wisdom from some inner fount, than
either of the two university professors—Mossbanker and
Eugenia Jones respectively—Jemima had recently encountered.

Proffy manifestly lived in chaos: his rooms at Rochester
had demonstrated that before ever she set foot in Chillington Road. Eugenia Jones' personal life seemed to bear the
marks of a kind of personal chaos: what with a disappearing
husband, in Jamie Grand's smart phrase "the ideal husband, one who was never there when she was wanted";
then there was the wanton daughter who had singularly
failed to live up to the heroic name of Antigone, but had
emerged from her academic background with her sights
determinedly set on a rich husband.

Jemima did not think she was merely carried away by
Professor Ho's mandarin appearance. That was as incidental
to her personality as Sister Suella May Mackintosh's colour
was to hers. Thus Professor Ho incarnated the intelligent
balanced English lady of a certain age, while Sister Mackintosh stood for the fiercely bossy—but golden-hearted—
Scottish nurse. (It was perhaps no coincidence that contact
with one lady had led Jemima, through a trail of experts, to
the other.)

"I wonder, Miss Shore, if you quite appreciate the
situation with regard to your Moses—I take it he's not in
fact Jewish by the way? So far as you know that is." Jemima
shook her head. Professor Ho continued in her measured
manner: "You see, you will not be able to tell him who he
is. You may be able to tell him who he is not."

Jemima sighed. "He's torn, our Moses. He's not a fool, in spite of behaving in a very foolish manner. Most of the time. On the one hand he was curious enough to latch on to the question of the blood groupings—to get some book out of the college library, Glaister I think it's called as I told you, and to ask me to take the matter a little further. On the other hand . . ."

"It would be a great shock to a young person," finished Professor Ho kindly, "to find out that he was in effect an adopted child—which is what Moses may turn out to be—having believed himself to be the biological child of his parents for twenty years."

"I think Moses wants some kind of certainty about his identity. I don't think, oddly enough, that he plans to make any kind of use of this certainty, given he can achieve it."

"Not so odd, perhaps. If by doing so he robs himself of a great deal of family money." Professor Ho's tone remained amiable. "Especially when he has been brought up to enjoy an extravagant lifestyle. At least that is the impression you gave me."

Jemima had a vision of Saffron, last seen lying in hospital offering vintage champagne; or Saffron the Oxford Blood, gyrating to the music of the *Liebestod*, at the Chimney-sweepers' Dinner, tickets £50 a head.

"An extravagant lifestyle covers the situation."

"The interesting thing about your Moses is that he does not let the matter lie."

Jemima hesitated. "I have the impression that it's to do with his inheritance, his true inheritance," she said after a while. "He's been brought up in this way, with such an emphasis on what he has inherited, or is about to inherit. Now the whole thing is cast in doubt. *Is* there anything hereditary about blood? Your kind of blood."

Professor Ho smiled, looking more like a Chinese Queen Mother than ever.

"In one sense blood is the most hereditary thing there is—my kind of blood, as you put it. Blood groupings. I take it you don't mean my ethnic Chinese blood. It's all to do with blood corpuscles and agglutinogens as you discovered from Glaister. You can have no agglutinogens present in the blood: that's called O. Or you can have A agglutinogens present, or B, or both A and B. As I've explained to you, everyone takes a bit from both parents. That is why your young man—and you assure me his grouping is definitely AB—falls into a comparatively rare category."

"It's AB. That at least is certain." Jemima had established this in conversation with Sister Mackintosh, in connection with a so far totally imaginary programme on the subject of blood donors and the National Health Service. The question of Saffron's blood group had been raised ostensibly in order to demonstrate a point she was trying to make.

"You see, to form AB, he must have one parent who is A and another parent who is B," pursued Professor Ho. "Now A is the most common category among white British people—O being the second most common. Forty-six per cent of the white British population are A, whereas forty-four per cent are O group. But B is relatively uncommon—eight per cent I think. I'd have to check it in Mourant." She tapped one of the piles of text-books which jostled with the flowers on her desk, then could not resist opening it. "Yes, eight point six per cent.

"If AB demands not only one B parent, but also B in combination with an A, you can see that the chances of an AB child diminish rapidly," she went on. "Three per cent of the British population according to Mourant's work on blood frequencies. Among the Mongoloid races, and thus among Chinese immigrants, B is much more frequent. As a matter of fact my own blood grouping is B." Jemima wondered whether this, for an expert on blood groupings, was a matter for congratulations, and whether she should proffer them.

Professor Ho continued: "I repeat, among white British people, B is comparatively rare. The reason I asked you whether the name Moses had any significance other than purely Biblical was because you also get a much higher incidence of the B blood group among Jewish people; it varies, but it can be as much as twenty-five per cent."

"As far as I know, Moses so-called is not Jewish. Not

Chinese either," Jemima added with a polite smile. Saffron with Jewish blood? In so far as it was possible to define the physical characteristics of Jewish blood, it could not be ruled out. With that black hair and faintly olive complexion, Jemima had felt all along that there was something of the Mediterranean about his appearance—as opposed to the copybook Englishness of his cousins Jack and Fanny for example. The conventional idea of a Jewish appearance in English terms was often no more than that—something of the Mediterranean or the Middle East, something which had come home to Jemima when visiting Israel and being frequently unable to tell Jew from Arab among the indigenous population.

"Higher too among Greeks—fourteen per cent as opposed to eight per cent in the UK. The increasing presence of Greek Cypriots in this country after the Turkish invasion means that the Health Service needs more B group blood donors than before. There's a particular disease called thalassaemia—Colley's anaemia—to which they're subject."

Greek? Greek Cypriot? Yes, Saffron could well have Greek blood, Greek Cypriot (or for that matter Turkish) if one was simply into some ethnic guessing game based on his appearance. All of this was however to do with who he was or might be rather than who he was not.

"At any rate what you're saying is clear," replied Jemima. "If Moses' parents are both group O, as his mother has stated, then they cannot be his *biological* parents. So I suppose it's back to me to try and establish that one way or another."

"It's really quite simple—or a case like that is simple provided you're quite sure about the parents. Since 1969 blood tests have been allowed in court cases of disputed paternity—to exclude a given father of course, from paternity. As Moses' father would be excluded in court from being the biological parent, given the circumstances: not to prove parenthood, only to exclude."

"How strange that these agglutinogens in our blood should be more strictly hereditary than anything else. After all, physical characteristics or talents like music are not necessarily passed on to children. You can have a red-haired parent without having a red-haired child, but you can't have a B group parent, without having something of B in that child, be it AB or I suppose OB. How strange that blood should be so important."

But Jemima saw from Professor Ho's expression that she did not think it particularly strange that blood should be so important.

"It's back to me," she said hastily, "and I've got to establish the truth of the parents' blood groups. Any suggestions how I should go about it?"

Professor Ho relaxed. "The mother is likely to be right about her own group, especially if she lost a number of children before this one. Three, you said. She might even be O Rhesus Negative to her husband's Rhesus Positive: the antibodies which clash produce a built-up and would account for the series of deaths. The first child should have been all right, did you tell me there was one live birth?"

Jemima shook her head. "Not as far as I know. No, wait, one born live who died about three weeks later. And it was the first child." She remembered the details of Nurse Elsie's story and from the peerage.

"That first child could have died for quite different reasons not associated with blood. After that the problem of Rhesus Negative and Rhesus Positive would build and build."

"And the father?"

"Is he old enough to have been in the forces in the war? People had to carry their blood group with them on a disc."

Lord St. Ives had been in the army: an MC came to mind after his name, and memories of the gallant war record which had made this otherwise somewhat austere figure acceptable to the Tory party in years gone by: "Ivo got all his men back from St. Nazaire, one of the few who did"—the words floated back to her from some television documentary compiled when he became Foreign Secretary. But she could hardly ring up the War Office to establish his blood grouping on the strength of this. The most inventive (and invented) programme for Megalith would hardly cover such an eventuality. No, wait . . .

One possible answer came to her.

"Professor Ho, could you just repeat to me what you told me about the Greek Cypriot community and that disease, the need for more B group blood in the UK as a result? I see a possible programme here. At least, one I could look into. That could be useful."

"Useful to your Moses? Or useful to society?" asked Professor Ho.

"Both," said Jemima firmly.

Not so much later Jemima, back in her flat, was pouring a placatory coup of champagne for a slightly sulky Cherry.

"Yes I know, I know darling, whatever will I think of next!"

"Are we *really* going to make this six-part series called 'The National Blood'?" enquired Cherry. "In which case I'm applying for a transfer." But she drank all the same.

"Why not?" asked Jemima with spirit, repeating to Cherry as to Professor Ho: "At least it's useful."

"You promised me a good time among the Golden Kids," Cherry grumbled, "and now you're talking about a lot of blood. Which reminds me that Cy is back, and according to Miss Lewis, after yours. Blood that is. Wants to know why shooting hasn't started on the aforesaid Golden Kids. That's because he's sold the programme in the States *and* another couple similar about the Golden Kids of France and Germany—I guess that has to be West Germany, but as Miss Lewis said, you never know with Cy, he could pre-sell a programme about the Golden Kids of East Germany when he's in the mood."

"Does he know about Tiggie Jones' engagement to Saffron? Now there's a piece of news for you." Jemima waited smugly to see the effect of her little surprise on Cherry. "You could even call it a Megalith romance since Tiggie was allegedly the researcher on the 'Golden Kids' programme. As to shooting, even Cy Fredericks can hardly expect us to shoot our hero in hospital having been beaten up with a boat hook. Not very golden."

"Saffron and Miss Tiggie! Engaged!" Cherry sounded even more startled than Jemima had expected. She really looked quite astonished, her eyes round as saucers. "Now that really does take my breath away."

"You mean—because of Cy?"

"That and other things."

Cherry looked at Jemima, began to say something more, stopped herself and then said with perhaps rather more vigour than the occasion warranted: "I never liked that girl." She went on: "Now tell me the questions you want me to ask about individual blood groups for this so-called programme." Cherry sounded quite kind.

A couple of evenings later Jemima found she also surprised Cass Brinsley with the news of Saffron's engagement. But then Cass was in the middle of a case and in that slightly captious mood she had come to associate with such situations. No doubt she herself was similarly abstracted— not to say irritable—when in the midst of shooting. All the same Jemima had to confess that his captiousness came as a slight disappointment when she herself had been looking forward quite eagerly, no really very eagerly, to seeing him following her return from Oxford.

"I always knew that girl would come to a bad end. Her lashes were far too long for perfect honesty," said Cass crossly.

"*Is* it a bad end to marry a very rich young man?" Jemima thought of Proffy and Eugenia Jones' rather similar objections to their daughter's match.

"It depends what you want."

"And what do you want, Cass?" It was quite a lighthearted remark but since it was already late, and they were sitting on the deep sofa in Jemima's flat, listening to *Don Giovanni* (Losey film version) Jemima half expected some romantic rejoinder. It was almost the end of the opera: with one ear cocked, Jemima heard the Commendatore dragging Don Giovanni down to hell, as the pious sextet rejoiced over his damnation. She rather thought her Don Giovanni might drag her down to bed. . . . Instead of which Cass answered quite seriously:

"What do I want, darling? Oh God, I wish I knew. Look it's late. Don G. has gone to hell and this case is getting to me. I'll call you tomorrow. OK?"

He gave her a quick firm kiss on the mouth, touched her lightly on the breast and got up.

A few minutes later Cass was gone. A few minutes after that Midnight came complacently through the cat flap and flumped himself down on Jemima's lap, purring loudly and stretching his black paws to her face. Midnight did not care to share Jemima's favours with other admirers.

Jemima once again felt oddly disconcerted, that Emma-at-Box-Hill feeling which had overcome her in the High Street at Oxford. Whatever the nature of their relationship—so carefully undefined—she had been looking forward to going to bed with Cass that night.

The presence of Midnight, large, furry and sensual nibbling at her cheek with his delicate tongue, only emphasized the absence of Cass.

Better to think about blood. Saffron's blood. Jemima found Mourant, the book presented to her by Professor Ho, the title: *Blood relations* and the sub-title "Blood groups and anthropology." Perhaps Mourant would send her to sleep. She began, rather firmly, to read the preliminary remarks about visible characteristics such as the shape of eye or colour of skin fixed solely or partly by heredity and came to the passage:

"In contrast to these visible characteristics, research during the present century shows that there is a class of invisible ones, fixed by heredity in a known way at the moment of conception, immutable during the life of the individual, and observable by relatively simple scientific tests. These are the blood groups. . . ."

Curiously enough, someone else was at that very moment also thinking dark thoughts about Saffron's blood. In a way these thoughts might have been benefited from the absolute clarity brought by Mourant; as it was, they consisted of a great swilling wash of anger brought about by the knowledge that Saffron was not what he seemed, seething like a tide in the basin of an uneasy brain without any possibility of escape. Relief would only come through the spilling of that same blood, the interloper's blood.

Bim Marcus had already paid the penalty for a mistake. The boat-hook incident had been a sudden impulse and as such had not really deserved to succeed. Planning was the essence of success. As Jemima restlessly put aside Mourant, and took up a P.D. James she had already read twice (its title ironically enough was *Innocent Blood*), the other person thinking about Saffron that night decided on what might turn out in the end to be the best plan of all.

CHAPTER TWELVE

•

Love and Hate

Jemima Shore woke up about five o'clock. Neither Mourant nor P.D. James had ensured heavy slumbers. At first she was surprised to find herself alone and murmured rather sleepily: "Cass." Midnight too was absent: some dawn prowl had claimed him.

An hour later, sleep being impossible, Jemima feeling remarkably discontented decided on a dawn prowl herself. The thought of Richmond Park in the early morning, green, quiet and empty, was suddenly extremely tempting. She pulled on a white track suit and filled a thermos full of coffee. She thought of a private breakfast picnic among the bracken; perhaps there would be deer; she could not remember which season it was which brought the deer to join the solitary picnickers.

Jemima driving fast—too fast—in her Mercedes, had forgotten the early morning string of horses and riders which usually filed into the park at that hour. She came to a rapid halt. Then at the traffic lights she found herself drawn up beside one especially magnificent glossy horse, a chestnut, which took its rider way above the height of the low sports car.

Jemima looked up. The rider was male, and like the horse, quite young and very glossy with thick hair not unlike the colour of his horse's coat.

She smiled.

"I like your horse."

"I like your car."

"Swap?"

"Horses are worth more than cars, even Mercedes. What will you give me to make up the balance?"

Jemima considered. The lights were changing.

"I could give you a cup of coffee, but then what would you do with your horse?"

"You know," began the rider, "you look rather like—"

The light was green and Jemima shot forward. What with Cass and Mourant and Midnight, none of whom had proved themselves to be particularly rewarding companions during the night hours, she began to wish that she had rather a different nature. Why not, for example, take off into the bracken with a handsome and unknown young cavalier and forget the cares of the world, or at least the cares represented by the foregoing three names for the length of one morning's idyll? Why not?

"Because I wouldn't have enjoyed it at all," said Jemima sternly to herself as she laid out her solitary picnic in the bracken, car abandoned, some time later. "That's why. What a perfectly ridiculous idea anyway. As it is, I'm already covered in bracken, so think what it would have been like . . ." Jemima drank her coffee and did think, just for a moment, what it would have been like.

Whether she was right or wrong about the anonymous cavalier would never be known, but she was still brushing fronds off her track suit when she entered Megalithic House. What was more, she was by now rather late, having encountered heavy traffic on her way from Richmond Park. The various traffic blocks gave Jemima plenty of time to ponder on a number of things, including whether there was a special God who deliberately sent down heavy traffic when you were late already and not for a reason that everyone in the world would consider a good one.

Cherry, looking remarkably appealing in a pink cotton boiler-suit, many top buttons left untouched and a tight belt to clinch her figure at the waist, gazed speculatively at Jemima as she entered.

"Messages first or a cup of coffee? You've just been having coffee? In Richmond Park? I knew it had to be something perfectly ordinary like that. Ah well, here goes. Cy of course. Three times, and I dare say Miss Lewis fended off some other of his reckless enquiries after your whereabouts before they reached me. Cass telephoned. Twice. Sounded agitated, if not as agitated as our Chairman. Says he missed you at home. And Saffron. Last but not least. First, he's out of hospital, back in his college. Second, the engagement weekend at Saffron Ivy has been fixed: bank holiday weekend at the end of May."

"Anything else?"

"Oh yes. A man telephoned. Nice voice. Wondered if you drove a white Mercedes sports car. He thought he might have seen you in Richmond Park this morning."

"What a weird enquiry!" said Jemima in her most innocent tone.

"That's what I thought. So I told him you drove an old black Ford and were anyway away filming in Manchester."

Cy Fredericks accepted with surprising equanimity Jemima's proffered explanation of a game of squash, and then a traffic delay driving from the squash club. It was the word club which seemed to soothe him.

"The Squash Club!" he cried. "Most exciting! Jemima, you must take me there sometime. Can one eat there late as well as early?" Luckily Miss Lewis entered before Jemima had time to sort out a suitable reply.

As to Cy's keen enquiries about the progress of the "Golden Kids" programme, Jemima was able to stop them at source by her double revelation of Tiggie Jones' engagement and her own invitation to Saffron Ivy.

"We'll be *shooting* there?" asked Cy in a specially reverent tone which he reserved for any conjunction of Megalith cameras and the more gracious aspects of English life.

"No, no, all shooting in Oxford." Jemima knew it was the moment to stand firm. "I've got the whole thing lined up." She took a chance. "You didn't read my memo. We centre round the Commem Balls at the end of June. St. Lucy's is having a big Commem this year—it's their turn—and Rochester is having an ordinary Ball, which I'm assured won't really be ordinary at all. We feature Saffron with Tiggie Jones, the future Lady Saffron, on his arm or anyway somewhere respectable like an arm, then the whole lot of them: the Golden Kids at play. Just what you wanted. Then

we move to St. Lucy's which is on the river: plenty of
punting. Remember how keen you were on punting."

Cy Fredericks looked uneasy but Jemima thought it was
more in reference to the unread (and as a matter of fact as
yet unwritten) memo than at the prospect of Megalith
cameras going punting. Which should actually have worried him more.

"Tiggie Jones to wed," he said at last. "I shall never
understand you English girls. Never." Jemima thought it
diplomatic not to probe further into that statement. Nor did
Cy Fredericks seem in any mood to amplify it. It was his
kind of obituary on the future Lady Saffron.

The ten days or so before the Saffron Ivy weekend were
spent by Jemima both at Megalith and Oxford in a frenzy of
official activity as the "Golden Kids" programme suddenly
became a reality—a hideous reality said Guthrie Carlyle in
one of his daring *sotto voce* remarks at a planning meeting,
and "that bloody programme" was heard on more lips than
just Jemima's. All sorts of questions had to be answered
rather quickly, ranging from the practical to the theoretical.

For example, was Spike Thompson (Jemima's favourite
cameraman and many other people's favourite man) avail
able? It was generally agreed that Spike would display an
unrivalled mastery over the shadows on the long grass and
Laura Ashley dresses and doomed youth and fingers trailing
out of punts and ancient stone walls and all that sort of
thing. He would also deal expertly with pop music, heavy
metal, rock music, and sundry other concomitants of the
modern world which Jemima, if not Cy, was well aware
went with a successful Commem Ball. Spike could also be
relied upon not to raise his camera—nor for that matter his
eyebrows—at some of the more lethal habits of doomed
youth, the exotic cigarettes to be puffed, the exotic white
substances to be sniffed. In short Spike Thompson was, so
far as Megalith was concerned, Thoroughly Modern Cameraman.

"Champagne yes, if it's around, the rest of it no,"
observed Guthrie Carlyle wisely. "You can't drink and
drug. At any rate not on a Megalith programme."

As for Spike's expenses: "Even Spike can't do much with
a lot of students' snack bars," suggested some optimist. For

Spike Thompson's expenses while on location were legendary; so that people sometimes swapped anecdotes about such trips at eventide in the Blue Flag, as Henry V predicted that the men who outlived Agincourt would recall St. Crispin's Day.

"I'm not sure we'll be moving exclusively in the snack bar set. The programme *is* called 'Golden Kids.'"

"But not 'Golden Cameramen,'" retorted the optimist wittily. Jemima exchanged glances with Cherry. It was in both their minds that introducing Spike to La Lycée—and how could it be avoided?—was rather like showing an Alsatian into a butcher's shop.

As to the theoretical side, it became increasingly obvious that there were two programmes here. One was the programme beloved of Cy Fredericks—the "Golden Kids mean Big Bucks" programme which was undeniably the type of programme he had successfully pre-sold in those parts of the world—the more luxurious parts—which he had recently visited. The other was the kind of socially investigative programme beloved of Jemima Shore and Guthrie Carlyle in which the lifestyle of the Golden Kids would be contrasted with that of the vast majority of the undergraduates eating in Hall, living off grants or, rather, struggling with inadequate grants, finding even coffee an expensive luxury and never touching a drop of champagne from one end of term to the other.

"This is where Kerry Barber is important," explained Jemima. "He's our link. For one thing, he's not only boycotting St. Lucy's Commem Ball but leading a protest outside it, a protest against the price of the tickets, that is. He thinks the money should go to the Third World and is prepared to say so to camera. He's also going to provide us with some undergraduates of the same way of thinking. We've got permission to film at St. Lucy's as well as Rochester, so the Barber protest should be quiet an effective contrast."

"Jem, my gem," began Cy Fredericks warmly, "you're doing wonders here as you always do. Rounded, human *and* humanitarian: I can see already how this programme is shaping. All the same, our motto here at Megalith has always been hard-*nosed* not hard-*grained* reporting." He paused, giving everyone at the meeting including himself just time to wonder exactly what the difference if any between these two terms might be, before he rushed on: "What I'm saying, and I think—Miss Lewis, is this right?— I *think* I'm quoting from my address to NIFTA last fall—the essence of interesting controversy on the screen is equality of protest."

Miss Lewis' silence being taken as assent, Cy beamed even more warmly, particularly as this last statement gained a great deal of muttered encouragement from all those present, delighted to have such an unexceptional sentiment with which to agree.

"So, my gem, please no uncouth types in blue jeans given our air time for their causes . . ."

"I'm afraid I can't guarantee the elimination of jeans from the programme altogether," interrupted Jemima sweetly, allowing her gaze to roam the room before resting briefly on her own designer-jean-clad thigh. "But I should tell you that the principal protestor at St. Lucy's on the night of the Commem will be Jack Iverstone, who is of course Saffron's cousin. Is that what you meant by equality of protest?"

Everyone agreed afterwards that it was a noted victory for the cause of the good in the perpetual—and not unenjoyable—war waged between Cy and Jemima on the content of her programmes. But as a matter of fact the victory, if it was such, had been engineered by Fanny Iverstone. In the course of her various expeditions to Oxford, Jemima had found no difficulty at all in securing the agreement of assorted undergraduates to appear on the programme promoting assorted views. But although the views were varied, the declared motive for agreeing to appear was generally the same:

"I thought I might go into television after I've gone down," confided the innocent. The more sophisticated eyed Jemima keenly and asked details of graduate training schemes at Megalith. It all came to the same thing: most people at Oxford, like Kerry Barber, were perfectly prepared to share what they imagined to be Jemima's forum of the air.

Nevertheless Fanny's approach took Jemima by surprise. Perhaps it should not have done. After all Fanny was an

indefatigable organizer. Saffron was really quite right to
compare his cousin to Mrs. Thatcher—except that the latter
had actually been at Oxford as an undergraduate whereas
Fanny, as she had cheerfully admitted on their first meeting, had had no education at all. The thought occurred to
Jemima as they sat in the dark plate-glass window of Bunns,
Oxford's most fashionable café. Fanny was drinking an
extraordinarily expensive cappucino while Jemima toyed
with an orange juice (equally expensive). In view of Fanny's
forceful character, it was tragic that foolish Daphne Iverstone had taken no interest in her education. With education, Fanny might have gone far. Correction: Fanny
would—somehow—go far; of that Jemima felt sure. The
question was, in what direction?

Jemima certainly could not imagine her married to her
cousin Saffron, although she would have made an excellent
Marchioness of the old-fashioned school; but the pair of
them would have driven each other to desperation. Jemima
only hoped that the dominating streak Fanny had inherited
from her father—at present concealed under the softness of
girlhood—would not lead her in the same political direction
as Andrew Iverstone.

It was Andrew Iverstone who constituted the problem for
Jack, confided Fanny. That and his political ambitions.

"Can you imagine what it's like for him, being the son of
Old Rabblerouse? For Jack who won't allow any violent
emotion whatsoever to surface? Quite apart from being
ambitious to save the world and all that sort of thing. So it's
twice as important for Jack to make his name as for anyone
else. You must feature him on your programme. Doing his
thing. This protest with that rather dishy tutor who eats
nuts, in his shorts and sandals. Just so everyone can see he
doesn't agree with Daddy. Please, Jemima."

"What about you, Fanny?" asked Jemima curiously. "Do
you mind being the daughter of Old Rabblerouse, as you
kindly term him?"

"It's different for girls, isn't it?" Fanny gave her confident
upper-class laugh which was possibly more charming now
while she was still young than it would be when she got
older. "I'll change my name when I get married. For me,
frankly, it's much worse being Mummy's daughter. All that

ghastly debutante stuff and the match-making! I ask you. In this day and age. Quite a relief when the Prince of Wales finally got married, I can tell you. If only the other two would follow suit. Prince Andrew, as you may suppose, is Daddy's ultimate idea of what a hereditary leader figure should be."

"I gather she even had cousin Saffron in mind." Jemima spoke carelessly.

"Who told you that?" Fanny sounded—and looked—quite put out.

"Oh just gossip!" said Jemima hastily. "Poppy Delaware, someone like that."

"She should talk. She's been after him for ages. Oh well, now Tiggie Jones has got him. For the time being. We've been bidden, you know, to the great engagement weekend. And Mummy and Daddy. All very feudal: political differences to be strictly put aside: blood is thicker than politics."

"For the time being?" questioned Jemima, catching at one of Fanny's seemingly careless remarks. "You don't think the marriage will last?"

Fanny gave another of her confident smiles. "Did I say that? I didn't exactly mean it wouldn't last if they did get married. I just meant that they're not married yet." But Jemima had the impression that this time Fanny's jauntiness was slightly forced.

"Many a slip between engagement and lip," Fanny went on, "or at least where that couple is concerned. Tiggie Jones is going to have to give up one or two of her bad habits, for one thing."

"Her universal displays of affection? Or as she put it herself once to me, I just love love. Is that what you had in mind?"

"Oh absolutely," replied Fanny in a tone of voice which made it quite clear that it was not.

It was noticeable that Jack Iverstone, whom Jemima interviewed about the programme in his rooms at St. Lucy's, took rather the same line about the engagement. Fanny was perhaps animated by a certain feminine jealousy. Jack had to be acquitted on that score. Nevertheless he frowned over the prospect, that deep rather weary frown which from time to time marred his cheerful face and made one see the anxious politician he would one day become.

"Trust Saffer to pick on the one girl who can be guaranteed not to pull him together."

"You don't like Tiggie?"

"Tiggie isn't someone you like or dislike. She's a perfectly idiotic force of nature, if such a thing is possible. I just think they're far too alike. That dreadful capriciousness of hers and those mad ideas of his—did he ever talk to you about his Marxism? Marxist! *Saffer*! Who even has his shoes cleaned by Wyndham, at least fifty years his senior. It's all part of his plan to provoke, and Tiggie, in so far as she has any plan, has roughly the same idea. You have to have one sane one in a marriage. It's terrible when people think alike and they're both wrong."

He stopped at Jemima's expression.

"Yes, I am thinking of my own parents, if you're interested. My mother's lifelong adoration of my father—they married when they were both twenty—it's one of his chief problems. No one at home has ever argued with him."

"Except you."

"Except me. And I don't argue, I reason. But you won't find me reasoning with him at the coming weekend. I shall rein it all in—keep it perhaps for your television programme," Jack said with a slight smile. "It's going to be grisly enough without a father-and-son confrontation. Cousin Ivo will be giving us his celebrated impersonation of a very parfait gentleman, as a result of which he was able to appear as our most popular Foreign Secretary for years, in spite of being quite a tough customer underneath it all. Cousin Gwendolen needs no impersonation to be the very parfait English lady." He shuddered.

"Such politeness all round! When we stayed there as children and my father was making all those terrible speeches about immigration in the seventies. Just *The Times* handed over to you at breakfast: 'Jack, your father's making the headlines again.' Perfect politeness, no reproach. I wanted to *die*. I was so embarrassed I couldn't read it and had to sneak into the library later. I used to be sick before coming down to breakfast in anticipation."

"And Fanny? The same?"

"Good God, no! Fanny's more straightforward. 'Has Daddy been spouting tosh as usual?' she'd say brightly. And help herself to the rest of the sausages. Fanny's one of the strongest characters I know. And I don't mean physically."

"I take it there'll be a great deal of politeness around this weekend. Including your father."

"Oh yes, you know Daddy's manners when he wants things to go well. At Saffron Ivy there'll be so much politeness about on the surface that we'll all be swimming in a great dish of rich cream. But what about the hatred underneath? You should worry about that, Jemima Shore Investigator."

Jack leant back in his large worn green armchair, the bottom of which was visibly sagging. He had installed Jemima in the only vaguely new chair in the room, something which had evidently arrived, but none too recently, from Habitat. His mantelpiece was crowded with cards of various societies, mainly of a political nature, amongst which Jemima noticed the official programme of the Union. The contrast with his cousin Saffron's mantelpiece at Rochester was marked: there she had glimpsed practically no traces of Oxford life at all (unless you counted Chimneysweepers' menus) but a number of rather grand engraved invitations to London parties. Her eye lit upon a rather pretty water-colour of a house hanging to the left of the fireplace, much the most attractive object in the room. Jemima recognized Saffron Ivy.

"Nothing that happens in a house like that can be all bad," she said. But afterwards she would always swear that even at the time some frission, some faint expression of her famous instinct, had warned her that these words were, like those of the Megalith spokesman on the subject of Spike's expenses at Oxford, absurdly optimistic.

CHAPTER THIRTEEN

•

Saffron Ivy

There were a number of cars drawn up in the sweep of the drive which ended with a flourish in front of Saffron Ivy like the dramatis personae of a play. Jemima saw a Rolls, not a new Rolls, at least fifteen years old Jemima guessed, but so beautifully kept and shining that it gave the impression of being a treasured yet still useful antique, like an immaculately polished dining-room table. Drawn up alongside was a sharp little mini, navy blue with tinted glass windows. Jemima thought the mini might belong to Fanny Iverstone. There was also a rather fine motor bike, probably a Harley Davidson, since it was remarkably similar to that owned by the legendary cameraman Spike Thompson and thus occasionally ridden pillion by Jemima Shore (amongst others). Next to that was a Porsche.

Then there was a dusty grey Cortina, looking like a poor relation: Jack Iverstone? Beside it Jemima recognized Saffron's car, a Maserati, dashing and rather too ostentatious like its owner; in case she hadn't, the final note of ostention was presented by the initial S on the driver's door and a coronet over it. The back seat of the Maserati had a jumble of cassettes on it and some white and frilly garments spilling about. Tiggie's presumably, not Saffron's. Would his car be unpacked as well as his suitcase? Jemima remembered Saffron's description of the chauffeur Wyndham "looking after everything in my car." That led her to Saffron's account of the original attack, the fixing of the car. Jemima shivered.

Above her head, above the surrounding flat but grace-fully wooded landscape, a vista of greens beneath an enormous bowl of grey sky, rose up the imposing shape of Saffron Ivy. To Jemima there was something menacing as well as palatial about its magnificent façade. She felt that the rich and newly respectable Iverstones, who dragged Robert Smythson from the employment of Bess of Hard-wicke to build the house, did not intend their robber baron origins to be entirely forgotten.

The front door opened and at the head of the steps stood a welcoming figure in T-shirt and jeans. Saffron. She assumed it was Saffron. The informality of his clothes was, she thought, in pleasing contrast to the formality of the late Elizabethan façade. The welcoming figure then trotted down the steps and revealed itself to be a good deal older as well as stouter than Saffron.

Slightly startled, Jemima put out her hand. Instead of taking it, the T-shirted figure deftly possessed himself of her car keys and before she could protest, was burrowing in the back of her car for her luggage. Her suitcase emerged with its conspicuous labelling (ordered by Cherry—but that was really no excuse) JEMIMA SHORE. Jemima found that she was gazing at the T-shirt, strained over an impressive chest, which also bore a piece of conspicuous labelling.

"I'M BINYON" she read.

The jean-clad figure looked down at her suitcase, tapped his chest and smiled even more broadly.

"Good afternoon, Miss Shore. We've both of us nailed our colours to the mast, as it were, haven't we? But then in a manner of speaking, we're both in the same line of business. If you don't think me presumptuous."

Jemima, even more baffled, smiled back, her beautiful smile of all-purpose sweetness which was particularly useful when total strangers accosted her, apparently confident of recognition.

"I'm Binyon"—the chest was tapped again— "Binyon the swinging butler."

Some vague memory stirred.

"And of course I don't need to be told who you are. Label or no label. You're just like you are on television. Very friendly." Binyon shepherded Jemima up the steps. "The

staff are so excited. What with his lordship's engagement
and your arrival."

To be accurate, thought Jemima, out of the two of them
it was Binyon who was the friendly one. And what was a
swinging butler anyway? Unless it was simply a butler who
wore jeans and a T-shirt in the afternoon. Jemima found she
was oddly disappointed; atavistic snobbery no doubt, but
she had been expecting the sort of butler you saw on
television—except that Binyon seemed to indicate that he
had been on television. Oh well . . .

"His lordship is in the library," said Binyon. At least that
was a conventional butler's observation. And the library,
the famous Saffron Ivy library founded by some intellectual
Iverstone in the early eighteenth century, was everything
of which a romantic might dream: tooled leather, dark
bindings, deep embrasures by the windows, heavy chairs,
a large globe, a beautiful deep desk, it was all here. So for
that matter was his lordship: not Saffron, however, but
Lord St. Ives, jumping up with extraordinary briskness
from his chair and lolloping to greet her, as though a
second's delay might indicate a fatal degree of impoliteness.

At the same moment, a large labrador, so pale it was
almost white, started towards her. The dog, unlike Lord St.
Ives, was remarkably fat which perhaps accounted for the
discrepancy in their respective gaits. The words "well-
preserved" might almost have been coined for Lord St.
Ives: he was so spare as to suggest that the familiar cartoons
which showed him as a series of narrow straight lines were
in fact portraits not caricatures.

While the dog sniffed slowly and cynically at Jemima's
high-heeled shoes, as though little that was good could be
expected from them, Lord St. Ives shook Jemima's hand
with a particular kind of energetic delight. Jemima found it
oddly familiar until she realized that she had watched him
displaying it on the television news, on numerous occasions, as he greeted world leaders when he was Foreign
Secretary. The more the ensuing talks were expected to be
"controversial" in the words of the newscaster, the more
pleasure Lord St. Ives evinced; he had the air of running
into a friend from his London club. How different, how
very different was the Cy Fredericks style of greeting! The

Chairman of Megalith was apt to welcome even those he knew well with a very slight air of unease beneath his rapture, as though they might have gone and changed their name or in some other way subtly betrayed him since their last meeting.

Then Jemima saw that Lord St. Ives had not been alone in the library. At the far end, an elderly woman was struggling out of a deep leather chair, similar to that from which Lord St. Ives had sprung with such trapezoid agility. Finally she was able to stand up with the aid of a stick, two sticks. Jemima, recognizing Lady St. Ives from Saffron's photograph at Rochester, thought that she actually seemed years older than her husband. This was partly because Lady St. Ives, like the dog, moved slowly and had pure white hair. She wore spectacles, secured with a cord round her neck; Lord St. Ives' hair on the other hand, in line with his general air of preservation, retained a kind of sandy colour which made Jemima suppose he must have looked much the same even as a young man. How old *was* he? How old was *she*?

The most surprising thing about Lord St. Ives was that even now he was actually an attractive as well as a charming man: something to do with centuries of having things your own way, thought Jemima suspiciously. But then Lady St. Ives must have had her own way too: perhaps illness had prevented her from developing this particular kind of allure; Jemima remembered Saffron's references to his mother's health.

In the meantime Jemima was being briskly guided to the far end of the library by her host; managing however to take in the famous Lawrence of "The Strawberry Children," which showed a little girl and boy holding a basket of fruit between them, on the way.

Jemima shook Lady St. Ives' extended hand which bore a number of splendid but slightly dulled diamond rings. (Was it *nouveau riche*, she wondered, to have one's jewellery cleaned? Jemima neither possessed a lot of precious jewellery nor coveted it—except perhaps the odd emerald; so far the offer of an odd emerald had not come her way.) Lady St. Ives wore a handsome diamond brooch pinned to her flowered dress, as well as three rows of pearls; the brooch was similarly dulled. The pearls looked superb.

"We're all so excited, Miss. Shore," Lady St. Ives echoed her husband's words. "And Binyon has been polishing the silver as he only does when the Queen comes."

"Rather more so!" exclaimed Lord St. Ives gaily. "He's been practically polishing us."

Jemima saw an opportunity to get at least one mystery solved: "Yes, do explain to me about Binyon."

"Oh we thought you might know him"—surprise from Lady St. Ives. "From the telly—"

"Nonsense, my dear, she's much too grand."

"Yes, but he's Binyon." Lady St. Ives turned to Jemima, quite eagerly: "Binyon, the singing butler."

"Oh *singing*, you said singing. Singing, not swinging." Puzzlement from Lady St. Ives.

"I don't think Binyon swings. What would he swing from? But he has a very nice voice. Rather like John McCormack, we always think."

Jemima was distinctly relieved to find that Binyon, jeans or no jeans, was no new breed of butler, but had simply entered an amateur talent competition on television. He had won a series of rounds culminating in an exciting final in which Binyon the Singing Butler had defeated Mirabel O'Shea the Crooning Cook.

"At least, that's how the papers described it," confessed Lady St. Ives. "But Mirabel O'Shea, while being an absolute darling, all twenty stone of her, we loved her, Binyon invited her down here afterwards with her children, there wasn't a father, all the same she wasn't exactly what you'd call a cook. She'd been frying bacon and eggs in a motorway café, you see."

"Nonsense, my dear, move with the times! That's exactly what you'd call a cook these days." Lady St. Ives did not answer her husband but instead displayed to Jemima an enormous and very ugly television set, facing her chair, to which they had all been glued during Binyon's weeks of fame. Above it hung an exquisite double portrait of a mother and child, the mother with a mass of powdered curling hair, the baby with its fat white arms thrown upwards; once again Jemima had seen so many reproductions of the picture that she found the sight of the original, sited so cosily above the television set, slightly disconcerting. The label read: "Frances Sophia, Marchioness of St. Ives and the Honble. Ivo Charles Iverstone."

Lord St. Ives followed the direction of her gaze. "Sir Joshua. We think ours is better than the one in the National Gallery. So did K. Clark, I'm glad to say."

"It's ravishing. *She's* ravishing."

"Oh, Frances Sophia. I'm afraid she was no better than she should be—you remember Greville's phrase."

"Of course. And the baby is delicious," replied Jemima firmly, who had never read Greville, but did not intend to be wrong-footed, at least not on that score, by her host.

"The baby—Ivo Charles—he grew up to be the corrupt MP, I fear. And a terrible gambler. Fox's friend."

"We used to think Saffron looked rather like him as a baby," volunteered Lady St. Ives. There was a small quite unmistakable pause: Jemima was quite sure about it. Then Lord St. Ives gave a light laugh.

"I do hope the resemblance is not carried through. As far as I am aware, gambling at least is not among my son's vices."

"But he used to love playing *Vingt et Un* as a child, when we all went to Bembridge." What further reminiscences Lady St. Ives might have produced of Saffron's childhood— the topic was after all not absolutely without interest—was not to be known, since the subject himself now arrived in the library.

Saffron was dressed in white cotton trousers, rather tattered, and ending as though more by chance than design at the knee, and a scarlet vest. He was browner than Jemima remembered and, she had to admit, looked remarkably handsome. He also had an air of health. It was difficult to believe that he had so recently been in hospital; in fact with his tanned skin, thick black hair, considerably longer, flopping over his face, and his slanting black eyes, he looked more like a gipsy than ever; a state gipsy from a musical comedy perhaps.

Tiggie on the other hand, in baggy khaki shorts and a mud-coloured shirt, looked for the first time drab, not a word which Jemima would ever have thought to apply to her in London. Compared to Saffron, she had the air of a hen bird: she had had her hair cut very short and her skin remained pale. The only sparkling thing about Tiggie on this occasion was the conspicuous ring on her finger. Diamonds, yes, and emeralds, or rather one great big emerald. This ring really did gleam and was either brand new or had been recently cleaned. But the nails on the small pale hand which bore the weighty ring were dirty. Jemima was surprised; she had the impression that the fairy creature she had first encountered at Megalith had been immaculately clean beneath her bizarre get-up.

Saffron gave his mother a light peck on her papery cheek; then he gave Jemima a kiss on both cheeks, followed by a hug. He was hot and sweaty like a young horse which had just run a successful race.

"Tennis, darling?" enquired Lady St. Ives, with a doting look, as though to explain this condition and at the same time boast of it.

"Fanny and I have just beaten Jack and Cousin Andrew."

"Andrew must have hated that!" pronounced Lord St. Ives with much satisfaction. "He used to be frightfully good. Didn't he play in doubles at Wimbledon, my dear?" Lady St. Ives looked rather vague as if the subject of anyone else's tennis other than that of her son's did not interest her.

"I don't think Jack liked it very much either," said Saffron. "He always used to beat me. But Fanny's terrific. Serving like Martina Navrati-what-not. Tremendous at net too."

"Oh darling, do you think you should—your head—"

"Oh Ma!"

"What about you, Antigone?" Lord St. Ives asked kindly. Jemima noticed he exhibited the same courtesy to the young as to the old, and was especially gallant to his future daughter-in-law.

Saffron answered for her. "Tiggie doesn't play." Tiggie cast down her eyes, so that the long lashes which Cass had admired, fluttered on her pale cheeks. "I hate games," she said in a voice which was scarcely above a whisper.

Saffron took her hand and held it. The pair of them were standing directly beneath "The Strawberry Children"—

subtitled: "The Honble. Miss Iverstone and her brother with a basket of fruit." Then he dropped the hand and turned to Jemima.

"Well, I love games. There's going to be a return match. Come and watch. Cheer me on. You're on my side, you know you are." Saffron's bold black eyes challenged Jemima: there was something febrile about him today, as new and marked as Tiggie's passivity. It was a sexual statement.

"My dear boy, I'm certainly on your side." Lord St. Ives put his arm around his son's shoulders. Jemima wondered if he had perhaps known what Saffron was up to, and decided that he probably had: not much passed by Lord St. Ives. Seeing them side by side for the first time, "father" and "son," she was struck by the similarity of their stance; Saffron had evidently copied his father's bearing, even some of his mannerisms, from childhood. Although physically they could hardly have been less alike, the one so dark, the other so typically English, Jemima ruminated on the interesting resemblances which "nurture" not "nature" was able to bring about. She had known other adopted children, come to think of it, who had grown to resemble their "parents" so strongly, that people sometimes refused to believe in the truth of their adoption.

"You're avenging all the times Andrew used to beat me," said Lord St. Ives.

"Quite apart from Jack beating *me*," replied Saffron. "All the cousins are terrifically athletic; or anyway they try very hard. To make up." Saffron sounded quite complacent.

"To make up for what?" Jemima asked innocently, although she knew the answer; but she felt an urge to prick the complacency, a radical urge which she instantly regretted when Lord St. Ives, who had not held Russians in play for nothing, picked up cudgels. Or rather, he appeared to gaze at the cudgels beneath his nose and find them instantly delightful.

"Why, to make up for being dreadfully poor of course, whereas we are dreadfully rich!" he exclaimed, with his usual zest. "It *is* unfair. Don't you think so, Miss Shore? Of course you do. That we should have all this—" he gave a wide gesture embracing not only the Reynolds, the

Lawrence, and several thousand books in their majestic bindings, but also Binyon who had at that moment entered and was standing, still clad in his eponymous T-shirt, at the door. "I expect you want me to feel guilty. Oh Miss Shore, I do, I do."

"Ivo, why are you being so silly?" Lady St. Ives suddenly enquired. "You know you don't feel guilty at all. The hereditary system is absolutely indefensible, except that it happens to work brilliantly. I've heard you say it countless times."

"Oh my dear, don't give me away," said Lord St. Ives tenderly. "I only say that in the House of Lords; you've been listening to my speeches which I really don't advise. Nobody listens to my speeches in the House of Lords."

Lady St. Ives continued to look gently reproachful.

"Besides, I think Miss Shore is referring to primogeniture, aren't you, Miss Shore? Why should I sit in glory here at Saffron Ivy while for example poor Cousin Andrew pigs it in Henley?"

"I did ask a question," said Jemima sweetly. "But I don't think it was exactly that one."

"But Ivo, Daphne and Andrew don't live *in* Henley, no one lives *in* Henley—" began Lady St. Ives.

"*Façon de parler*, my dear, *façon de parler*. I have to admit that one good defence of the hereditary system does seem to me the fact that I live here and Cousin Andrew doesn't. But then I'm prejudiced. Now what about that tennis?"

"The players are on the court, my lord." It was the solemn voice of Binyon, once again sounding, if not looking, like the butler of Jemima's dreams. "Mr. Valliera is playing with Miss Fanny in place of Lord Saffron."

"No he bloody isn't!" exclaimed Saffron. And so they all went and watched the tennis, leaving Jemima with various images in her mind, some of them concerning Saffron, some Tiggie, some both; and some thoughts about Lord St. Ives and the hereditary system. She did not think that Lord St. Ives had been altogether joking when he defended his inheritance on the grounds that he was worthy of it, whereas his cousin was not. That substitution all those years ago . . . she had expected to find it quite implausible in the face of Lord St. Ives' famous courtesy and "parfait" manners, in the words of Jack. But Jack was right: there was something quite steely there underneath it all.

The last thing she had learned concerned the passionate affection which was borne towards Saffron by his parents— not only Lady St. Ives, but Lord St. Ives as well. There was something quite naked about the devotion he had momentarily exhibited when he put his arm around Saffron's shoulders. Jemima dreaded to think what would happen to this elderly couple if anything happened to him. And this time she was not pondering on the fate of the Iverstone inheritance.

CHAPTER FOURTEEN

•

Tennis Is About Winning

It came as relief after these subterranean fears, to watch the open rivalries of the tennis court. When the St. Ives party arrived, Proffy and Eugenia Jones were sitting in two ancient deck chairs beside it. Their heads were close together.

Jemima had the impression that some rather earnest colloquy had been interrupted, certainly not of an amorous nature and probably not connected with the tennis match either. Both stood up as Lady St. Ives, walking with difficulty, arrived. Eugenia Jones looked extraordinarily melancholy and, unlike Lady St. Ives, in no way conveyed that kind of indulgent affection towards Tiggie which might have been expected on such a celebratory occasion. More than ever she seemed dependent on the ebullience of Proffy who gave the air of cosseting her, as a bear might protect some smaller breed of animal. This kind of possessiveness in public away from home was no doubt intended to make up for his defection to the side of Eleanor in marriage.

On this occasion Eugenia simply ignored Tiggie and walked in the direction of St. Ives as though to speak to him. In a neat manoeuvre, Proffy somehow managed to outflank her:

"A word—" he began.

"Later, later. After tennis. I know words. They lengthen into sentences. To say nothing of speeches. Then we shan't get any tennis."

"Oh Ivo, are you going to play?" cried Lady St. Ives.

"If anyone will play with an old man like me," replied Lord St. Ives genially. "A geriatric doubles, perhaps, after this dashing match is over." He settled himself down, as though the matter was decided. Jemima was nonetheless left with the impression that the tension within Eugenia which Proffy had in some way tried to relieve, had not subsided.

The tennis court itself, Jemima was amused to note, was more in the tradition of Lady St. Ives' jewellery, antique splendour now much dimmed, than of anything more professional. Andrew Iverstone did indeed allow himself some fairly barbed references to the superiority of the court in—or rather near—Henley. Lord St. Ives bore it all with great humour as he sat in a deck chair, itself not in its first youth, his face shaded by an aged straw hat, whose faded ribbon doubtless proclaimed membership of some exclusive club to which Andrew Iverstone had never belonged.

"Can't you get your people to look at this court, Ivo?" shouted Andrew Iverstone eventually, when he failed to return a modest lob from Saffron which landed in one of the more obvious craters.

"What people, my dear chap? I don't have any tennis people, I fear. This court was made before the war. *En-Tout-Cas.*" He gave the name exquisite French pronunciation. "I must say it's lived up to the name. Until today that is."

"I'll give you the name of ours," grunted Iverstone, smashing a good low forehand drive from his daughter unexpectedly to Saffron's backhand and thus winning the point.

"Such charming people" fluted Daphne Iverstone in the vague direction of Gwendolen St. Ives. "Old-fashioned manners which I think make such a difference—"

"Be quiet, will you, Daphne, when we're playing." Andrew Iverstone's politeness, in its own way as much a part of his public character as that of Lord St. Ives, evidently did not stretch as far as the tennis court. Some of the other young sprawled temporarily by the court. They included Bernardo Valliera who proved to own both the Harley Davidson and the Porsche (how had he transported *both* to Saffron Ivy?). The dusty Cortina however did not belong to Jack who said cheerfully he could not afford a car, but to Proffy. The smart little Mini was a recent present from Saffron to Tiggie. Then the young departed for the croquet lawn which lay at some distance, sufficiently far for the gales of laughter which punctuated play to have a charming rather than irritating effect upon the ear.

Iverstone was at net where he made an imposing bull-like figure, his great red forehead gleaming with sweat; there was no doubt that he was still a formidable tennis player, and Jemima could well imagine that he had once been in the top class. In spite of his weight—in any case much of it still gave the impression of being muscle—he looked fit enough. Jack looked quite puny beside him and was, as he wryly admitted, still regularly beaten by his father on that immaculate Henley court.

"Since Daddy is a master of the chop shot, the slice, the top spin and all other similar ploys."

"Tennis is about winning, my dear boy" was Andrew Iverstone's comment on this. All the same, Jack was a good player, with style and ease.

Jemima glanced at the spectators. It was odd how Eugenia Jones kept her glance quite rigidly fixed on Andrew Iverstone and to a lesser extent Jack, her tension if anything increased. She remained silent throughout. Proffy on the other hand took an active interest in the game, shouted encouraging comments, applauded, and generally revealed himself in the rather unlikely role of a tennis buff. Although his ceaseless chatter might have put off some players, it was in a way preferable to Eugenia Jones' unhappy silence. Jemima turned back to the court itself.

The wonder was that Saffron and Fanny had taken the first set; perhaps knowledge of local conditions, in the form of the court's bad patches, had helped them, Jemima reflected wryly. If Saffron in his tight white breeches and red vest looked like a stage gipsy, he played tennis more like a stage bullfighter in the sense that his tennis had the air of being conducted largely for the benefit of the spectators. There were frequent smashes, many of which landed against the rusty old netting at the end of the court, rather than anywhere more conventional within the white lines.

At any rate Andrew Iverstone and Jack took the second set quite easily, six–one. Although Jemima could not help noticing that Iverstone took advantage of every doubtful ball to call the score in his own favour, without any interference from Jack: it was so characteristic of the man. Even when the Iverstones were leading four–love against Saffron and Fanny, Andrew Iverstone insisted that a particular ball of his daughter's had been out although Jemima could have sworn that there was a tiny puff of chalk from the bedraggled court. Jack did nothing. After all, what was there for him to do? Only Saffron, with a deliberate swagger, carefully dropped the next few balls which came his way just over the net.

"Just to make sure, Cousin Andrew." It was in fact this method which secured Saffron and Fanny their solitary game, since it defeated both Iverstone at the back of the court and Jack who waited for his father to take them.

None of this seemed to make much impact upon Tiggie, sitting on the grass at the side of the court and wearing a large flowered cotton sun bonnet—where had she found it?—which accorded oddly with the rest of her khaki outfit. She was totally docile, to the extent that Jemima wondered if she was actually aware of the play in progress.

The third and decisive set began. It did not seem likely that Saffron and Fanny would find their original form again. Tiggie's head in its large bonnet drooped. But it so happened that Saffron and Fanny, having gone a long way down at the start of the set, with Andrew Iverstone (and to a lesser extent Jack) grimly determined to pulverize every ball, now began to pull back.

This was partly due to Fanny's steady strong play: Saffron's comparison to Martina Navratilova was perhaps going a little far, but there was certainly something of the same determined masculine style about Fanny's tennis. Jemima discerned for the first time a distinct resemblance to her father in the stance of the well-muscled but shapely legs, for example, which were not particularly long but twinkled across the court at an astonishing pace to bat balls down the tramlines beyond her father's reach.

Saffron's smashes were also beginning to find their mark just inside the court instead of a yard outside it; and similarly his first service actually produced some aces, as well as the usual ration of ineffectively hard shots which left the aged net shaking as they slammed into it.

The score in games was now five–four to Saffron and Fanny, Saffron having just held his service with a triumphant last ace. Now Andrew Iverstone himself was serving, with Jack a slightly deferential figure at net. Jack's air of deference was in part due to the fact that his father's service had become just slightly erratic with age: although Iverstone was still capable of delivering balls with an amount of top-spin which made them highly challenging to return, he was equally capable of an apparently inexplicable double fault. In such a case, Iverstone's temper, like his service, could be erratic.

Now a series of these double faults from Iverstone had brought the score to deuce. Then Fanny in the right-hand court passed Jack at net with one of her well-placed drives. Andrew Iverstone glanced briefly and very angrily at the ball: for one moment Jemima thought he might actually call it out—although the ball was in by inches. Instead he said nothing. It was left to Saffron to sing out the score:

"Advantage Lord Saffron and Miss Iverstone, that popular young couple. Set point. Don't feel nervous." Jemima thought it singularly tactless of him. After all, everybody realized it was set point. Nobody else commented. Saffron, still very much at his ease, crouched slightly to receive Andrew Iverstone's service.

It was at this very moment that Tiggie, for no particular reason that anyone could see, suddenly jerked into life. Her head came up and she stared at the court. Then she started to laugh and clap with uninhibited frenzy:

"Saffer, Saffer, ooh Saffer," she clapped again, "I've got something for you, Saffer."

Jemima realized rather belatedly that Tiggie had to be stoned; not necessarily stoned out of her mind, but certainly stoned beyond the permissible level of a spectator at a tennis match. The symptoms which Jemima would soon have identified in metropolitan London had been so alien to the mellow environment of Saffron Ivy that she had failed to recognize them. Pot? Cocaine? Probably the latter, since Tiggie now seemed to be miming some form of sniff for the benefit of her fiancé. Jemima wondered what Andrew Iverstone's reaction would be. It was not likely that this kind of interruption would be tolerated for very long by a man who had told his own wife to be quiet when he was playing a point. And at a crucial moment in the match.

Afterwards it was difficult to decide whether Tiggie's frenzied clapping, her cries of "Saffer, oooh Saffer," had actually caught Andrew Iverstone in mid-serve. As a matter of fact, he had probably already delivered the serve when she broke out into her little birdsong. All the same, fairly or not, the fact that the ball went into the net on the first service seemed not unconnected with Tiggie's cries.

Immediately Iverstone served again, too quickly perhaps. That service too foundered. In this low-key fashion the third and decisive set had been won by Saffron and Fanny.

In the prevailing silence—no one dared clap—Tiggie gave a loud titter: "Oooh, there it goes again. Into the net. End of the set."

At this point three things happened more or less simultaneously. Saffron flung up his racket in a whoop of triumph (the racket, unlike the net, was gleaming new): "Six–four to the good guys. Well done, Cousin Fan."

Lord St. Ives went with great speed behind Tiggie's chair and started to help her up with the words: "Come along, Antigone my dear."

And Andrew Iverstone, with astonishing viciousness, aimed a ball hard at precisely that bit of wire netting which protected Tiggie's frail figure from the game's onslaught. "Little bitch!" he shouted.

That in itself might not have mattered so much had the Saffron Ivy netting been of the high quality of, say, the Iverstone court at Henley. Only too clearly, it was not. The impact caused a large section of the blackened netting to fall to the ground, amid an unpleasant hail of rust. The ball itself struck Tiggie just as she was obediently rising to Lord St. Ives' command. Shock, more than pain, must have caused her to give a short scream. Tiggie opened her large eyes and sucked her finger.

Jemima involuntarily looked towards the court. Andrew Iverstone stood panting and flushed as though struggling to master himself and resume the mantle of his manners. And on Jack Iverstone's face she saw a surprised look of absolute disgust, presumably at his father's behaviour, so strong as to amount to something close to hatred.

Jemima sighed. She pitied him.

"Daddy, don't be such a bad loser." Fanny's bracing voice came as a positive relief. Jemima watched, fascinated, as the mask of impassivity came down again on Jack's face; there was now no trace of the strong emotion he had exhibited only a moment before.

"I'm terribly sorry." Andrew Iverstone's voice was musical in its apology; he made a theatrical gesture with his hands. "How could I be such an oaf? Fanny's quite right. I'm the most awful loser." He made it sound as if this was a charming eccentricity on his part. "Antigone, are you all right?"

But Tiggie was being helped towards the house by Lord St. Ives—"I'll be back later for my game"—and Saffron, whose high spirits were quite unimpaired by recent happenings, was busy trying to do a breakdance on the court.

"Jemima, can you do this?" he called. Saffron made no attempt to follow Tiggie, nor for that matter did her mother. When Lord St. Ives finally returned, dressed in ancient white flannels which in no way diminished his air of battered elegance, it was to find the little party at the court, spectators and exhausted players, waiting in a silence which still had a great deal of awkwardness about it.

"Now for the Golden Oldies!" cried Saffron, whose gyrations were by now quite unnerving.

"Personally, I need a fast runner for a partner, one who's going to take every shot in the front of the court. My dear boy, if *you're* to fill that role—" Lord St. Ives looked pointedly towards Saffron, who was still standing on the top of his head "—do take care."

"We'll take you on, Ivo. Fathers and sons. Jack and I against you and Saffron." Andrew Iverstone stood up. He still looked heavily flushed. Jemima could understand why Daphne Iverstone began a tremulous protest.

"Oh darling, you know what the doctor said—"

She expected Andrew Iverstone, in spite of his state, to administer a sharp snap to his wife. Instead of which Iverstone hesitated, then smiled affably and sat down again. "Damn it, she's right. Doctor's orders. Three sets and no more. As I intend to play tennis vigorously for the rest of my life, I have to pay attention." He added pleasantly: "I'll umpire. Take my revenge that way."

That left Lord St. Ives looking for a fourth player in the direction of Fanny, or perhaps Jemima. But Jemima, although she secretly rather fancied her tennis, thought that the opportunity for observation on this occasion was not to be missed. Tennis as a guide to character was a favourite preoccupation of hers. (Cass and Jemima for example had an on-going singles match in which Cass beat Jemima by strength and Jemima beat Cass by stealth.) She thought that she might get to know a little more about the character of Lord St. Ives in the game which followed. The ruthlessness which must lie beneath the charm might perhaps be more clearly exhibited under the pressure of the game.

Who then was to be the fourth? Fanny and Jack together, it was felt, would make rather an uneven game: there were more polite references from Lord St. Ives to his geriatric tennis. At which point Proffy suddenly stood up and said: "I'll play."

For the first time Jemima realized that he was wearing white tennis shoes (one black lace, one brown) with his loose grey flannel trousers for a purpose: she had imagined this detail to be further engaging proof of his absent-mindedness. Eugenia looked startled, gave the air of being about to say something: a third feminine protest to be joined to that of Lady St. Ives which had failed and that of Daphne Iverstone which had succeeded. Then she sat back again in silence without speaking.

Proffy gambolled on to the court, looking more than ever like a bear that had lost its way: but he was obviously prepared for the game quite apart from the shoes, for he produced a pair of gold-rimmed, plastic-lensed glasses from a pocket which he substituted for his habitual black-rimmed ones. Jemima remembered her original estimate of Proffy as a man whose absent-mindedness merely applied to those details of life which did not interest him (such as his wife's Christian name) and decided it had been correct.

She focussed her attention on the game. Yes, Lord St. Ives could be said to be a ruthless, or at least competitive, player: although to be fair he was not nearly as competitive as Proffy, some of whose line calls were strangely reminiscent of those of Andrew Iverstone in the previous match— or perhaps the gold-rimmed spectacles were not as efficient as they looked. Otherwise she noted that Lord St. Ives had a quick rather old-fashioned way of serving, with no great throwing up of the ball; true to his promise, he left all the running to Saffron; lastly his net play was lethal.

Jemima watched Proffy's surprisingly hard forehand drives being killed time and time again by Lord St. Ives at net in a way that left even Jack—a fast runner and a fit one—no opportunity to reach them. Proffy's way of dealing with this was simply to hit harder—but he still aimed straight at Lord St. Ives, as though mesmerized by the tall spare figure at the net. And Proffy's despair was comical.

"Insane, insane," he kept muttering. "Can't help aiming at him, can't help it."

Since Lord St. Ives continued to despatch these balls within his reach, Saffron twice won his service, erratic as its style remained. Jemima thought that Lord St. Ives looked more like a gun at a shoot, polishing off driven grouse, than a tennis player. Then she remembered that he had been a noted shot in his day: no doubt an excellent eye explained his lethal performance, even at the age of seventy.

At this point a hard ball sent by Proffy actually hit Lord St. Ives on the shoulder. As Proffy began to lumber forward, apologizing profusely, and Saffron galloped towards his father, Andrew Iverstone suddenly called out from the sidelines: "That's your point, Proffy."

"For heaven's sake, Daddy," began Jack.

"Of course it's their point, Andrew. I'm aware of the rules. And I'm perfectly all right. No, Gwendolen, please do not call Binyon." But for once Jemima had actually seen Lord St. Ives' genial surface ruffled.

After this incident, there was a distinct rise in the level of the game's tension, which Jemima attributed directly to the presence of Andrew Iverstone sitting implacably, still rather flushed, behind the court's rusty netting.

Jack and Proffy were now leading five games to two, these two games representing Saffron's service. The games however had been closer than the score indicated: Lord St. Ives in particular had played with still greater keenness following Proffy's blow and Andrew Iverstone's intervention. Proffy's own shots were getting wilder and rather less hard, as if the blow had upset him far more than his host, and something of the edge had gone off Jack Iverstone's play, possibly for the same reason. Lord St. Ives and Saffron were definitely the improving couple, and only lost the seventh game after a series of deuces and a call from Proffy which was to say the least of it dubious.

It was Lord St. Ives' turn to serve.

"He wants to win," thought Jemima, "or rather he does not want to lose."

Then Andrew Iverstone called Lord St. Ives' second serve out, just as Proffy, playing in the right-hand court, took a swipe at it. The swipe went into the net.

"Out," he repeated.

"Balls," said Saffron in a tone which was clearly audible.

"I must say I thought it was in," said Jack in a mild tone to no one in particular.

Proffy panted and said nothing.

Lord St. Ives said nothing either but simply crossed to the other court and prepared to serve again. The score was now love–fifteen. Lord St. Ives served a double fault—very quickly, both balls delivered and into the net almost before Jack was ready to receive them.

Love–thirty. He recrossed, and served once again, too low, too quick, and straight into the net. But the second serve, surprisingly fast and also surprisingly deep, actually hit the white line close to Proffy's feet and Jemima herself saw the puff of chalk. The ball, both its pace and depth, obviously took Proffy completely by surprise; for one thing he was standing far too forward. He made no move to hit it.

It was this lack of movement which encouraged Andrew Iverstone to call out again from his deck chair: "Out."

"Was it out?" asked Lord St. Ives in quite a sharp voice. He spoke to Proffy.

"Oh yes, absolutely out, absolutely. Wonderful serve all the same." Proffy, apparently unaware of what was going on, spoke with great enthusiasm. "Wonderful serve, but out."

Love–forty. And set point.

Then Lord St. Ives picked up a tennis ball and with much more grace than his cousin Andrew Iverstone at the end of the previous match, but with very much the same intent, hit it in a high parabola above the net. The ball bounced somewhere way outside the court. In no sense could the shot be interpreted as a serve.

"Set and match to you," said Lord St. Ives. "Or rather we'll give it to you. I shan't bother with my second service." He handed his racket to Saffron. "Carry that for me, will you, old fellow? My shoulder is a bit painful."

He walked off the court.

"You're quite right, Andrew," were his next words, said with extreme good nature to the MP, still sitting in his deck chair. "We really must get our court seen to. Will you give Gwendolen that address?"

Tennis, thought Jemima, was not the only game being played at Saffron Ivy. Some grimmer, more secret contest was also being played out.

CHAPTER FIFTEEN

•

Drawing Blood

Tiggie reappeared at dinner. She sat beside Saffron. She looked terrible and spoke not at all. It must have represented a considerable effort, Jemima thought, to have come down to dinner at all under these circumstances. Above the heads of the affianced couple hung another Lawrence, a sketch for the big double portrait of "The Strawberry Children" in the library, two youthful heads: compared to Tiggie, the Honble. Miss Iverstone looked healthy and enchantingly pretty.

There were eighteen people at dinner, stretching down the long table, with its weight of glass and silver; the latter included a rococo silver centrepiece which on close inspection proved to represent a tortuous grove of trees, liberally entwined with the ivy which formed the family's crest. Ivy was also to be found on each separate dinner plate, together with the Iverstone family motto, whose Latin caused Jemima a moment's earnest but ultimately useless concentration.

"It means something like 'Like the ivy, I protect my own walls,'" said Lord St. Ives genially, noting the direction of her gaze. "Which is of course absolute nonsense, since ivy, if anything, pulls walls down."

"A good motto, nonetheless. Haven't you rather lived by it?" Seeing Lord St. Ives look slightly taken aback Jemima added with a politeness to match her host's own: "As Foreign Secretary, I meant."

Binyon, serving dinner, was assisted by a young man

called Stephen, wearing a dark suit which did not fit, and an elderly man wearing a similar suit which did. Retainers. Assisting Lord St. Ives—and Binyon—to protect the walls. To Jemima there was something faintly distasteful about an elaborately served banquet at which most of the guests were in their late teens and early twenties: the sight of the elderly retainer bending low to proffer a soufflé dish to Saffron with the words—"Haddock Soufflé, my lord"— struck her as against the natural order of things in which youth should minister to age.

"Come on, Saffer, don't take it all," said a rather jolly young man simply called the Gobbler sitting opposite him; the Gobbler's interest in food was one of the running jokes of the Saffer set, Jemima observed, so that even the simplest remark of this nature issuing from his lips was greeted with gales of laughter. Everyone felt very disappointed if the Gobbler did not fill his plate to overflowing; just as the Gobbler showed equal disappointment if those around him did not try to seize the food back off his plate. Jemima had inadvertently contributed to the fun before dinner by mentioning a new series about gourmet food to be mounted by Megalith in the autumn.

It was pure courtesy which had led her to mention that there was an opening for a researcher on this particular series when the Gobbler made the more or less obligatory enquiry about openings in television, since she could hardly imagine the Gobbler or indeed any of those present at Saffron Ivy (except possibly Fanny) being able to hold such a job down.

"Is that the sort of thing that interests you?" The question was quite innocent. But as a result, when the hilarious laughter died down—Jemima thought Poppy Delaware would literally choke, she laughed so much—an extra running joke was added on the subject of the Gobbler and his television career.

"The Gobbler must do some research" became a rallying cry at the sight of any dish, to the untiring amusement of all the Oxford Bloods. From Jemima's point of view it was a relief to contemplate the only two outside guests, both male, both Cambridge dons, one quite young called Shipley and one very old called Leek. (Jemima dreaded to think what the Oxford Bloods would have made of such names, had they been the slightest bit interested in anybody's concerns at the dinner table other than their own . . .)

The dons were sitting at the other end of the table, on either side of Lady St. Ives. The function of Shipley was to make conversation to Eugenia Jones about classical tragedy. The function of Leek, less exhausting, was to listen to Proffy who addressed him about the problems of the Albanian Resistance in World War II over the head of a passive pretty girl called Nessa, last seen at the Chimneysweepers' Dinner, who seemed to be loosely attached to Bernardo.

Jemima surveyed the table and took a deep breath. She thought that the presence of the two dons, loquacious and silent respectively, would make the next stage of her investigation easier than the reverse. All the same, there was a certain risk in what she proposed to do. It was not a question of Cherry's briefing: she trusted Cherry to the hilt, even though Cherry's enthusiasm for the subject had not matched that of, say, the Gobbler, for gourmet food. No, the problem was Saffron. In order to carry out her plan, she had had to enlist his help. Even if she had not, he would soon have guessed her intention, so that to take him into her confidence was in another sense essential. All the same, she hoped that Saffron would keep a cool head.

Jemima had come to agree with Kerry Barber about the quality of Saffron's intelligence, even when it was cloaked with some deliberate affectation of idiocy. Yet there was nothing very cool about him this evening. On the contrary, he was in dangerously high spirits: she thought that already he had drunk more than most people would drink in a whole evening. Saffron drunk and indiscreet was capable of wrecking the whole plan.

At that moment, Saffron leant forward and in a voice which was almost perfectly casual asked: "I say, Jemima, what's next?"

"Next?" Jemima excused herself politely from a conversation with Jack Iverstone about the possible unification of the SDP and the right wing of the Labour Party.

"When you've finished with us Golden Kids—" an audible groan from Jack "—all right, holy cousin, *we* didn't call ourselves that. We're Marxists, as you know, or we were last term."

"Oxford Bloody Marxist!" said Jack which for him sounded quite rude.

"We're anarchists now, Saffer," Poppy Delaware interrupted sternly. "Don't you remember that night after the Talking Heads concert? We got out our manifesto." Poppy looked ravishing in a loose but extremely well-cut white linen dinner jacket, wing collar and narrow black tie; the only thing which was visibly anarchistic about her was her wildly streaky hair, in which silver and orange were only a few of the colours visible. Jemima knew that it was despicably sexist on her part but she could not summon up enormous interest in Poppy's political views; on the other hand, she would like to know where she got the dinner jacket.

"Anarchists, OK, yah. Well, what are you going to do next, Jemima?"

Saffron was not to be deterred.

"Now for something totally different. I'm working on a programme about blood as a matter of fact. No, not noble blood this time. Everybody's blood."

She was conscious of the presence upstairs of that invaluable text-book, *Blood Group Serology*, 5th edition, procured by Cherry, together with Mourant's *Blood relations*. What had the maid thought when she unpacked them? (They were placed conspicuously on her dressing table next to her make-up instead of beside her bed with the other books, as though of a vaguely pharmaceutical nature.) Jemima launched into her theme. Blood transfusions . . . The need for more and different kinds of blood in the National Health service . . . blood groupings . . . ethnic frequencies . . . types of formerly rare blood becoming more frequently needed in a society in which immigrants play an increasing part . . . to say nothing of the whole new problem of AIDs.

Once again Saffron played up admirably. He referred to his own recent blood transfusions at Oxford and even managed to make the announcement of his own comparatively rare AB group sound like a characteristic boast.

"It's surprising how few people do know their own blood group." Daphne Iverstone was a helpful if unexpected ally. "I remember working for St. John's—we all thought it should be compulsory to carry it on you."

"Had to be in the war, of course," grunted Andrew Iverstone. "But I'm not sure we want any more bureaucratic rules here, do we?" It was noticeable how his wife brought out the worst in him, his normal courtesy perceptibly flagging. But he was also badly placed at the table: the preponderance of males brought about by the presence of the two unattached dons meant that he had ended sitting next to the Gobbler—scarcely a marriage of true minds; he had Eugenia Jones, still being lectured by Shipley, on his right.

Daphne Iverstone hesitated; Jemima saw her struggling with natural reluctance to contradict her husband on anything. It was Fanny on the Gobbler's other side, who came to the rescue. She leant forward.

"Don't be silly, Daddy. When it saves lives. Think of accidents and things like that. I learnt all about it with the Guides. You can't give someone any old blood transfusion, you know. You have to be sure of the group first."

Daphne Iverstone took heart.

"And precious time is wasted while you take a test. But if you know the group—"

"So what is your group, my dear Fanny?" Andrew Iverstone was once more sounding gallant.

There was general laughter as Fanny hesitated. Finally she burst out laughing in her turn.

"How awful! I've forgotten. I promise I knew once."

Jemima pursued the opening.

"This is one of the things I'll be considering, of course. Should we carry cards? As servicemen did in the war. For example, let's see how many people, if any, round this table do know their blood group, A, O, B or AB. And as a matter of interest if we get enough figures, whether the pattern conforms to the national average." She started with her new ally, Daphne Iverstone.

"A—A positive actually. That means I'm Rhesus positive." The nice young man next to her called Ned who was said to be a wonderful cricketer shook his head, bemused by the turn the conversation was taking. Fanny, opposite, came back gamely with A.

"I'm sure it was A. Is A rare too?" she enquired hopefully.

"A and O are the two most common English groups." Daphne Iverstone sounded delighted to be able for once to put her daughter down. In so doing she did Jemima's work for her.

"That's really one of the points of my programme. Groups like B, which used to be comparatively uncommon, under ten per cent, are becoming more common with immigration; hence the need for more blood of these rarer groups within the National Health Service."

Andrew Iverstone, whose ears had evidently pricked up at the sound of the word immigration, leant forward in his turn.

"How very interesting, Miss Shore. I don't think I'd appreciated that, in spite of my special study of this kind of subject. Isn't this an example of the way British society is simply not able to *cope* with large influxes of alien races, whose very blood cannot mix successfully?"

But Fanny, for one, was having none of that.

"Oh, come on Daddy, let's go round the table," she interrupted brightly. "I think it's a fascinating new kind of game. Maybe we should all go off and have blood tests or something."

Jemima's eyes met those of Saffron across the table. This was not quite going the way they had intended. Or was it? As she hesitated, Bernardo Valliera, sitting next to Fanny, suddenly and surprisingly volunteered that his own group was O. There had been some accident playing polo as a result of which he had derived this information. Jemima, remembering from one of the maps in Mourant that virtually the whole of the South American population were group O, felt a glow of pleasure that Mourant was working out so exactly: she beamed at Bernardo.

"Now we go round the table," said Fanny. "Tiggie, you next."

But Tiggie, unsurprisingly, did not know her blood group. All she did when asked was sink her head on Saffron's shoulder with the words: "Ooh, horrible. I hate it when they take your blood, don't you? I hate needles. They should be like vampires. They should *suck* it. Sucking is lovely—"

This time it was Saffron who effected the interruption, passing the question on to Poppy who said she had absolutely no idea, but offered the fact that she was a Pisces as being an alternative and perhaps preferable line of enquiry. . . . At which point Saffron interrupted even more firmly, as a dangerous babble of zodiacal chit-chat could be heard coming from Tiggie, which Poppy showed every sign of picking up.

Luckily the elderly don called Leek did know his blood group—O. Nessa next to him smiled, fluttered her eyelashes and said nothing; she seemed not to believe that any serious question could possibly be addressed to her. Proffy, who was rattling away, paused just long enough to pronounce: "A, A, pure Alpha" before rattling on again. Lady St. Ives, suddenly grasping the subject at discussion, plunged into it with some enthusiasm, much as Daphne Iverstone had done, based in her case on her presidency of the local Red Cross.

She confirmed that her own blood group was O and pointed out that when in doubt in an emergency, O group blood was administered since it contained no clashing agglutinogens. Then she went on to talk about the difficulties experienced with new ethnic groups who had immigrated to the local towns, especially the east coast ports: "We need more B blood."

This time Jemima did not look at Saffron. She was desperately anxious that the question should continue to run on round the table to where the object of the whole exercise sat at the head, listening to proceedings with his usual air of impartial benevolence. So that she was not much disappointed when first the don called Shipley and then Eugenia Jones passed, neither betraying any particular enthusiasm for the subject, before returning to Shipley's disquisition on classical tragedy.

Andrew Iverstone, however, threatened to wreck the whole show. He had been frowning, first at Daphne, then as he listened to Lady St. Ives' own little lecture.

Finally, when asked the question, he said lightly: "Oh something thoroughly British. A, I think."

"No, it isn't, darling!" cried Daphne Iverstone. "B. Definitely B. B negative. I remember because when the children were born, and there was some question, there might have been difficulties."

"Oh Andrew," Lady St. Ives sounded quite enthusiastic. "Maybe you will give us some of your nice B blood."

There was some laughter from those who realized the significance of what had just been said. Andrew Iverstone joined in.

"Serve me right. Patriotism is not enough. You have to have the right blood too. Daphne, my dear, thank you. Your frankness may save my life in a car crash."

The question was passed to the Gobbler whose mouth was full and who did not attempt to answer it.

Fanny had already answered. It was Jack's turn.

"I don't know. But I can easily work it out having done biology at A-level. If Daddy is B and Mummy is A then I must be AB. And so must you, Fanny."

Again Professor Mossbanker paused just long enough in his peroration to Leek to say: "He's quite right, quite right," before rattling on again.

Oddly enough, nobody commented on Jack's statement, although Jemima nervously thought that someone at least might have worked out its implications as regards Saffron with his O group mother. But perhaps she overestimated the guests' interest in the subject.

"My own group is A, A positive like Mrs. Iverstone," said Jemima quickly. "And now Lord St. Ives—"

Her host sat back in his chair, eyes half shut, and sipped his claret in a leisurely manner as though trying to decide on the vintage, information he must however already have had at his fingertips.

"My blood group? Oh, I'm afraid I've no idea, no idea at all," said Lord St. Ives.

Jemima's heart sank at his answer—had all this charade been for nothing, other than to establish that Andrew Iverstone was full of "non-British" blood which might be good for his soul but not helpful to her investigation? Then there was a discreet cough from her left shoulder.

"Excuse me, my lord, Wyndham says your blood group is A. He remembers from the war." It was Binyon. Jemima saw the elderly retainer at his elbow nodding with satisfaction at having preserved this precious information for so many years.

"So it was. If Wyndham says so. He was my batman in the war," Lord St. Ives confided to Jemima.

"And Miss Shore," continued Binyon loftily. "My own group is A, like your own. Wyndham's is O. Stephen from the farm doesn't know his," he added apologetically. "Now I've made that five Os and five As, counting the servants, which I hope you don't think irregular, in your little experiment. Mr. Andrew Iverstone is of course B as we have learnt from Mrs. Iverstone and there are the ABs—"

Someone had to say it. "Like readers of *The Times*," broke in Jack, "I'm delighted to be an AB."

"Since we're brother and sister, I suppose I'm one too," said Fanny. "I suppose it's a family thing."

Brother and sister.

Jemima looked across at Saffron, sitting on the opposite side of the table under the Lawrence portrait of the Iverstones. A family thing. She suddenly realized something, in that heightened atmosphere of relationships based on blood, an overwhelming and obvious truth, which had been hovering just outside her consciousness for so long.

It was strange. Once this truth was apparent, not latent, it seemed so obvious to her that she was amazed that she had not seen it, or at least suspected it from the first. Unfortunately for Jemima Shore Investigator it was a truth which, far from helping to unravel the mystery of Iverstone family life, only served to entangle it further.

As Jemima put it to Cass, when the events of the weekend had passed into history, unhappy history: "It was the picture which gave it away. That on top of Fanny's words. And the definitive discovery that Saffron was not his parents' child. An O and an A can't produce an AB—It's in *Blood Serology*. I looked it up later. Their children must be either A or O: AB and B are what is called 'impossible phenotypes.'"

"You certainly drew blood there, Jemima Shore Investigator. To coin a phrase," commented Cass. "Congratulations."

"But it was the picture really," pressed on Jemima. "'The

Strawberry Children': you know the one, you know the picture if not the name. All red fruit and pink ribbons. You've seen it reproduced all round the world. Miss Iverstone and her brother. He's not named for some reason: I asked Lord St. Ives and they think it was because he died shortly after Lawrence painted the picture. But his name was of course Saffron."

"They're brother and sister," said Cass, who was talking about the picture.

"They're brother and sister," repeated Jemima, who was not. "I looked across at them at dinner and it was quite clear. They were sitting next to each other because they're engaged; there was some joke about it: apparently it's the old-fashioned thing."

"Saffron and Tiggie Jones!" exclaimed Cass incredulously. "Brother and sister!"

"Half-brother and sister, to be accurate. It has to be so. And then of all extraordinary things—almost as if she read my mind, Eugenia Jones leant forward and said to me down the table in that rather gruff voice of hers, disconcerting coming from such a little woman: 'If you're really interested in statistics, I believe my blood group is B as well, I believe that of many Greeks is so.' And of course that figured too. One of Saffron's parents had to be B."

"So you sat there—"

"I sat there in that incredible dining room—that's where the Holbein is by the way, much smaller than you'd expect but even more powerful—being handed endless food by Binyon. I sat there and I looked along at Eugenia Jones in her red velvet dress, same as she wore at the Chimney-sweepers', and I *knew* they were both her children. It changed everything."

"You mean, it should have changed everything," replied Cass sombrely. But then he was speaking after the weekend was over.

CHAPTER SIXTEEN

•

A Tragedy Must Take Place

Up till the night of the dinner party, Jemima had never thought of Saffron as being somebody's child; only as being nobody's child, unless of course he was the lawful child of his parents, something which had now been ruled out. Suddenly he had a mother: that gipsy look, how marked it was in Eugenia! And it was Greek of course, not gipsy. Jemima had been right: Saffron did have something of the Mediterranean about him. Eugenia's classical scholarship had distracted her from the fact that she had actual modern Greek blood.

Not only did he have a mother, he had a half-sister. Did Eugenia Jones know she was gazing in her sad abstracted way at her own son? Jemima, remembering her horror and dismay at Tiggie's impetuous announcement of her engagement, believed that she did know.

Under the circumstances, this reaction and the look of despair which Jemima had surprised on the face of Proffy, to say nothing of the melancholy which possessed Eugenia here at Saffron Ivy, were easy to understand. All that fell into place. Eugenia's evident apathy made Jemima wonder what steps she now proposed to take. Was it possible that she was actually going to allow Tiggie to marry her own half-brother, something which was considered genetically dangerous in the modern world, and even worse in the world of classical tragedy which Eugenia Jones might otherwise be deemed to inhabit. Was classical tragedy the clue? Did she feel there was a dreadful inevitability about these events, that a tragedy must take place . . . ?

But then how was Eugenia Jones to stop the match? Only by telling her daughter the truth, and that meant, in effect, telling Saffron the truth.

That also meant telling Lord and Lady St. Ives the truth, or rather Lady St. Ives, if one accepted Nurse Elsie's story of her ignorance. And there was a further consideration: how was such a secret to be kept? How, for example, was Cousin Andrew Iverstone to be kept in ignorance of news which left him, and Jack after him, heir to the Marquessate of St. Ives with all that implied? It might be that Eugenia Jones, seeing her son in a position of vast wealth and privilege, had hesitated to deprive him of it. In that case she had indeed found herself between Scylla and Charybdis, the mythological rock and the whirlpool dreaded by ancient mariners.

On the one hand she sacrificed her daughter, like a Greek maiden to the Minotaur; on the other hand she dispossessed her son . . . there was doubtless still some further mythological comparison amid the plethora evoked in her mind. It was at this point that Jemima became aware that Binyon, impeccably coated in a tailcoat and striped trousers, was offering her asparagus, with the air of one who had been doing so for some time.

"Our own asparagus," he said confidentially; for Binyon, as Jemima had observed, seldom missed even the slightest opportunity for conversation with those he served. "In case you're wondering, Miss Shore,"

"Wondering? Yes, I was." Jemima helped herself with an automatic smile in the direction of the butler, now in full butlerian fig. But that hardly seemed the right thing to say to Binyon, who accepted her remark with a discreet, a very discreet but still perceptible, air of surprise.

She corrected herself. "I meant, I was *hoping*."

Binyon passed on to Daphne Iverstone; he now looked, with equal discretion, satisfied.

It struck Jemima that throughout her stay so far Binyon had treated her not only as an honoured guest, but also as an ally—an ally from their shared television world. So that in a subtle way he was both anxious for her behaviour to be correct and gratified when it was.

Then this was forgotten as the full implications of her

discovery—or rather her intuitive flash concerning Tiggie and Saffron, flooded over her.

Poor little Tiggie, how wan she was, how woebegone, how unlike the odiously affected but high-spirited creature who had seduced Cy Fredericks, engaged the admiring attention of Cass Brinsley and driven Jemima mad at Oxford. Did she have some inkling that her glorious destiny was about to be snatched from her? Jemima recalled her words at the Mossbankers' house: "I'm going to be Lady Saffron. And I'm going to be really really rich. . . ." She remembered also those other revealing snatches from Saffron about Tiggie: "We think alike. We want the same kind of life."

It was as though Saffron, in all the atmosphere of hereditary claims in which he had been brought up, had felt himself claimed by his own family, and mistaking one thing for the other had been impelled to bond Tiggie to him.

Who knew? The question reverberated in her mind as she gazed across at the Strawberry children opposite with their dark eyes and high cheek-bones, so similar to those of Eugenia Jones. Then there came another more startling thought, distracting her sufficiently to take another enormous helping of the home-grown asparagus, so that Daphne Iverstone, did she wish for more, was left lamenting. Jemima was assuming all along that her own intuitive discovery meant the end of the projected marriage. What on earth had led her to that conclusion? For one thing, she had no proof, only surmise; for another, even if proof were advanced—an admission of the truth by Eugenia Jones for example—was she, Jemima Shore, about to play God, an avenging god at that, as Cass had pointed out right at the beginning *a propos* Nurse Elsie's revelations? "Justice is for Almighty God"—Sister Imelda's words. Jemima had entered the fray out of curiosity, not to right a wrong. She had stayed to investigate—and protect Saffron.

In any case was it really so terrible for half-brother and sister to marry? Stranger things must have happened in the history of the aristocracy, to say nothing of the history of the average country villages. Memories of delving into the history of birth control before her programme *The Pill: For or Against* came back to her: there had been long ages, almost to the present day, when the absence of effective birth control of any sort must have led to such embarrassing problems on more than one occasion.

Jones. Who *was* Jones? Tiggie was older than Saffron, a fact on which the gossip columns had not failed to comment, when printing rumours of the impending engagement. If the mysterious Jones was the father of Tiggie, who then was Saffron's father? She gazed down the table at that great progenitor, Professor Mossbanker. Was *that* possible? Ironically, enough, Proffy's blood group—A, which fitted— now became as interesting to her as the blood group of Lord St. Ives had formerly been.

At this moment, the rest of the meal having passed in a kind of daze for Jemima while she accepted food in continuing large quantities as a method of covering the desperate sorting of her thoughts, she was aware of a soft voice at the end of the table trying to engage her attention.

"Miss Shore," Lady St. Ives was saying, leaning down the table. "Isn't it lovely? Binyon will sing for us after dinner." Jemima realized that Lady St. Ives was actually doing that old-fashioned thing of catching her eye; as a result of which the ladies of Saffron Ivy were expected to abandon the dining room to the gentlemen.

The sight of Lady St. Ives' pale drawn cheeks, her thin throat hardly concealed by the rows of pearls, and a green silk evening dress, rather grand, the colour too bright for her complexion, reminded Jemima that the truth, if disclosed, would cause pain to far more people than merely Tiggie and Saffron. It would be a vicious stone to throw into any pool, and pain and astonishment and shock and scandal and fear would spread in rings.

Fear. The word recalled her sharply to the original reason for her visit to Saffron Ivy. Someone was trying to kill Saffron. How and where did the surmise of his true parentage fit into this scheme of things?

With a purpose which she hoped was not too apparent, Jemima sought out Eugenia Jones in the White Drawing Room as the ladies settled themselves down for their period of ritual planned waiting. It was noticeable how the style of the White Drawing Room rendered some costumes so much more appropriate than others. Lady St. Ives, settling her wide emerald green taffeta skirts and picking up a large bundle of embroidery, possessed an unconscious grace which she had not displayed throughout the day. Fanny Iverstone, in a pale pink dress with a wide white collar which owed a great deal to the current fashions of the Princess of Wales (although their figures were markedly different), suddenly looked elegant; her healthy plainness vanished. But Tiggie, in a white chiffon dress, no petticoat but a trail of sequins laid across it, and a bedraggled feather in her hair, looked like a little ghost. There was no place for her at Saffron Ivy.

"Gommer's dress," exclaimed Fanny, as though she read Jemima's thoughts. "I've got it. You're wearing Gommer's court dress, Tiggie." She sounded quite angry. "And you've torn it."

At once Tiggie, in her chiffon, stood and sketched an impertinent little dance in front of Fanny; she did it all without speaking, like some chiffon-draped Squirrel Nutkin in front of a conspicuously irritated Brown Owl. But she was much hampered by her shoes: battered white satin court shoes, several sizes too big. The long white kid gloves, with their pearl buttons, were also too big.

"Doesn't the dress look charming on Antigone?" enquired Lady St. Ives to the world at large. "It belonged to Ivo's mother," she added into the general silence. "Darling Gommer. How we all loved her." Her voice trailed away.

"We used to be allowed to dress up in her clothes as children. On special occasions. If we were very careful." Fanny still sounded sulky. "Such a pity if it were ruined now."

Daphne shot Fanny a look in which the warning was unmistakable. It was the look of the poor relation down the ages. The look meant: don't overstep the mark. It's Tiggie's dress now—or it will be. And one day, who knows, we will depend on her favour to come here. If we come here at all.

The full dislike which both ladies harboured for Tiggie was equally unmistakable.

Jemima was just thinking how ironic it was that Tiggie's dress, deemed by her so inappropriate, had actually turned out to be, as it were, the dress of the house, when Tiggie

made her first pronouncement since they had entered the
White Drawing Room.

"I think I'll just go and have some sleepy-byes," said
Tiggie. She half danced, half stumbled towards the door,
catching her foot in its battered white satin shoe with the
pointed toe in the train as she did so. (Gommer St. Ives'
shoes? Presumably.) There was a tearing sound.

Fanny cast her eyes up to heaven. Daphne Iverstone
hummed. Lady St. Ives kept her eyes on her embroidery.
Jemima, seeing her opportunity, sat down hastily beside
Eugenia Jones, who, as ever where she was concerned, had
not sought to intervene or even speak to her daughter.

"She's very like you—" Eugenia Jones creased her lips
slightly. "To look at, I mean," continued Jemima. "But then
I suppose one always thinks that, if one knows only one
parent."

Eugenia Jones inclined her head.

"Perhaps Tiggie is after all very like her father?"

Eugenia Jones looked at Jemima with her enormous dark
hooded eyes, eyes which despite being surrounded with a
network of wrinkles, were still beautiful. She wore no
make-up whatsoever: the effect was in one sense to make
her look haggard beyond her years; but in another way the
untouched olive skin, if one ignored the lines, the full
mouth and fine firm chin, were ageless and might have
belonged to a much younger woman.

"Tiggie's father died before she was born. I was never
able to compare the two."

The words were sufficiently abrupt to encourage Jemima,
rather than the reverse. She felt some kind of advantage
coming her way.

"How sad."

"Sad?"

"For you of course. But I actually meant: how sad for
Tiggie never to have known her father."

"At the time—I was very young—it seemed more important that I did have her, than that she did not have a father."

"And now?"

"Don't you find, Miss Shore, that being stuck with the
decisions we make when we are too young to understand

their possible consequences, is one of the most disagreeable aspects of middle age?"

Then Eugenia Jones unexpectedly gave Jemima a most ravishing smile which eradicated the heaviness of her face and transformed it.

"What am I saying? You are so much younger than I. What do you know of these things?"

At that point, before Jemima could answer, the gentlemen appeared at the door of the White Drawing room, preceded by Binyon bearing a tray which bore three categories of glasses: heavy tumbles of whiskey, delicate champagne glasses and smaller tumblers which appeared to contain barley water. The choice of drink proved something of a test of character, even if it was not so intended. Both Lord St. Ives and Andrew Iverstone took whisky, both Lady St. Ives and Daphne Iverstone refused altogether. Saffron took three glasses of champagne, deposited one dexterously in front of Jemima and then preceded to sit at her feet nursing the other two. Fanny Iverstone and Poppy Delaware, and most of the other girls, took champagne; Jack Iverstone, alone of the young men, chose barley water.

A little later all were once more concentrated on the figure of Binyon as the butler, standing in a position of advantage in the middle of the drawing room, began to sing with that mixture of melody and confidence which had once held fourteen million television viewers enthralled. Binyon, like the great John McCormack on whom, according to Lady St. Ives, he modelled himself, had a tenor voice. And Jemima (who had once been presented with a McCormack record by Jamie Grand, a self-acknowledged expert on the subject) could see that the resemblance had been cultivated. It amused her to find this McCormack of the eighties dominating the after-dinner scene at the noble house of Saffron Ivy with his performance, so that there was no possibility of conversation, and all on the strength of his telly triumph. It was a splendid butlerian triumph of the times in which Downstairs finally succeeded in subjugating Upstairs (Jemima, for example, was longing to continue her conversation with Eugenia Jones) through the medium of television, just because they both shared it equally.

"Fear no more . . ." sang Binyon, his fine chest rising and falling.

Jemima looked round. Fear. Saffron had settled his back comfortably against Jemima's knees which she found slightly embarrassing but not disagreeable. Tiggie had not reappeared. On a particularly sentimental song, Daphne Iverstone took her husband's hand: he did not disengage it. Jack and Fanny sat slightly apart from the rest of Saffron's friends, although Fanny at least had been very much part of the Oxford group in all the earlier festivities.

Fear. She felt it. Someone in this room was frightened. Was it Eugenia Jones, frightened by the whirlwind which she was now reaping? Lord St. Ives? His part in all this remained an enigma, if one that Jemima was determined to solve in the future. But she could not imagine pure fear as such ever holding this man in its grip. Proffy? He had placed himself beside Eugenia Jones on arrival in the drawing room; now he was leaning back and was either fast asleep or shamming sleep. Jemima remembered that Proffy like Eugenia Jones was a passionate lover of opera: it was possible that he did not regard the singing butler with, for example, the same indulgent approval as Lady St. Ives. As for the lady in question she was definitely asleep: quietly dozing over her embroidery.

> "Golden lads and girls all must
> Like chimneysweepers come to dust."

Jemima shivered. How odd, how morbid, that Binyon should have chosen that particular song on which to end his recital, in view of Saffron's unpleasantly publicized involvement with the club making use of that name. Perhaps it was innocent. Or perhaps it was deliberate: perhaps Binyon, no more than the rest of the world, did not love his employer's wild young son for the extravagances of his privileged youth, having witnessed them first hand.

Binyon gave a ceremonial bow. There was a flutter of applause. Lady St. Ives gave a slight start and clapped in her turn. Proffy had clapped loudly from the beginning. His eyes however remained shut. Shortly after that the evening broke up. That is to say, the bright young things, including

Fanny, proposed to vanish to some distant ground-floor billiard room now fitted up as a music room where it was understood they would play their "horrible tunes"—Lord St. Ives' cheerful phrase—out of earshot, as late and as long as they liked. Only Jack said he would prefer to go to bed.

"Oh *Jack*!" exclaimed Fanny. "Just for once, why don't you unwind?"

Jack gave a comic shudder.

"Unwind to the sound of Saffron's thousand-pound amplified torture chamber? I shall be fresh for tennis—and revenge—in the morning."

"I shan't be long," remarked Fanny rather vaguely as though some explanation was due to her brother.

"I'll be along later," said Saffron. "Bernardo—the key—" He tossed across a large key. There was something almost too carefully casual about his voice. "Something I have to do."

All in all, Jemima was not totally surprised when, about fifteen minutes after she had entered her vast dark bedroom, with its canopied bed, the door opened silently.

Saffron entered. He was still dressed in the white ruffled shirt he had worn beneath his dinner jacket, but had taken off the tie. The shirt was open to the waist. His black eyes glittered. Jemima thought he was rather drunk.

"To what do I owe this honour?"

"The West Bedroom? I thought you were in Lady Anne's Bedroom. You might have told me. I've just been invited rather sharply to leave by Cousin Daphne. As if I should want to seduce *her*."

He was definitely drunk.

"Your luck is out. You're about to be invited equally sharply to leave the West Bedroom."

"It's pretty, isn't it?" said Saffron inconsequentially, touching the faded chintz in a pattern of wisteria which was hung everywhere in the room. "I think this is the room where I had my first fuck—"

"Saffron—"

"Or was it the Elizabethan Bedroom? Do you know, I think I've had someone in every room in this house. Except the servants' bedrooms, of course. And even one or two of those—"

"Saffron, will you spare me? Your reminiscences. And your boasting. Both."

"Sorry. Gone too far. Really very sorry."

Jemima said nothing.

"Don't you fancy me, Jemima Shore? I rather thought you did. Don't fancy the bastard?" Saffron put his arms around Jemima from behind and held her for a moment, pressing himself against her. "A bastard. That's what I am, aren't I? You know it's true. We discovered it. You and I. The blood thing doesn't work. I am a bastard. Rather romantic in literature. I'm not so sure in real life. *Don't* you fancy me?"

Jemima still said nothing.

"Wouldn't you like to be in that bed with me? Cheer me up? I'm drunk of course. But not that drunk, not *too* drunk. Just say the word and I'll come back. I'll creep in. Lights out. No one will ever know. Go on. Say I can come back. Don't worry. I'm not going to force myself on you. Rape isn't my thing, you know."

Jemima, Saffron's arms still around her, feeling the dreadful possibility that the treacherous flesh might somehow betray her, remained silent. It was the best she could do.

"Don't say anything then. I'll come anyway."

"*Don't*," she said at last.

"You don't mean that."

There was another pause.

"Yes, I do." Then she added: "But Saffron, I'm *sorry*."

"I know you are. Bless you for that anyway." He sounded more sober all of a sudden. "You go to sleep in your great big bed," said Saffron gently. He kissed her and this time she did not resist, but kissed him back, a consoling, passionless kiss. He went.

All the same, long after Saffron had gone, Jemima found herself lying awake. Worse still, she discovered that oddly her ear was still slightly cocked for the discreet click of an opening door.

Her door did not open. But sometime in the night hours, she did hear the distinct noise of a door opening and shutting somewhere else along the corridor of the big silent house. Jemima surmised, sardonically, that Saffron might be trying his luck elsewhere. Or might just conceivably be joining his lawful if thoroughly stoned fiancée, Tiggie Jones, in her drugged slumbers.

Jemima finally fell asleep.

In her dream she was aware of a body, a warm body, sliding into bed beside her. Somebody was pulling up the thin silk of her nightdress. Someone was touching her. She felt a hard, hot body against hers . . . she had no idea what the time was when out of the mists of sleep, Jemima was aware that somewhere along the way, her dream had turned into reality. Someone was touching her, but touching her on the shoulder, on the cheek. Someone was pulling at her, whispering to her.

The light snapped on.

Jemima found herself gazing at Saffron. He was wearing a red towelling robe and nothing else. He looked ghastly.

"Jemima, please come, please help me. It's Tiggie. Something's happened to her," he was saying. "You must help me. I think—I think she's dead."

CHAPTER SEVENTEEN

•

Two Unlucky Lives

Jemima followed Saffron in his red towelling robe down the broad darkened corridor, oil paintings of bygone Iverstones dimly glimpsed, nearly to the end where a big uncurtained window looked onto the park. Tiggie's bedroom—inconsequentially Jemima noticed the name "The Butterfly Room" on the open door—had one light burning by the bed. The bed was smaller than Jemima's, canopied in soft white material on which butterflies were lightly printed.

On the walls there hung various pictures made up of brilliant butterflies, pinned down in deep frames. On the bed lay the little butterfly, Tiggie Jones, with her hand stretched out as though in appeal. She was naked except for a pair of tiny white briefs; her body was so thin that she had the air of a naked child asleep in a picture. Her eyes were shut. There was no sign that she was breathing.

Jemima ran forward and felt her pulse. There was no pulse that she could find. She felt her flat infantine chest; it was still. Then Jemima stumbled on something at her feet. It was a syringe. She pushed it aside, then, more carefully, picked it up between finger and thumb and put it on the table. The syringe lay next to a glass paper-weight containing a butterfly whose spread wings were the colour of viridian.

Tiggie's body was not cold, but it was not completely warm either. There was a cool damp feel to it.

Jemima pulled one of the sheets over Tiggie's body,

leaving her head still exposed as it lay half on, half off the white pillow.

"A doctor. Saffron, you must get a doctor at once."

Saffron turned, hesitated.

"Tigs. Is she dead?"

"I don't know."

"She is dead."

"Get a doctor for God's sake! He'll tell you."

"Yes, yes. I'm sorry. Look—"

"I'll stay here. In case—"

"OK. And—thanks."

It seemed to Jemima an age before Saffron returned although probably not much more than fifteen minutes had passed while she sat in a low embroidered chair beside Tiggie's bed in the Butterfly Room.

Twice Jemima touched Tiggie again and felt if there was a pulse. She could find nothing. She believed the body was growing cooler. She began to try and order her thoughts a little.

Tiggie was dead. Jemima had not much doubt of that. But Tiggie had not been dead long. How had she died? Her eyes were closed. Had she administered some fatal dose by mistake and in the mists of a narcotic dream passed from life into sleep and from sleep into death. Or . . .

When Saffron came back he was dressed: jeans, an old green jersey and trainer shoes. That reminded Jemima that she was only wearing her silk nightdress and a thin kimono over it; she was barefoot. Grey light was beginning to steal through the thick curtains, chintz patterned in butterflies. Jemima like Tiggie was growing cold. It seemed another age in which Saffron had put his warm arms around her and tried to take her into bed.

"He's coming. The doctor. I've told Pa. He'll be along. He's dressing and waking Binyon to let in the doctor. We're letting Ma sleep."

"What happened? To Tiggie."

"She's still . . .?"

"I'm afraid so. What happened? After you left me."

"I was drunk. You know that. Christ—" Saffron put his hand to his brow. He had dressed but he had not combed his hair; the effect was to make him, like Tiggie, look very

young. "It's odd, I don't feel at all drunk now. Anyway,
what happened? First, I went back downstairs to the old
Billiard Room and drank a good deal more. A lot of
champagne. A lot of whisky. We watched this horror video
which Ned brought. Called *The Girl-eating Ghouls* or
something like that. Did somebody have some coke?
Probably. I was too drunk to care. At some point they all
went to bed. I roamed about a bit. I like this house at night.
Even as a child—look, the point is I don't really remember.
I think I attempted to pay a social call on Nessa, rather
forgetting that old Bernardo was here, but he *was* here, or
rather he was there, and they didn't seem to welcome the
idea of a party. Then I went back to the old Billiard Room.
It was empty. Played some music, *The Clash*, *Thriller*, that
kind of thing. I may have ended on Wagner. Then back up
here. A call on Tigs. When I found her."

"You saw no one else? When it was late, I mean." Why
was she asking him these questions?

"No one. No, wait. How odd. I did see someone else. I
saw Fanny."

"*Fanny*? What on earth was she doing? Or was she just
paying what you call a social call, like everyone else?"

"Fanny? I doubt it. She's quite prim, Cousin Fan. No,
she was carrying a pile of sandwiches of all ridiculous
things. She said it was to put outside the Gobbler's room.
As a joke."

Then Lord St. Ives arrived, and almost immediately after
that the doctor accompanied by Binyon. Jemima, after a
discreet explanation of her presence, judged it the moment
to withdraw.

Soon the telling would have to begin, first of all the
telling of Tiggie's mother—would she be found in the arms
of Proffy? Did it matter? Did anything make it any worse or
better now that her child was dead? Then the telling of the
house-party, followed by its disbanding. Then the telling of
the world.

The worst moment, the very worst moment of all, so
Jemima told Cass afterwards, was the next morning when
Eugenia Jones broke down and started screaming.

"She chose Lord St. Ives as her target—words like 'your
bloody, bloody family'—but I felt it could well have been

anyone there, anyone in the house, the house itself. She became like one of her own Greek characters, Medea perhaps."

"Except that Medea killed her own children. And Eugenia Jones' child killed herself!" Cass pointed out.

"Or did she? I don't know. *Did* she? Oh Cass!" Jemima felt herself starting to cry again. "That poor little girl. I should have done something. I knew something was wrong. Something was wrong about the whole weekend. But then, what with the proof, if you call it that, that Saffron was illegitimate, and the discovery and I do call it that, about Eugenia Jones being his mother—"

Cass hugged her again.

"You'll find out what happened. And at least there'll be some justice."

"Justice! Where was the justice in a twenty-four-year-old girl killing herself by—or possibly being killed by—an enormous overdose of heroin acting on a great deal of alcohol." Jemima, in spite of herself, found the tears coming again.

"I keep thinking of her, her little interventions at the tennis match. That evening in her white dress. Like Ophelia."

"Come on. Who could have done it? Think of that. Are you sure she didn't kill herself."

"Not sure. The police, by the way, are quite sure that she did. Accidentally. Not suicide. They say they have much experience of these things, alas, and you can't expect drug addicts to behave rationally or self-preservingly in any way. They gave me the impression of having a pretty poor opinion of the said addicts, including, I may say, poor Tiggie."

"But you don't agree?"

"It's Saffron," said Jemima slowly. "He's positive that Tiggie didn't use heroin all that much, plenty of cocaine however, and when she did, she sniffed it. She hated needles. I remember her saying it about blood tests. Why couldn't blood be sucked out instead? You see, there were no other syringe marks. Even the police admitted that."

"How did they account for that?"

"There had to be a first time. And this was it. It was unhelpful that Tiggie had been in such a daze all day. All her friends agreed about that: the police talked to them. And she had been taking a lot of coke: they all had to agree about that too. So the combination was lethal, with the drink as well."

"Where did she get the syringe?"

"That was rather unhelpful too. Only her prints on it. Wait. No, that's odd, isn't it? Why no prints of the person who sold it to her?" Jemima felt her spirits revive. "But if the syringe was wiped clean after she was killed—injected with this enormous dose, that is on top of a lot of cocaine— the murderer had only then to plant her prints on the syringe with her hand."

"The Press has been ghastly, hasn't it?" interjected Cass. "Poor Lord St. Ives. Poor Lady St. Ives. I even felt sorry for Saffron, something I never expected to be. The engagement weekend: the stately home. The dashing, now tragic, young lord with his handsome face and his evil reputation. It's all been jam for them."

"The Press! No worse than Eugenia Jones' denunciations, and in a way better, because more impersonal. There and then in the great hall the next morning, the young gathered forlornly with their suitcases. Binyon trying to organize them into their cars like a portly sheep dog. Both the girls, Poppy and Nessa, were crying. Fanny looked frightful and I thought Jack was going to be sick."

"Then Eugenia Jones comes flying down that great wooden Elizabethan staircase, feet clacketing as she came. I thought she was going to slip at first, black hair all over the place—yes, you're right, she was like Medea. Then she starts on Lord St. Ives."

"Didn't anyone try to stop her?"

"Lord St. Ives stood for once like one frozen. Nobody else had the wit or courage. Perhaps Binyon might have had a go—but he was lugging suitcases outside. So she went on and on. Saying things like: 'You should have done something' over and over again, 'You should have stopped her.' Finally Proffy appeared and put his arm around her. He said something to her. I think it was in Greek. He sounded very tender. And he took her away. I didn't see her again."

"I'd like to say something tender to you, in Greek if you like, and take you away. Jemima, why don't we have a holiday? I'll talk to my clerk. I'll take you to Greece—"

"I've got to solve it," said Jemima doggedly. "Beside, believe it or not, I've still got to make this programme: 'Golden Kids.' Yes, Cy Fredericks thinks it has become something called sociologically reverberating. That's the next stage up after being socially relevant, it seems. To compensate, I'm going to solve the mystery of Saffron's birth if it kills me."

"Because it has killed Tiggie?"

"In a way. And probably that boy at Rochester, Bim Marcus. And nearly killed Saffron. Can I bear that holiday in mind to see me through?"

"You can. And now let me give you something else to bear in mind to see you through."

They went into Jemima's bedroom. It was a reunion, but unlike most reunions it was all sweet not bitter; both Jemima and Cass wondered afterwards as they lay in the huge white bed with its airy views of the tops of the Holland Park trees why they ever found it necessary to try other views of other trees in other bedrooms and elsewhere. But neither of them gave voice to the thought. It was not in the contract.

Immediately after Cass left, Jemima, who had been half-feigning, half-feeling sleep, leapt up and pulled on her honey-coloured robe. Action would blot out all such reflections which unlike the reunion were half sweet, half bitter. Cherry. Cherry and Jamie Grand, in that order. Cherry, superbly efficient (unless her love life was in chaos) could be entrusted with this new mission over the telephone, but Jamie Grand needed more dulcet treatment.

To Cherry, Jemima outlined her latest task, only to be greeted by a most un-Cherry-like gasp.

"But it's only a birth certificate, Cherry," pleaded Jemima. "You've done this before. Don't you remember that case we had? The little girl. You were so brilliant, darling darling Cherry—"

"What do you mean, Jem, done this before? Who has

ever looked for a birth certificate for a baby born probably under the name of Jones somewhere in London?" Cherry spluttered. "When I've got this new wonderful fellow in his late forties, just getting over his third marriage, and his third wife's cooking, all he wants is to eat out, hold my hand, and forget."

"All that food should strengthen you," replied Jemima soothingly. "Which reminds me that I've got a new contact for you at Oxford, to do with the 'Golden Kids' programme. He's called the Gobbler, but don't let that put you off. I think you're going to have a lot in common."

"Jemima—"

"After all, you do know the baby was a boy. And the date of birth, twenty-eighth October 1964."

"Isn't that fantastic? We know he's a Scorpio. The sexy sign. But I daresay you knew that already, didn't you?"

Jemima maintained a short dignified silence; Cherry had a feline ability to discern the possible direction of Jemima's fancies which simply could not be encouraged.

Then she said in her most winning voice, which she knew would not fool Cherry for an instant: "I have found out one or two other things which will be helpful. London is certainly the place, Nurse Elsie definitely mentioned London—she did talk of the other mother being 'not far away.' You see Saffron was officially born in the St. Ives' London house, which was then in Bryanston Square— they've sold it long ago of course. Hence Nurse Elsie as the private midwife, hence the opportunity to practise the deception which couldn't have been carried out in a nursing home, let alone a hospital. Nurse Elsie had also delivered the other mother very recently, Eugenia Jones we now think, when Lady St. Ives' labour started prematurely. Start with the local Registry office for Bryanston Square."

"And work out. Start with Jones and work—where do I go from Jones, Jemima? Smith, Brown, Robinson—"

"Concentrate on the date. Children have to be registered by law within six weeks of their birth. So the time span isn't too large. Also the new baby, the illegitimate baby who is now, we think, Saffron, can't have been much older otherwise somebody would surely have smelt a rat. As for the name, I think she almost certainly did use her own name: its very anonymity must have been attractive. And it is after all an offence to register under a false name. You can get into all sorts of trouble."

"Let's hope the Joneses of the world weren't in an especially productive mood in October 1964" were Cherry's last gloomy words.

Jamie Grand was invited by Jemima to lunch at Monsieur Thompson's on one of those frequent forays to London from Oxford which his interpretation of a sabbatical year as a visiting professor did not preclude. Unlike Cherry, Jamie was highly responsive to Jemima's request for information, especially when she prefaced invitation with the words "This is about gossip not literature, Jamie."

"What a relief," he sighed down the telephone. "There was a time when Oxford itself was more like that. I'm trying to use my short stay to re-educate them. Serena of Christ Church is a nice girl but she will keep asking me about W.H. Auden. . . ."

"Eugenia Jones. The life and loves of Eugenia Jones."

"Beyond Proffy?"

"Before Proffy. Jones, the mysterious Jones. What happened after his death, which actually occurred, Eugenia told me, before Tiggie was born."

"It won't be difficult just at the moment. Everyone's terribly sorry for her. She's totally shattered, one hears. Added to which Eleanor Mossbanker is pregnant. Again." ,

"An unlucky life."

"Eugenia or Tiggie?"

"Both, I suppose. Two unlucky lives . . . I actually meant Eugenia."

A few days later Jemima's impression of Eugenia Jones' unlucky life was thoroughly confirmed by the tale spun out—not without a certain rueful relish, it had to be admitted—by Jamie Grand at Thompson's.

"Your friend Marigold Milton was a great help. That woman has a talent for gossip which is very much under developed. She remembered a number of absolutely vital rumours about Eugenia twenty years ago which even I had quite forgotten."

Over exquisite portions of fish in various delicate vege-

table sauces, Jamie Grand talked of passion, passion and
Eugenia Jones.

"A very passionate undergraduette. Was one still permit-
ted to use that word in the fifties? Perhaps not. At all
events, a brilliant mind, a brilliant career ahead and an
astonishing capacity for indulging in the most hopeless love
affairs on the side. She might have been a man, her capacity
for divorcing her judgement at work from her judgement in
bed was so absolute. Names? I could name a few—"

Jemima allowed him to amble on. One loved or loathed
gossip, but in Jamie's company one simply had no choice
but to share his preoccupation.

"But then something more serious started," pursued
Jamie. "We're now at about nineteen sixty. An affair with a
married man. Something she didn't talk about, something
which obsessed her. She was in London by then, working
on her first book, travelling a good deal to Greece. A
slightly different circle of friends. Her movements were
much less circumscribed. You know what Oxford's like, or
should be like. Not much individual freedom there, freedom from gossip. There was even one rumour—here
Marigold Milton was useful—that Eugenia, with that fine
classical mind of hers which always seems to excite ama-
teurs of secrecy, was mixed up in some kind of intelligence
work."

"A spy? Eugenia Jones?" At one level all this was difficult
to reconcile with the Eugenia Jones she knew, or had at
least encountered quite frequently over the last traumatic
months. And yet she had to recall that mysterious sense of
power which Jemima had sensed in her from the first, that
feeling of impenetrability—only a rare public flash of
anguish after her daughter's death.

"Nothing so crude as a spy," went on Jamie. "At least
according to Marigold Milton. Perhaps a report here, a
mission. Greece in the late fifties—an interesting place.
It was odd the way Tiggie came along, and the mysterious Jones was married and killed off all in a short space of
time."

"You think he never existed?"

"That's what everyone thought at the time. It was fiction,
a graceful fiction, to have this child by her lover and bring

her up, but not unduly challenging the Oxford authorities by unmarried motherhood. To which place she now returned. And settled down. Little Antigone at her knee."

"Is this when she meets Proffy? Proffy we know was in intelligence in the war—he's never made any secret of it. As a scientist he was much in demand. There may have been a connection there." Jemima was aware of a strange unaccountable feeling of disappointment. This meant that Proffy, father of so many, was also Saffron's father. Why was she disappointed? Why was she surprised? It was surely the logical explanation, had always been the most logical explanation of Saffron's parentage, given that Eugenia was his mother. She already knew that the blood groups fitted.

"I guess so. She certainly met him. Sooner or later he must have replaced the original married lover and become the new obsession. The only thing about that is that Proffy didn't marry her, Eugenia. Why did he wait, except out of sheer absentmindedness, and then marry Eleanor some time later?"

"No time off?" Jemima had to cross-question Jamie if she was to establish the truth of Eugenia's movements throughout 1964. But she had no intention of confiding to him the reason for her interest; that would be altogether too much jam, too irresistible for Jamie, too unfair to Saffron himself. "No intervening love affair?"

"No new love affair that I could discover. A change of pattern. After all she was married, well, widowed by now. A small child. But there was time off. One more year taken off, or six months perhaps to write a book. But the book never appeared."

Jemima tried not to show her relief, or her excitement. "And that year was?"

"1964 or 1965. Around then."

"Jamie, you're an angel," cried Jemima with a warmth which surprised both of them. "If only I was ten years younger and at Oxford."

"Oh Jemima, you're absolutely no use to me," said Jamie Grand in mock horror. "W.H. Auden is the least of your demands. So what's it all about? I'll have some more of this excellent Puligny Montrachet while you answer," he added.

"Oh gossip, Jamie, gossip. Just gossip ancient and new."
And Jemima called the waiter.

Jemima was still in a good humour, and in a state of
excitement when she walked back to her flat from Monsieur
Thompson's. Midnight greeted her with a reproachful rub
round the legs and shot savage looks at his cat bowl—which
happened to be full, having been filled to bursting by Mrs.
B. Midnight however never failed to imply that there could
be yet further supplies or fresher supplies of food, if
Jemima really cared.

As Jemima went to scratch him, the telephone began to
ring.

It was from a call-box.

"Jemima," began Cherry in an urgent voice. "I think I've
found something very odd. You see, slogging my way
through the Joneses, and a fertile lot they were, I fear, it
suddenly occurred to me we were looking in the wrong
place."

"Not London?"

"London all right. But not births. Deaths not births. One
child died, right? The real St. Ives baby died. And the false
baby was put in his place. So there had to be a death
certificate for the real baby. Only it would be under the
false name. Are you with me?"

"My God, Cherry, I *am* with you!"

"So listen to this, Jemima. I then went through the death
certificates at the same time. Male babies called Jones. Not
at all difficult. No luck at Marylebone, but when I got to
Kensington, guess what I found?"

"One dead male baby called Jones. Who died on or about
twenty-eighth October and was born shortly before."

"No. Not one dead male baby called Jones. One dead
male baby called Saffron. Saffron Jones, to be accurate.
Born on twenty-sixth October and died on twenty-eighth
October 1964. Mother's name Eugenia Jones. Now guess
the father's name."

"You're the investigator. You tell me." Jemima held her
breath.

"Ivo Charles," said Cherry in a voice of triumph, "Ivo
Charles, as in Ivo Charles Iverstone, Marquess of St. Ives
in the big red peerage. Ivo Charles. Get it?"

Into the silence came the pip, pip sounds of the call-box phone and Jemima was left gazing at the instrument in her hand as the harsh burr of disconnection eventually replaced them.

CHAPTER EIGHTEEN

•

Your Father

"My father!" said Saffron uncertainly as though trying out the words for the first time. Then he repeated with more strength: "My father. My father."

Finally Saffron laughed. "This is ridiculous, isn't it? What you're saying, quite simply, is that my father—the father I've known all these years, Ivo Charles, Marquess of St. Ives, is actually—"

"Your father," completed Jemima in her turn. "Your naturally biological father. As well as in a weird kind of way, also your adopted father. I've worked it out now. The birth certificate, or rather the birth certificate and the death certificate, thanks to that genius Cherry Bronson Investigator, began the unravelling.

"It goes like this," she continued. "There were two babies. One was your mother's, I mean Lady St. Ives' baby, this is getting confusing but you know who I mean—"

"It's definitely too late to think of Eugenia Jones as my mother," said Saffron firmly. "Go on."

"This baby dies at birth on the twenty-eighth of October, but is smuggled away by Nurse Elsie, and buried under the name of Jones—Saffron Jones, as it happens. They used *your* real date of birth and its own date of death for the certificate. Then there's the true Saffron Jones—that's *you*—who was born to Eugenia on the twenty-sixth of October and substituted for the dead baby. So it—he—you grew up as Lord Saffron."

"Both of them my father's sons." Now Saffron sounded

almost angry. "The most shocking thing about all this, more shocking than anything else you've told me is that my father, the most upright man in Britain as he is famously regarded, my father had an affair, a long long affair with Eugenia Jones. Including when my mother was having a last desperate stab at having a baby."

He stopped.

"Oh Tiggie. Oh Christ, poor Tigs—is what you're saying that Tiggie was my sister?"

Jemima nodded. "Your full sister. I thought at first she was your half-sister. But now I think that there was never any Jones, ever. Just a hidden love affair. And a child. And then—perhaps when the affair was nearly over, another child."

"*Christ*. It's unbearable. The hypocrisy of it."

They were in Saffron's rooms at Rochester. A huge poster-size picture of Tiggie, panda eyes and all, taken by some fashion photographer Jemima guessed, gazed down at them. Someone—Saffron?—had written RIP underneath it.

The room had a desolate feel to it. There was a pile of unopened letters and notes on the table and some books. None of the invitations on the mantelpiece looked particularly recent, nor were there any empty champagne bottles to be seen; the cricket bat still reposed in the corner of the room with the tennis rackets and the squash rackets. They were neatly stacked, and did not look as if they had been in recent use. The sight of an enormous golfing umbrella, open and sodden, spread across the hearth rug reminded Jemima that outside the Hawksmoor quad was equally desolate, with driving squalls of cold rain, of the sort that Cy Fredericks for one would never believe could belt down in Oxford in June as the summer term reached its climax.

What were they to do if it rained throughout Commem week? Could even the legendary skill of Spike Thompson create idyllic punting on the river, the balm of a summer night, the rising luminosity of an Oxford dawn when rain was beating down on all parties concerned? "No long shadows," had been Cy Fredericks' firm instructions. Like King Canute, Cy Fredericks might have to bow to the inexorable force of the English climate.

Saffron, hunched in a T-shirt bearing some message of vaguely revolutionary—or perhaps satirical—import, and torn white track-suit trousers, bare feet (his soaking sneakers put to dry by a small smoking fire) now looked merely depressed as well as angry. The resemblance to Eugenia Jones that fatal weekend at Saffron Ivy, was marked. And his height came from his father. The B blood and the A blood. Ah well, thought Jemima, at least he gets his brains from his mother. A for aristocratic blood and B for brains. She still found it irresistible to think in terms of blood grouping.

On the other hand one could hardly suggest that Lord St. Ives had no brains, no intelligence, no cunning, no shrewdness. . . . She wanted to tell Saffron about her recent lunch with Lord St. Ives then decided against it. Saffron had enough to bear, enough to sort out.

Lord St. Ives had responded to her invitation to lunch with his usual enchanted—and enchanting—courtesy. In spite of Jemima's determination not to be put in thrall by the old fox's charm, as she put it to herself, she found herself believing that her invitation had totally transformed a rather dim day at Saffron Ivy.

"How delightful . . . we never did get to know you . . . tragic weekend . . . how *is* my son? I assume you've seen him at Oxford since the funeral that is."

"I will be seeing him."

"Good, good . . . Such an admirable influence." The flattering phrases flowed on, then: "Gwendolen would so much like to meet you again"—but I didn't ask her, thought Jemima in a panic—"however, as you know, she never comes to London these days . . . Her health, alas . . . Another time at Saffron Ivy . . . When you feel ready . . ."

Curiously, Lord St. Ives showed no signs of asking Jemima what the lunch was about. It was only when Jemima suggested Le Caprice that Lord St. Ives exhibited some degree of interest. Le Caprice was convenient for what she conceived to be his Mayfair/St. James's/Whitehall orientation and she wanted to be on her ground not his.

"Le Caprice? The smartest restaurant in London! That does sound exciting. I expect my son goes there. Ah no, alas. Please excuse the selfishness of an elderly man, Miss Shore, but I'm afraid I must insist on being the host at this luncheon. For one thing it's much too late for me to learn to be paid for by a lady; I should be in the most dreadful state throughout, wondering what I dared eat and drink without ruining you. No, I'm sure your salary is enormous. But secondly you must indulge me and allow me to be seen with a pretty woman somewhere where it will add enormously to my prestige. What a fillip it will give to my reputation to be seen with you!"

Lord St. Ives suggested Wilton's. Jemima, feeling out-manoeuvred, agreed.

As smoked salmon followed by lamb cutlets (Lord St. Ives) and dressed crab (Jemima) were brought with a stately courtesy equal to Lord St. Ives' own, by waitresses like ageing family nannies in white overalls—here at last were the traditional retainers of her dreams—Jemima wondered desperately whether the whole lunch would pass without her being able to step out of this warm bath of politeness.

In the end it was Lord St. Ives who turned the topic of conversation from a mixture of gardening and Tory politics ("what kind of roses do you suppose Mrs. T. admires? Huge strong-growing hybrid teas, I fear.") to something more personal. First he waved on the raspberries:

"Yes, yes, you must—raspberries for Miss Shore, a nice large helping and lots of cream. Some Stilton for me."

Then he looked at her directly. She thought for the first time that Lord St. Ives had a very sad face in repose. She still could not see Saffron's features in his, Saffron having the full mouth of his mother, Lord St. Ives the narrow mouth beneath the straight nose of the crusader. But those mannerisms which she had once thought "nurture not nature" and the figure, the long legs and narrow shoulders, all these Saffron had inherited from his father.

"My son, Miss Shore," said Lord St. Ives in a gentle voice, "I think you want to talk about my son. He *is* my son, you know."

"I do know that—now."

"But you doubted it." There was a long pause. Then Lord St. Ives went on, still in the same quiet tone: "Nurse Elsie, Miss Shore. A very indiscreet woman, at least when she was dying. She told my wife she had seen you. Without saying why: just that you were interested in her story. Gwendolen passed it on to me. I—shall we say I held myself in readiness, Miss Shore? Then things began to fall into place. Your interest in Saffron, for example. Other things: that conversation about blood groups at dinner; altogether too pat, too convenient. Am I correct?"

Jemima nodded.

"That wretched woman." Lord St. Ives heaved a sigh. "But then who am I to judge someone dying of cancer?"

"Who wanted to make her peace with God," concluded Jemima. "I'm not a Catholic, but who are we to judge her harshly for that?"

"'Never trust a Catholic servant,' Gwendolen's mother, old Hattie Wiltshire, a frightful dragon, used to say. 'Sooner or later the Pope starts giving them orders instead of you.' That's going a bit far perhaps, but in this case perhaps justified. Nurse Elsie's peace did cause a great deal of strife for the rest of us, didn't it?"

"At least the truth is known. That's a good thing." Jemima sounded more convinced than she felt.

"Is it? I envy your certainty, Miss Shore. A lifetime in politics has taught me that truth can be just as damaging as lies. A depressing conclusion, perhaps. Ah well—you are not here to listen to my political reminiscences. Who knows this particular truth? You know it. Does my son know it? Andrew and Daphne Iverstone?" He gave a slight grimace.

"Nurse Elsie told Saffron the first part of it. It was terribly upsetting for him, naturally. He half believed it, half rejected it. I think it was partly responsible for him going off the rails. All that business with the restaurant." She tried not to let an element of reproach creep into her voice. "Now I can tell him the second half of it. The other Iverstones—no, they don't know." Jemima devoutly hoped this was also the truth. "I'm going down to Oxford to see Saffron."

"Do you judge me very harshly? I see you do. Before you go down to Oxford, Miss Shore, let me tell you a story. A love story if you like, a love story of long ago. Or perhaps a story of guilt."

Then Lord St. Ives, in quite simple language, his

affectations of enchantment and enthusiasm dropped, told Jemima the story of the married man, the rising Conservative minister, who encountered the unmarried young woman, the beautiful and intelligent young woman, quite unexpectedly, by one of those improbable coincidences which should never have happened, might never have happened, in the course of their shared work.

"The Ministry of Defence. I was Minister for Defence in the late fifties, not for long, but long enough. And Eugenia, you've probably heard this, worked for them for a period. Someone from another world. I'd never really known anyone, any woman that is, like Eugenia before. Such wildness, such passion. There'd been occasional—well, flings—Gwendolen always in the country, no, I don't want to apologize for them—but never love. I'd always wanted to love someone: and then I loved her."

"You loved her. Did you also want to marry her?"

"There was never any question of that. I could never leave Gwendolen. How could I?.An innocent woman. What had she ever done wrong?"

"Did Eugenia want—"

"She said not. I don't know. At any rate she accepted it was impossible. I took her once to Saffron Ivy: a risk, that. My mother-in-law was dying. Gwendolen went to be with her. The excuse was to look at the library, that's what the servants were told. I've no idea if they believed it. Oddly enough, I think it was then that Antigone was conceived. And then Eugenia insisted on having the baby. I helped her. Jones was invented of course: a convenient fiction, his birth and equally convenient death."

"I worked that out."

"It was after that, after Antigone's birth, we parted. Did you work that out too? Gwendolen was so terribly unhappy. She knew."

"She knew about Eugenia?" Jemima was startled.

"Not in so many words. She knew something was up. Don't people always know that sort of thing? But someone told her something: I've always suspected Daphne Iverstone, as a matter of fact. So we parted, Eugenia and I."

"But then—Saffron—and the other baby which died.

Very much the same age. Born within forty-eight hours of each other."

"Wasn't it odd? Almost as if it was fated. By chance once more, I met Eugenia again. I was Foreign Secretary by then. There was some visiting Greek dignitary, some banquet. Gwendolen was in the country. We took the chance, the risk. One night, not even a night. I went back to Saffron Ivy full of guilt. And a few days later—need I go into this further?—the other baby was conceived. Gwendolen had lost so many children. But she was determined to have one last chance. Even the doctors didn't want her to try."

"That baby died."

"I nearly went mad. Gwendolen was hoping for so much in spite of the doctors. And it was then that the idea came to me. Nurse Elsie was looking after Eugenia too: in a way it was strangely easy. You see, Eugenia once again refused to have an abortion. I couldn't make her, I thought it was a mistake. The affair was over, she was making a new life. She was just beginning to see Proffy; he had, I think, just fallen in love with her. The baby was going for adoption. I was half crazy, I admit it. All Nurse Elsie had to do was tell Eugenia her child had died."

"So Eugenia didn't know what had really happened to her child." Jemima was astonished.

"Not then, not for years. Our paths didn't cross. We took care in fact to avoid each other. Myself in London or Saffron Ivy; Eugenia in Oxford; we never had any friends in common, that was part of the fascination, I suppose. It never occurred to me that Antigone's path would cross with Saffron's: the one thing I never thought about. And yet somehow, by another kind of strange fate, they seemed drawn to each other."

"When did Eugenia know? I got the impression that she did know. That she regarded the engagement with horror as a result."

"Nurse Elsie. Told her too on her deathbed in her grand confessional mood. She sent for Eugenia after sending for you."

So that was the other woman, thought Jemima, who

came on the last day of all to the Hospice. I suspected Daphne Iverstone.

"As for the engagement," pursued Lord St. Ives, "we were both appalled. But separately. I tried to speak to Eugenia about it, but Proffy wouldn't let me meet her. He's quite jealous of her in his Pasha-like way. So I wrote to her: a carefully guarded letter, because for one thing I did not think the truth should be committed to paper, suggesting that the matter would be sorted out at Saffron Ivy. My plan was to put them off without revealing the truth: they were both so young, so capricious, it could happen naturally. This engagement came from nowhere, one of Saffron's schemes. We could sort it out. I could sort it out."

Jemima thought: and in its own tragic way, it was sorted out at Saffron Ivy. But she did not say so.

None of this did she think it right to pass on to Saffron.

There was one last question for Lord St. Ives.

"Forgive me, your wife? You said people always know. Did she know this too?"

"There was a time: he was such a dark little baby, she used to comment how odd it was. Then a time came when she never mentioned the subject of his looks. After that she began pointing resemblances to Saffron in the Iverstone family portraits, almost as if she wanted to reassure herself. They say a mother always knows. But then, Miss Shore, to me she *was* his mother."

"As you were his father."

"In exactly the same way," concluded Lord St. Ives firmly. "In exactly the same way."

"And in addition to saving your wife, you saved your estates. So you protected your own walls."

"Like the ivy, in the family motto? That's also true. But now, Miss Shore, would you have wanted Saffron Ivy to pass to Andrew Iverstone?"

"A nice liberal dilemma. But now there's Jack of course. He's a decent fellow."

"Very decent. Almost too decent I sometimes think; as though he was repressing quite different feelings. But I could hardly have expected Andrew and Daphne to have a son like Jack, could I? Heredity is certainly a very odd thing."

It was Lord St. Ives' last word on the subject of the
Iverstone family.

To Saffron in Oxford, Jemima said:

"Don't judge him too harshly—your father."

"I don't want to judge anybody!" exclaimed Saffron
fiercely. "And I don't want to be judged either. Let him try
to come the heavy father on me now, lectures about my way
of life, no way, that's over." He laughed angrily and leapt up
with a kind of furious grace, which reminded Jemima of his
antics on the tennis court.

"Let's have some champagne."

Jemima shook her head. "I don't want any. I'm meeting
the cameraman and the director, down by the river at St.
Lucy's. Much need for Megalith mackintoshes."

"Oddly enough, I don't want any either. You may not
believe this, Jemima, but I'm absolutely fed up with all that
shit. Golden Kids and all that. I'm thinking of going
straight. Cousin Jack will be amazed. He's always given me
moral lectures about waste and the family honour. I'm
actually thinking of *working*." He made it sound as unlikely
an activity as going to Xanadu.

"And one last thing, Jemima, I'm not taking part in that
fucking programme. You can tell Megalith Television to go
and stuff themselves. Let the others get on with it: there are
plenty of Golden Kids in Oxford. The Gobbler, Poppy and
the rest of them. No lack, whatsoever. But you can include
me out, in the immortal words of Sam Goldwyn."

Saffron stopped. "So what do you think of that, beautiful
but icy Jemima?"

"I'm not icy. Just cold. I find I prefer Cy Fredericks' idea
of Oxford with golden sunshine playing on the arcades
rather than puddles: dreaming spires, not spires teeming
with rain."

"You look icy. Icy towards me."

"As a matter of fact I feel quite warmly towards you."

"Not disappointed about your programme?"

"It's only television," said Jemima lightly, hoping that the
lightning, dispatched by Cy Fredericks, would not come to
strike her dead. "As a matter of fact, I think it's probably the
first sensible decision you've made in your life."

"I'll come to the Commem. I mean, I'm not aiming to

become a monk, for God's sake. It's my own College, I've got the tickets." He paused. "But I haven't got a partner, have I?" There was a silence. "Jemima—"

"I'm working, Saffron," said Jemima hastily. "You may have opted out of 'Golden Kids' but some of us are not so lucky. Do you realize that if I don't make this programme successfully, this darling of my boss's heart, he could send me to the Siberian equivalent of the saltmines, which in Cy's case could be making a six-part series of programmes about Common Market attitudes to the EEC?"

"I thought the Common Market was the EEC."

"That's my point."

"Not as much fun as a programme about the Radical Women's Settlement. To which I was once going to give some money if you acted as my private investigator." Saffron hesitated. "Jemima—have you thought about all that?"

Jemima wondered what she should say. She had indeed thought about "all that." She had gone through over and over again both in her head and with Cass the various murderous attacks, one successful but hitting the wrong target and one failed. Bim Marcus who died on Staircase Thirteen, Saffron attacked with the boat hook at the Chimneysweepers' Dinner. And then there was Tiggie, fatally injected with a massive dose of drugs, Tiggie who feared the needle and yet had died by it. She was beginning to see a connection, in terms of the various people who had been present on all three occasions; the names of those who had the opportunity led her inexorably to the motive, the obvious motive. Envy.

But these thoughts too she did not wish to repeat to Saffron. A taste for murder was said to grow, like other tastes. Tiggie was gone but Saffron still lived. She wished that she could pen her suspects together, pin one of them down, abandon the others; at the moment it was still risky to see them as more than a group, those who had had the opportunity on all three occasions.

Bim Marcus' death could have been encompassed by anyone in Oxford at that time; they only had to walk into Rochester—which was not difficult—and then lie low until the dead of night. The murderer or murderess could then lurk somewhere else in the college, and leave easily, at leisure, when the college gates were open.

If envy was the key, as she had felt all along, then the Iverstone family certainly had the strongest motive. Had Nurse Elsie possibly confided the truth about Saffron's parentage to one of them as well as to Jemima and Eugenia Jones? Daphne, Fanny, or even Jack. Andrew Iverstone was a ruthless man, no one denied that, and she had glimpsed his naked hatred for Tiggie as he slammed the tennis ball at her. Andrew Iverstone had been in Oxford at the time of Bim's death, and at the Chimneysweepers' Dinner and at Saffron Ivy. So for that matter had Daphne Iverstone, although it seemed even more far-fetched to suspect her, twittering innocent as she appeared. No, of the two Andrew Iverstone was the far more likely. Technically, Fanny Iverstone had had the opportunity, having been present on all three occasions. But while Fanny was slightly more plausible as a killer than her mother, she was also demonstrably very fond of Saffron, and she surely had to be ruled out on those grounds alone.

As for Jack Iverstone, he had to be ruled out for two reasons: first he had not been present at the Chimney-sweepers' Dinner, and secondly sheer niceness must make him the least plausible member of that Iverstone branch to emerge as a murderer.

Nothing more could happen. Or so Jemima had confidently told Cass in London. Inwardly she was by no means so sure.

Jemima took a decision.

"I'll come with you. Or rather, you'll come with me. Stay with me. You'll be good cover for my sizzling exposure of the *jeunesse doré*, particularly now you've elected to leave their ranks. You'll protect me."

Her unspoken thought was: And I'll protect you.

CHAPTER NINETEEN

•

Supper à Deux

Megalith's luck was out. Or at least as far as the weather was concerned. Tantalizing sunshine succeeded the rainstorms early in the week, and then the day of the St. Lucy's Commem and the Rochester Ball—and the first filming for the "Golden Kids" programme for that matter—was marked by a downpour in the morning.

Jemima thought there was after all a kind of beauty about the rain-washed spires, and the heavy blue thunderclouds looming over the dome of Christ Church and Magdalen tower had some kind of Constable effect; but the huge marquees in the quads of those colleges which were about to have, or had just had, a ball, conveyed all the cheerfulness of a rained-out fête, as rain fell persistently on the canvas. The boats, both punts and canoes, drawn up and chained by St. Lucy's, had an especially depressing air; a young boatman was bailing them out with a misanthropic expression.

Traditionally a Commem Ball ended with punting on the river at breakfast time as the sun rose on the tired revellers—an idyllic scene which Spike Thompson had absolutely promised to get in the can for the benefit of Cy Fredericks' romantic sensibilities concerning Oxford. With a gloom worthy of the boatman's, Jemima wondered whether rain would stop play.

She met Fanny Iverstone in the hairdresser's.

"Oh, it'll be all right on the night," said Fanny confidently, reaching for a copy of *Taffeta* and adding it to the pile of glossy magazines on her lap. "It always is, isn't it? I've been to dozens of Commems. God just does this to frighten us. I've got the most groovy dress, Brown's, it cost a fortune, Mummy paid, she approves of Commems, I think they remind her of her youth. She definitely brightens up at the thought of them, as though they were the last bastions of civilization."

Fanny laughed: "Which is quite funny, really, when they cost a packet, the dinner's disgusting, you generally quarrel with your partner or lose him more likely or fancy someone else's partner, they last forever, and end up at six in the morning with everyone totally pissed and, worse still, most people sick as dogs. Some civilization."

Jemima shuddered. Could Spike Thompson be trusted to make this unpromising material into something more like an advertisement for, say, an upmarket shampoo?

She could not resist asking Fanny: "Then why go?"

Fanny looked at her in surprise, her blue eyes opening wide. "Oh, one has to *go*," she said. "It's just that one doesn't expect to enjoy oneself very much. That's all." And she turned her berollered head happily back to the cosy vitriol purveyed by *Taffeta* magazine.

Jemima thought it was time for an urgent conference with her director and her cameraman. Guthrie Carlyle had vanished but she found Spike Thompson at St. Lucy's in the rooms of Rufus Pember, who turned out to be Chairman of the Ball Committee, with Nigel Copley, as a committee member, also present. She had not seen Rufus, except fleetingly in the High, since the night of the Chimneysweepers' Dinner when he had appeared with Nigel Copley from the river. The memory of that secret expedition upstream—even if Rufus and Nigel had to be acquitted of the attack on Saffron, on the evidence of Fanny Iverstone—stirred in her momentarily other thoughts about that night and the possible movements of other participants in the drama. The police, after some initially strenuous inquiries, had for want of any real evidence against anyone, abandoned the investigation. Privately Detective Chief Inspector Harwood gave it as his opinion that it was a typical piece of undergraduate folly which had gone wrong. He did not exactly say: "Let them lay about each other with boat hooks, if they like, so long as the honest citizens of Oxford are left in peace." But Jemima got the impression that the thought lay somewhere at the back of his mind. . . . Then her attention was distracted by the merry sight of Spike Thompson and Jimbo, the sound man, recording as they put it, "some useful wild track of champagne corks popping."

"Who pays?" enquired Jemima sternly.

"Jemima! You ask me that! These lovely boys are paying, aren't you, boys?" Spike seemed to have had a hypnotic effect on Rufus and Nigel, or else they were already glazed with champagne-tasting on behalf of the Ball Committee, for they nodded agreement.

"This is going to be the greatest Commem Ball ever. And that's official. Right, boys?" Rufus and Nigel nodded again. "You name it, they've got it. Bands. They've got bands. All the big names: Glenn Miller—"

"Style of Glenn Miller," interrupted Rufus Pember, showing a moment's anxiety at the enthusiasm of his new friend. "Glenn Miller's dead." He paused. "Isn't he?"

"Of course he's dead! But he lives again in the person of this fabulous guy with this fabulous band. Then there's Boy George and the Culture Club—no, sorry mate, the *new* Boy George and the *new* Culture Club. This lot's going to be big, right Rufe? And the latest reggae band. What's the name of the latest reggae band? It doesn't matter. They met a man who met Bob Marley; they have to be good."

Rufus nodded more happily, as Spike Thompson reeled off the names of a further five or six famous bands or groups or singers ending with one singer whose sex Jemima never did quite work out since he or she was described as looking rather like Mick Jagger's younger brother, but sounding more like Marlene Dietrich.

"Something for everyone," said Jemima diplomatically. But Spike Thompson was not finished yet.

"And the fireworks! And the sideshows! There are exotic sideshows: strip-tease; both sexes. No, correction, all three sexes. Correction again, this is the eighties, all four sexes. A disco, a dancing bear—"

"No, the bear can't come. It's got a previous engagement," put in Nigel.

"Pity. I was planning the shot. Anyway, all-night videos in the Junior Common Room, videos of an advanced nature, I take it. As for the Senior Common Room, God knows what will be going on in the Senior Common Room, some of these professors are ravers."

"*We* organize this Ball, you know," said Rufus, slightly stuffily. "The undergraduates. It's nothing to do with the dons. We do it all—our committee. We organize everything from the champagne"—he looked pointedly at the bottles, now empty—"to the security, to keep out the gatecrashers."

"Of course you do, mate, no offence meant. And it's all going to be recorded by Megalith Television. Immortalized."

Jemima wondered when the moment would come to break it to Spike that whatever turn his nocturnal activities might take, he was not expected to bring back shots of "advanced" videos to Megalith Television. . . .

"And all this for one hundred guineas a double ticket," ended Spike brightly. "I mean, it's given away, isn't it? I'm surprised you have so much trouble with gatecrashers. You'd think they'd be glad to pay." Ah, that's my boy, thought Jemima. For a moment Spike had had her slightly worried. The price of the ticket reminded her that she needed to discover the final details of Kerry Barber's demonstration outside St. Lucy's against the price of the aforesaid tickets and in favour of aid to the Third World. She looked into Jack Iverstone's rooms. Instead of Jack, she found Kerry himself, scribbling a message on Jack's desk.

"His father's ill," Barber told Jemima cheerfully over his shoulder. "They've telephoned through. Some kind of attack brought on by high blood pressure. It almost makes a rationalist like me believe in God when the bad guys start getting it."

Under the circumstances, Jemima saw no need for any conventional expression of sorrow. Nor was she particularly surprised, remembering that sweating flushed bull-like figure on the tennis court. Playing competitive tennis, even limited to three sets, was certainly no way to combat high blood pressure.

Jemima was more surprised when Jack Iverstone arrived that evening at her suite at the Martyrs Hotel, just as she was changing for the ball—or the programme—and announced that he was carrying on with his protest.

"No, I'm going through with it. It's important to me. My chance."

"But Jack," protested Jemima, "your father—"

"It's a put-on. Fanny agrees with me. She's carrying on with her plans. We had a frightful row on the subject of Kerry Barber's demo. He said I was making a fool of myself. I said I could live with that. Then he changed tack and said I was making a fool of him. The idea of me appearing on television riled him, you see; he thinks he has the media all sewn up. Now he produces this convenient attack and I'm supposed to come running."

Shortly after Jack Iverstone departed, Saffron himself arrived. In his dark green tail coat with its white facings—the mark of an Oxford Blood—he looked extraordinarily handsome; the slightly gaunt appearance he had presented since his accident, and still more since Tiggie's death, suited him. With the thick black hair flopping across his forehead, slightly too long for the conventional idea of one who wore a tail coat in the evening, Saffron looked for a moment more like a musician, a young violinist perhaps, than a rich young undergraduate come to escort a lady to a Commem Ball.

Because Jemima was wearing a ball dress of roughly the same colour—bottle-green watered taffeta, off the shoulder, with flounces and a very full skirt—she had to admit to the mirror that they looked curiously well matched. Even her white shoulders matched the white facings of his coat.

It's a great pity I'm not into younger men, thought Jemima, as Saffron kissed her quite hard on the lips. This is all very well, but I've got more serious things to do like make a programme. And more serious people to kiss, for that matter. All the same, she responded to the kiss with an enthusiasm which took her—and perhaps Saffron too—by surprise.

After a bit, they broke apart; green eyes met black ones. Jemima patted her hair, in a gesture she only used on television when she was extremely nervous.

"Eyes like a cat," said Saffron. "Do you scratch like a cat as well? I have a feeling you might."

"Dinner, Saffron. You're taking me to dinner. We queue for our dinner tickets, right? And then take our places in the tent. It's all in with the ticket, I gather, which it jolly well should be. We're not going to film that, so there's plenty of time." She was speaking too quickly. "The demo doesn't get going till about eleven. That's where I catch up with Spike. And you're not coming to that with me."

"I thought we'd have some pink champagne in my room at Rochester first, supper *à deux*," said Saffron carefully. "And some lobster. I've studied your tastes. We're having our own ball, as you know, but I've bribed a member of the committee with an extra bottle to let me keep the key to my own room. All the rooms are supposed to be doled out to the eight hundred jolly people as sitting-out rooms but I didn't fancy that very much. As for the official Commem dinner, why don't we give that a miss? Not exactly an inspired menu, with Rufus Pember at the helm, and another eight hundred people at St. Lucy's milling about in a tent like the vegetable show at the Spring Fair at Saffron Ivy."

Saffron took Jemima over to Rochester under the shade of an enormous black umbrella. Even so, her long green taffeta skirts swished in the puddles of St. Giles and she feared for her very high-heeled green satin sandals. Then Jemima went swishing up the winding staircase of Staircase Thirteen and climbed to the top, past Proffy's door (the oak, she noted, was firmly sported) all the way to Saffron's room at the top. It was in half darkness; then Jemima realized that the top of the vast tent which filled the Hawksmoor quad, on which the rain was gently rattling, obscured the window, through which she had once been able to look down on the green sward, the fountain and the Fellows' Garden beyond.

Saffron slammed the heavy door.

"We don't want any interruptions from eager beavers of this college, male and female, having their first and only night out of the year."

He opened the pink champagne and poured it into a silver mug which looked like a christening mug—Jemima turned it round and saw the engraving: Saffron Ivo Charles 28 October 1964. She also saw that the room was filled with white roses, Virgo, the kind of greenish-white rose she loved.

"More study of my tastes." She drank. She wondered whether he would get the date on the mug changed to the twenty-sixth, and thought he probably would not. She drank again.

Afterwards Jemima blamed the champagne (a thin excuse however from a champagne drinker, so perhaps it was the scent of the white roses) for the fact that after a while Saffron persuaded her that her taffeta dress was really too wet to be worn, that the dress needed hanging up to dry if it was to feature properly on Megalith Television in a couple of hours' time, and really all Jemima needed to do was to step out of it, and then the problems of the world would be solved, or at least for the time being, and even if they weren't, the evening would be off to a very good start. . . . So Jemima did step out of the green taffeta dress, which left her, roughly speaking, in her stockings and high-heeled green shoes, all of which Saffron much appreciated, and shortly after that Saffron and Jemima adjourned to his bedroom, a small untidy cell off the sitting room, with a scarcely made bed, none of which made any difference to the pleasure and variety of what followed, the endless pleasure, the remarkable variety.

"Christ!" exclaimed Saffron, a good while later, sitting up in bed with his black hair in chaos. "There's somebody trying to unlock the bloody door." There was a good deal of other black hair all over his body, and as he jumped up and snatched at the red towelling robe, Jemima was reminded of how at Saffron Ivy she had thought he looked like a gipsy; no longer like a musician, he was much more like a gipsy, a healthy, muscular young gipsy. Saffron ran into the other room, leaving her in the little cell. Jemima sank, sensuously, beneath the duvet. Then she thought in her turn: "Christ, my *dress* is hanging up in there."

She heard Saffron say: "My dear Proffy, I've got special permission."

"From the Dean, Saffer?"

"Have some lobster, Proffy," was Saffron's reply. "And some pink champagne!"

It seemed a very long time indeed before Saffron returned to the bedroom, in the course of which Jemima had begun to wish she had not also left her little gold bracelet watch in the sitting room, as well as her green crystal drop earrings (all of which must be extremely conspicuous, unless Saffron had had the wit to conceal them). The watch became increasingly vital. If the worst comes to the worst, thought Jemima, the programme comes first, and if I ever doubted it, witness the fact that I'm going to have to stalk into the sitting room starkers except for a pair of green sandals, and assume my clothing as graciously as possible, under the watchful eye of Professor Mossbanker as he guzzles the lobster, in order to get to St. Lucy's on time to film Kerry Barber's demo.

But it did not come to that. Saffron returned.

"Proffy! He sure has a nose for a party. And for lobster. And for champagne for that matter." Saffron heaved a sigh. "Most dons give the Commems wide berth. But I believe the old boy was simply moseying about the Staircase looking for refreshment."

Jemima did not enquire about the dress. She only hoped that Proffy's legendary absent-mindedness extended to overlooking a ruffled green taffeta ball dress swaying gracefully in the window of Saffron's room. She was busy trying to replace Jemima, happily reckless lover of Saffron, with that other Jemima, presenter of Megalith's "Golden Kids" programme.

As Jemima and Saffron sped, under the great black umbrella, from Rochester, down the Broad and Long Wall to her rendezvous with Spike outside St. Lucy's, they passed a series of other revellers, the men in dinner jackets—wing collars were clearly in fashion, and the occasional tail coat—the girls all in long dresses which would have satisfied Cy Fredericks.

"Gatecrashers!" pronounced Saffron with pleasure. "The serious fun starts once dinner is over. In fact that is the only real fun of a Commem, gatecrashing it. Rochester's security is hopeless—anyone can get in if they want to—but St. Lucy's is a good challenge: you can swim across the river, carrying your clothes in a plastic bag, I did that to Magdalen one year. On the other hand they're wise to the river. St. Lucy's roof might be better: where it touches the botanical gardens; the chapel is too steep. There's a rumour that they're going to use hoses on the roof, which makes it even more fun. Added to which there's another rumour that Nigel Copley's brother was in the SAS, so that they're going to use SAS methods, or borrow the SAS on an amateur basis to keep out gatecrashers—which makes it even more fun, and more of a challenge. In fact I rather think I'll have a go—"

Jemima stopped.

"Saffron, whatever your plans are, you can gatecrash Buckingham Palace for all I care, but don't tell me. I've got a programme to make. In short, this is where we part. Do I make myself plain? If I see you, I don't acknowledge you. It's Falstaff and Prince Hal, only you're Falstaff and I'm Prince Hal."

"I know thee not, young man?"

"Precisely."

"You knew me."

"I did. And you knew *me*. Very lovely it was. Goodbye, Saffron." She kissed him on the cheek, then turned and crossed the road to St. Lucy's.

Saffron called something after her: "I'll be there. It's a promise. Meet you at Pond Quad at dawn. A definite rendezvous."

Jemima looked back. He was waving and blowing a kiss. "See you," then she called back: "Take care!" It was her last sight of Saffron, vanishing back up Long Wall in the direction of Rochester.

CHAPTER TWENTY

•

Dancing in the Quad

As soon as Saffron was gone, Jemima was caught up totally in the concerns of Megalith Television, beginning with the filming of Kerry Barber's extremely visible demonstration, which straddled in front of the great mediaeval archway gate of St. Lucy's. The effect, in view of the fact that Kerry Barber and his fellows were wearing T-shirts, jeans, baggy trousers and suchlike whereas the revellers visible inside were in formal evening dress, was to give the impression of peasants demonstrating against their feudal lord. The demonstrating peasants included not only Jack but an older woman, chic in khaki dungarees, whom Jemima guessed to be Kerry Barber's admirably teetotal wife Mickey. Then there was a girl Jemima dimly recognized and only pinned down later as Magda Poliakoff, she who had given evidence at the Bim Marcus inquest.

"All this," said Jemima to Guthrie Carlyle happily, "is going to look very good on our programme." There was a brief interval while two would-be gatecrashers, both male and rather small were unceremoniously evicted from St. Lucy's.

"I told you it was no good saying you were from the *Observer*," Jemima heard one say to the other indignantly. "Who cares about the *Observer* at a Commem?"

"You said you were from the *Daily Mail* and you got slung out too," hissed back his companion. "On account of the fact that there are eighty or ninety people from the *Daily Mail* there already."

Then Megalith, in the guise of Guthrie and Spike Thompson, was able to set to in earnest and film some splendid shots of Kerry Barber's banners—most of which mentioned the price of a Commem ticket—ONE HUNDRED PIECES OF SILVER was the most effective—in contrast to the plight of the Third World. The rain made it even more effective.

Jack Iverstone was unaccustomedly tense during his brief interview on camera with Jemima—with a background of St. Lucy's, plus a banner reading ONE NIGHT'S FUN FOR YOU, ONE YEAR'S FOOD FOR THEM. Either he was suffering from anxiety about his father or else the medium of television had robbed him of his habitual ease of manner. Jemima was relieved when the interview was over. Jack vanished, possibly depressed by his performance, and did not rejoin the demonstration. Then Megalith was able to move inside the defended portals of St. Lucy's and mingle with the lawful—or mainly lawful—crowds as they danced sedately to the new Glenn Miller, jived to the new Boy George, swayed to the people who once met a man who met Bob Marley, twisted (and shouted) in Luke's Disco, admired (and cat-called) at the strippers of all four sexes or repaired to the Junior Common Room for the sake of the advanced videos. Or simply vanished into the sitting-out rooms for the sake of wine or women, song being freely available outside in all varieties.

In all of this Jemima never spared a thought for Saffron. She was busy, doing a job, if not the job for which she had been sent into the world, at least a job which she enjoyed doing. She talked to Fanny Iverstone (who looked very pretty in her Brown's dress) and to Poppy Delaware (whose dress, at least by the time Jemima met her, was falling down, but she also looked very pretty in it or out of it). She did not talk to Muffet Pember (whose partner had cut his hand on some glass, thus convincing Jemima that Muffet, or at any rate her partner, was in some peculiar way accident prone).

She found the Gobbler, preparatory to interviewing him, only he was in the pond under the statue of St. Lucy's at the time consuming gulls' eggs on a plate as the fountain played on his fair and foolish face. So the programme had to be

made without the spoken views of the Gobbler on being a
Golden Kid. There was only this striking illustrative shot of
the Gobbler at play which many people afterwards thought
was the finest shot in the whole film, and a still version of
which was used on the cover of the *TV Times* and a whole
host of other magazines but for which the Gobbler's
parents, who turned out to be Very Important, were still
trying to sue Megalith Television long after "Golden Kids"
had picked up the last of its many inevitable awards.

All of this was to come. Jemima and camera picked their
dainty way past rather a lot of people who had just been or
were just going to be sick, particularly as the evening
progressed, but the cameras avoided all of that, unlike the
sight of the Gobbler at play. For one thing it was not really
very socially relevant or as Spike Thompson sagely observed: "Who needs Golden Kids losing their Golden
Dinners out of their Golden Gobs? What's happened to the
smashing bird in a red dress who promised to dive into the
pool starkers once we get that fat boy out of it?"

Copulating couples were however not utterly ignored.
As Spike observed to Jemima: "This might be a witty
voice-over situation for you, my love."

"Sex in, sicks out," was the way Guthrie Carlyle summed
it up.

In the early hours of the morning the rain stopped and
the fireworks went up into the night sky.

For the first time Jemima, gazing at them restlessly—she
hated fireworks in principle as dangerous and wasteful yet
found them irresistible—thought of Saffron. She wondered
if he had indeed tried to gatecrash St. Lucy's and if he had
succeeded. There had been no sign of him. Of those she
knew, Jack Iverstone had never reappeared, and Fanny
Iverstone, glimpsed early on looking rather flushed in her
Brown's dress dancing in Luke's Disco, had long since
vanished.

At about two o'clock a great cry went up in Pond Quad:
"Ahoy there!" Then: "They're on the roof!" Then to the
delight and excitement of all those lucky enough to be
inside St. Lucy's, two figures in black hoods and darkened
clothing were glimpsed on the sloping roof of St. Lucy's
chapel. The invaders' situation looked perilous enough

already, but then the firehoses began to play upon them. Although some of those at the Ball also got drenched—"Oh fuck off!" shouted an indignant girl of elfin appearance wearing a sprigged muslin crinoline, when the water sprayed her—it was thought by the rest to be a small price to pay for the fun.

The invaders slid ignominiously down the roof.

Saffron? Jemima rather hoped not.

It was only later that she learnt that the so-called invaders had actually been security men, the recriminations about the hosing down afterwards being so violent as to lend some credence to the theory that they were out-of-hours SAS men.

It was not until the dawn, a luminous dawn, with mist rising off the river, and the first intrepid revellers climbing into the punts, reckless of the rainwater, and the pretty skirts—or perhaps they were sufficiently dishevelled anyway—that she began to wonder seriously where Saffron was.

Jemima leant her head on Guthrie's shoulder.

"Breakfast, my love? You look as if you could do with kidneys, bacon, sausages, kedgeree, scrambled eggs, and whatever is the rest of the menu which I have in my pocket. Spike's going to take some shots of the river now the boats are out. He doesn't need you any more. Then an overall picture of the aftermath."

St. Lucy's was beginning to look like a battlefield, as recumbent bodies, the survivors, lay about, sleeping, unconscious, twined round each other. Bottles were everywhere. Somewhere one of the bands—or was it Luke's Disco?—was still loyally playing.

"No thanks, I have a previous engagement. I think I'll wander off." Jemima looked again at the scene of mayhem before her, more like Dutch peasants at the kermis, than anything more classically graceful—no shades of Poussin here.

"I wonder who won this battle? And who lost?"

"We won it. Megalith Television won it," said Guthrie smugly.

"There seem to be a great number of losers," Jemima pointed to the inert bodies, corpses as they seemed, strewn around them. "One wonders whether some of these will ever wake again."

I must look for him, she thought. Then: Saffron—he broke his promise. Why? Did he fail to gatecrash after all? Then with more urgency: Saffron: why didn't he come?

For the first time since she had parted from Saffron, she thought of the possible dangers to him in this great Oxford night of rout. Where were all those who might wish ill to Saffron? Where for that matter was Saffron himself?

At Rochester College, there was the same feeling of the battle lost and won, the same slightly morbid impression of corpses, as Jemima, now wrapped in a vast Chinese shawl against the cool of the morning, stepped her way through the quad to Staircase Thirteen. She had received, with Saffron, a pass to leave Rochester and return: finding she had lost it, Jemima expected the man at the gate to raise an eyebrow; instead she was waved on with a resignation singularly at variance with the paranoia recently exhibited at St. Lucy's. If security was the standard by which a successful Oxford ball was rated, no wonder Rochester's was considered to be inferior.

As she clambered up the high winding stone staircase, Jemima wondered if she would find Saffron too in some kind of passive state of post-revelling (and post-coital) contemplation. Perhaps he had merely gone quietly back to bed after leaving her at St. Lucy's. Or perhaps he had found the other possibilities for enjoyment at Rochester. . . . Nevertheless the sense of unease which had oppressed her since dawn at St. Lucy's became stronger as she reached the top of the stairs and saw that Saffron's door was open. She noticed that several of the other doors on the staircase were shut (although Proffy's on the ground floor was for once open; perhaps he had finally gone home to Chillington Road, having sufficiently slaked his appetite for lobster and champagne).

Jemima went into the room. It was empty. She went through into the tiny bedroom and stared. Saffron was lying on the bed, dressed in his white evening shirt and black trousers, only the white tie had been undone and lay loosely round his neck. His eyes were shut. One sleeve had been rolled up. Otherwise the resemblance to the body of Tiggie was uncanny.

Jemima ran forward and supported his head, realizing as she did so, that Saffron, unlike Tiggie, was breathing; his body was warm. But the pulse, when she felt it, was very faint.

"It's not true!" she cried aloud and started to pull at Saffron's body, slapping his cheek, tugging at his shoulders. Once Saffron's lips opened a little but otherwise there was no movement. He was in a coma, a drug-induced coma, Jemima recognized that only too well. The question was, how did she reverse it? What should she do, now, immediately? Did she dare leave him and fetch help? After that, she would work out how on earth he had got himself into that coma.

"Saffron," she said aloud again. "Saffron! Wake up, Saffron, you've got to hear me."

There was a very faint noise behind her. Jemima realized for the first time that she was not alone with Saffron.

She whirled round. There standing in the doorway of the tiny room, watching her and blinking slightly in his usual mild manner behind the black-rimmed spectacles, stood Professor Mossbanker.

"Proffy," she began, "thank God. We've got to get help. Will you telephone—you've got a telephone downstairs? We've got to save him—"

Then she stopped. She saw that in his hand Proffy was holding a syringe.

"You found that?" she questioned, still feeling confused. "What are you doing here, Proffy?" she said in a stronger voice. "What are you doing with that syringe?"

"I didn't expect you to be here," Proffy spoke with an odd kind of detachment. "Why did you come?"

"I came *back*," Jemima spoke urgently, "and thank God I did. And now we've got to get help, we've got to save him."

"Oh you'll be able to save him all right." Proffy continued to speak in the same casual tone. "If you think he's worth saving that is."

Then Jemima for the first time fully understood.

"You!" She hesitated and then said in an uncertain voice: "You—the murderer?" Jemima took a step backwards. She was not sure at the time whether it was a protective move towards Saffron or a defensive one on her own account.

"Precisely. Rather an unexpected discovery on your part, I fancy." Proffy spoke in his familiar rapid unemphatic tone; he continued to stand there blinking behind his spectacles. He might have been congratulating—or reproving her—on some slight matter of scholarship. Then he put down the syringe and removed his spectacles. For a moment his eyes, his whole visage, looked naked and rather innocent. Then she realized how cold his real manner was, had perhaps always been behind the friendly bumbling veneer.

Jemima felt an instant of pure panic. Proffy had tried to kill Saffron or was preparing to do so. He had—she grappled with the thought—killed poor little Tiggie. Her thoughts went further back as she struggled with the implications of it all: he had probably also killed Bim Marcus. Proffy: a double murderer. A would-be triple murderer. Was it likely that he would now spare her?

Yet Proffy still made no move towards her. In a way his stillness, his air of ease, was more sinister than if he had displayed openly the violence which must lie within him. She supposed that she ought, nonetheless, to prepare herself for self-defence, some kind of defence. She was tall and quite strong: Proffy was on the other hand, if a lot older, a lot taller and a lot heavier. On his own testimony he was a killer, even if the weapons he had chosen hitherto had been secret ones.

Jemima took a deep breath.

"Why?" she asked crudely. She had some vague memory that hostages were supposed to engage terrorists in conversation in order to defuse a violent situation. Even stronger was her obstinate desire to know the truth—if it proved to be the last thing she ever found out.

"Why?" replied Proffy, twisting his heavy spectacles in his hands. "I suppose I thought the world would be well rid of him."

"Wasn't it a case of being well rid of—*them*?" To her own ears, Jemima's voice sounded distinctly tremulous. Above all, she wanted to give an impression of calm authority.

"Ah yes, them. So you worked that out. Very good, very

good." There was the same surreal atmosphere of academic congratulation.

"The deaths of Tiggie and Bim Marcus. Aren't I right? Wasn't it all part of the same—" she hesitated again. "The same plan," she finished.

Proffy ignored the question.

"Why?" he repeated, instead. "Why indeed? A long story, a long story from the past. But not, I think, the story you anticipated, Jemima Shore Investigator. My impression was that you were altogether too carried away by other aspects of it all. . . . Ah well, it doesn't matter now."

Proffy put his spectacles on again and gazed at her. "You look frightened, I see. Not surprising I suppose under the circumstances. All the same, no need to be frightened, no need at all. It's over, all over."

"Why?" demanded Jemima desperately.

Proffy continued to consider her. "Yes, I daresay the enquiring mind ought to be encouraged. In theory if not in practice. Since it no longer matters to me, I will indulge myself—and you—by explaining. We might go downstairs."

Much later, Proffy said to Jemima: "While you're waiting for the police I think you'd better let me have the syringe." He blinked at her one last time. "I shall go outside. I've always been fond of parties, you know. Give my love to my wife and—" he stopped. Then: "Eugenia" he pronounced. It was not quite clear whether he was aware of his surprising triumph in getting the names the right way round.

Outside in the College, once the sun was fully up—too late for the ball, it was going to be a beautiful day—strong and competent men in the shape of the porter's workforce, started moving purposefully about. Plates and glasses, innumerable bottles, were collected and packed away, from innumerable suppers, breakfasts, in tent and quad, arcade, staircase and endless sitting-out rooms. It was now time to persuade the few last revellers of Rochester that the Ball was now well and truly over. As Jemima had suspected, one or two of the bodies, whether single or entwined with each other, were extremely reluctant to awake, and even more reluctant to move. One in particular was hard to rouse, the dark head sunk on the chest, a body lying in the corner of the big tent in the main Rochester quad.

"Come along, sir, come along. Time to go now, sir. Come along."

The porter shook the recumbent reveller by the shoulder without effect and passed on to the next body.

Twenty minutes later there was a call from one of his associates. "Fred—can't seem to get any reaction out of this one. Out for the count."

The head porter called back: "We'll put him to bed, then. If he's one of ours."

"Fred, come over here will you. I don't like this. He's—well he's cold. Quite cold." There was a new urgency in the voice.

"Who's cold?"

"It's the professor! Professor Mossbanker. Fred—I think we'd better get an ambulance. Quick. There's this syringe!"

"OK, right then. You go and telephone for an ambulance. That's the second time this morning. Well, we once had three after a Commem. I asked you. And they call it fun."

"This is serious, Fred. I think he's dead!"

To some of the revellers walking unsteadily in the streets of Oxford, on their way to the river, on their way back from it, the wail of the ambulance passing down the Broad, bearing Proffy's lifeless body on its ride to the hospital, was like the last music of the long night.

CHAPTER TWENTY-ONE

·

Purple for the Rich Man

Afterwards, back in London safely reunited with Cass, Jemima still shivered at the thought of what followed. But it was the thought of Proffy's strange mild calm which caused the revulsion.

"He seemed quite fatalistic about everything. Oddly dispassionate. All he really wanted to do was get it over— my questions—and then as we now know, go outside and kill himself. I got the impression that he was hardly interested in me; I certainly don't think I was ever in any danger."

"I'm glad of that." Cass put his arm around her shoulders.

"You see, for him the game was over: the *party* was over. He answered my questions, almost with a shrug. Said that he'd drugged Saffron when he came to drink the champagne." Jemima forbore to mention to Cass the question of the green dress. How ironic, she reflected privately, that Proffy the cool murderer, the former secret agent, the chemist who knew how to kill, should have failed to deduce from the presence of a ball dress hanging up in the sitting room that Saffron was entertaining its former occupant in the bedroom. . . . She thought of his formidable mixture of jealousy, ruthlessness and absentmindedness which had defeated her investigation for so long and turned her in the direction of the Iverstones, more especially the ever-decent Jack. Or perhaps Proffy was so used to female clothing draped round Saffron's rooms and even his car (she remembered the Maserati at Saffron Ivy bestrewn with white frilly underclothing) that he paid no special attention to one dress. It was after all part of his picture of Saffron, the careless sexuality of arrogant youth, the picture which he had determined to destroy.

"And now he was coming back to finish off the job. Just as he killed Tiggie," Jemima said aloud.

"Envy!" exclaimed Cass. "All that in the name of envy!"

"Envy after all can kill," said Jemima. "Can be destructive as well as self-destructive. He warned me, and that was his own piece of arrogance, on the night of the Chimneysweepers' Dinner. He was talking about the parable of Dives and Lazarus. What makes you think Dives wasn't happy? he said. Purple and fine linen: who wouldn't want to be dressed in purple and fine linen! What makes you think Lazarus didn't envy Dives his lot? That gave me the clue to the attacks on Saffron—a killing hatred based on envy was at the bottom of them. But I was obsessed by the hereditary element in it all, the fact that the Iverstone family were bound to envy Saffron and, if anyone, would want him removed. That tension I felt at the tennis match—the tension which was really between Proffy and Lord St. Ives: I was determined to put it down to Andrew Iverstone's jealousy of his cousin. Andrew Iverstone, Daphne, Fanny, even the ever-decent Jack—they were all present at the various attacks and had an opportunity—"

"But Jack wasn't present at the Chimneysweepers' Dinner," objected Cass.

"Yes, but he too could have canoed up river, as did Rufus Pember and Nigel Copley. That wouldn't have been impossible. What I knew all along, but failed to connect, was that Proffy had the best opportunity of all. Saffron's car, for example, the original attack, parked outside Rochester and in various car parks near the college; who had better opportunity than Proffy to fix it? And then the death of Bim Marcus: Proffy was even able to report finding the body with perfect impunity. No one needed to enter Rochester and lurk till the small hours, when the murderer actually lived there—right on the same staircase, Staircase Thirteen."

Cass frowned: "Why the washing machine? That always struck me as being so odd. If it was Proffy, why didn't he just do the deed and retreat back into his rooms? Why set the machine on and alert everybody to his presence?"

"Of course I should have realized all along the importance of that clue," agreed Jemima. "I felt instinctively at the time as you know; thought the police were a little too easy about it all—the machine was on, with Bim's prints on it; ergo he set it off. No, that was Proffy's cunning way of distracting our attention from his presence. The machine was put on deliberately to give him the perfect excuse to discover the body. Any prints or awkward traces he might have left—all taken care of."

"In view of his feelings about youth—by the way, who said he liked the idea of children and hated the young?"

"Tiggie," said Jemima.

"Perceptive. In view of these feelings it must have given him sardonic pleasure to use the legend of his own intolerance concerning the machine. Everyone knew he hated being woken up by it. But let's go on. Saffron Ivy, yes, I see he had every opportunity there. You said that he never shared Eugenia Jones' bedroom." Cass frowned again. "But the Chimneysweepers' Dinner! Didn't he take a risk there? You mean he just went from your side, attacked Saffron, and returned. A cool customer, indeed. Not only at the end."

"Till the very end. He encouraged me to telephone for a doctor from his room. Outside we still heard the music playing, and the sun must have been coming up, except the shadow of that huge tent blocked the light. I saw the photographs: Eleanor Mossbanker and all those towheaded children and a huge photograph of Eugenia Jones. Those dramatic looks she handed on to her children—to Tiggie, and to Saffron."

"Why did the attacks start *then*? Surely he had always known about Saffron and Tiggie—"

"No, no that's the whole point. He never knew. It was the Nurse's story which gave it away."

"Nurse Elsie strikes again."

"She did indeed. She told Eugenia about Saffron's—her baby's—actual whereabouts, Eugenia having believed for twenty years that the baby died shortly after birth. That was such a shock that Eugenia confided in Proffy simply for the sake of sharing the shock with somebody. But of course at the same time she had to tell him about Lord St. Ives being the father of Saffron. Otherwise none of it made any sense—the switch of the babies I mean. Proffy's a very jealous man you know, *was* a very jealous man. Up till Nurse Elsie's revelation he'd always imagined that the baby which died was his child, because it was conceived just at the start of their relationship. Eugenia, knowing his feelings on the subject, let him believe it."

"What about Tiggie?"

"Oh that was before he knew Eugenia. Proffy went along with the original story concerning the mysterious Jones. And now, with one fell swoop he learnt that his mistress had betrayed him sexually at the very beginning of their affair. What was more, she had in effect lied to him for twenty years. Worse still, it was clear that she must have always preferred Lord St. Ives. You see, it was Eugenia who had refused to marry Proffy, not—as I'd always imagined—the other way round. Lord St. Ives was the great love of Eugenia Jones' life; or the perfect masochistic emotional situation if you prefer it, the one man she could never hope to marry, the man who would never leave his wife. . . ."

"So now Proffy found that this boy, this arrogant rich privileged boy, where his own children were poor and numerous, was not only the son of his mistress, but also the son of his mistress *and* her lover."

"Exactly. Instead of hating Eugenia, as might have been logical, he transferred his hatred to the boy. So that it was easy for him. And he decided to kill him. Eliminate him from Eugenia's life."

"Purple and fine linen—and death—for the rich man," commented Cass. "With the compliments of Dives."

"Except that poor little Tiggie was the one who got killed, Tiggie and the wretched innocent Bim Marcus, killed for the coincidence of one wasted day of high life. Tiggie did for herself when she got engaged to Saffron. I suppose the spectacle of Tiggie, Eugenia's daughter, about to become rich and famous, as she herself boasted, to enjoy all that wealth, that house, those possessions, everything that belonged to the man Eugenia had preferred, was too much for him. Proffy reckoned he could make that death look like suicide, knowing the amount of drugs that Tiggie took. As with Saffron. Who would seriously question it? A death from drink and an overdose of drugs on the night of a Commem Ball—all too probable, especially with Saffron's reputation."

"The hatred of the old for the young. Must be all too easily encouraged by life at Oxford. If it's there in the first place." Cass shivered.

"Don't forget that the Kerry Barbers of this world, who are also to be found at Oxford, are a much larger part of it in fact," Jemima pointed out. But Cass, for the time being, was not thinking of the Kerry Barbers of this world.

"Finally he killed himself. And you let him do that. You got a doctor for Saffron, but you didn't get the police for Proffy. Was it to save the scandal? Was it for Saffron? Or did you think you wouldn't be able to convince the police?"

Jemima took Cass' hand. "No, not for Saffron. Nor even for the St. Ives family. As for the police, I would have tried my best, although it might have been difficult. No, it was for her, Eugenia Jones. She'd made a mistake, if you call love a mistake, twenty years earlier. And that mistake came to cost two lives, three if you count Proffy himself, and it nearly cost the life of another, Saffron. She had to live with the knowledge that her lover had killed her daughter and tried to kill the man she now knew to be her son."

"Did she suspect *anything*, anything at all before it happened?"

"There were a good deal of strong emotions floating about at Saffron Ivy that weekend, which fooled me at the time," admitted Jemima ruefully. "That is, I picked up the emotions and attributed them to the wrong people. Not only at the tennis match. Eugenia Jones is another example: that night when the butler was singing, I felt fear in the room, fear very strongly present. I thought it was Lady St. Ives' but that must have been Eugenia's fear for her daughter."

"So she knew?" asked Cass.

"Maybe she didn't know. But she feared. It was the thought of what she must have feared, as well as what she endured later, which made me think that she had the right now to come to terms with it all in secret. To recover her peace of mind, if she ever can, outside the baleful light of public scandal."

"The peace of mind Nurse Elsie sacrificed at her death."

"Peace of mind is for God to give: that's what Sister Imelda told me originally. I'm beginning to think she was right. I'm not sure who else but God, about whose existence I remain anxiously doubtful, will give it to poor Eugenia Jones. Whatever she may have suspected before, she now knows the full truth about Proffy. It's been hushed up for the rest of the world, a simple suicide while the balance of his mind was disturbed etc. There's no proof of what happened, after all, and of the various parties concerned, including Saffron, none of them want the truth to be exhibited to the world. Then there's poor Eleanor Mossbanker and those wretched children to be considered: suicide is better for them to live with than murder."

"You saw Eugenia Jones?" asked Cass.

"In Oxford. Briefly. She asked to see me. Said it wouldn't take long and that she wanted to ask me a question. She came to the Martyrs."

Jemima thought of that last interview. Eugenia Jones looked quite haggard. She also seemed to have shrunk in height. In her black clothes—official mourning for Proffy?—she resembled a middle-aged Greek peasant woman more than a distinguished academic.

"Did I do wrong?" asked Eugenia Jones abruptly. She refused to accept a drink or even coffee, and sat quite stiffly on the edge of her chair in the hotel suite. "It began with love. Was that wrong?"

"Why do you ask me? Of all people."

Eugenia Jones smiled faintly. She had a charming smile; Jemima had noticed before how it lit up her heavy features.

"You know all the facts. There's no one else I can talk to. Besides, you seem remote from love. I thought you might have a detached view."

"I can't and won't judge anyone in all this," said Jemima Shore honestly. "Except Proffy, and he's beyond all our judgements. Certainly not you."

Eugenia Jones stood up. "No absolution then."

"No need for it, as I can see it."

"Wise girl," commented Cass, when Jemima related this

(although she chose to omit for some reason that comment on her remoteness from love). "So now Saffron goes forward to be the next Lord St. Ives."

"And that's right too," said Jemima staunchly. "That's justice. He *is* his father's son after all. And his mother's son too—at least that's the line he's taking. I mean Lady St. Ives. He doesn't want to see Eugenia Jones and she doesn't want to see him. I daresay he'll be reconciled to his father in time, if only for Lady St. Ives' sake. It's over: the past will be left in peace, or at any rate that bit of it."

"How are they all? Your suspects. Your former suspects, I should say."

"I haven't seen Jack Iverstone since his father's death; I still feel guilty at having wondered at the end whether a jealous murderer's nature lay beneath that decent exterior."

"Jack—I wonder if he's glad or sorry that he finally revolted on that last night and chose to demo with Kerry Barber when it must have been fairly clear that his father was dying," mused Cass.

"Being Jack, he'd be sorry, very sorry. No, correction, the new Jack is probably deep down rather glad. Otherwise his father would have died and Jack would never have proved to himself that he *could* revolt. Except publicly, of course. But being a member of the SDP was nothing compared to his inability to speak up when his father was actually present. Think of that tennis match, for example. Now that Andrew Iverstone's off the scene, he can happily pursue that moderate political career for which he is so eminently suited. But Fanny, believe it or not—I'm taking Fanny into Megalith Television. As a secretary in the first instance; I'm sure she'll rise rapidly. I'm determined to save her from the twin curses of a right-wing background and an inadequate education."

"And Saffron?"

Jemima smiled. "Recovered. He has nine lives, like Midnight here, even if Proffy has used up a good few of them. He swears he's going to work next term. No more Oxford Bloodiness." She bent to stroke the cat, feeling for some reason that it was necessary to add: "I haven't seen him recently you know." She was aware that she was very slightly embarrassed.

At the same moment, Cass was producing a sentence, which exhibited a similar awkwardness; nonetheless Jemima got the impression he had been rehearsing it for some time. "Jemima, I've got something to say to you. First I think you should know, I don't know quite why I think this, but I do—that Tiggie and I, once or twice, you know, while you were in Oxford—she was so wild, sweet but crazy, it meant nothing. Not to either of us."

"Cherry must have guessed," he added, "or at least suspected. Because I had to ask her for Tiggie's telephone number. I take it she didn't tell you?"

Jemima thought of Cherry's slightly odd, even strained reaction to Tiggie's engagement, one of those things she had filed away at the back of her mind to be explained one day. Now she must either reward Cherry with flowers for her discretion or—that too was something which could be filed away for a later discussion; on the whole Jemima thought she would probably send Cherry flowers.

Cass seemed to have nothing more to say.

There was a long silence while Jemima, her head bent, continued to stroke Midnight as though his life depended on it; after a bit his heavy raucous purr filled the silence. As a matter of fact, during the silence Jemima was not thinking of Midnight at all but was reminding herself of fairness, justice, equality of opportunity, personal freedom, individual liberty, possessiveness-is-theft, and many other fine concepts, all in an effort to prevent an enormous wave of furious indignation and jealousy sweeping over her and knocking her right off her elegant perch on a rock, as she saw it, way above such horrible human passions.

To break the tension, Jemima jumped up and pressed the button of her cassette player. The melody from *Arabella* filled the room: "Aber der Richtige . . . The one who's right for me . . ." Jemima switched it off again.

Finally she said as lightly as she could manage: "Investigating the past is not always a good thing. As witness all the fearful troubles caused by Nurse Elsie's efforts to bring it to rights."

"Jemima, leave that damn cat alone," said Cass, putting

his arm round her. "That's only the first thing I have to say to you. The second thing is: if the past is best left alone, and I agree, how about, as you might put it, investigating the future? Our future, to be precise. I am proposing a new arrangement."

"Had you in mind some *legal* arrangement?" enquired Jemima cautiously. She still gazed steadily in the direction of Midnight, but allowed herself to rest against Cass.

"Why not? I am a lawyer," replied Cass.

"Then I shall investigate it."

"Is that a promise?"

"No promises at the beginning of an investigation," said Jemima Shore.

ABOUT THE AUTHOR

ANTONIA FRASER is the acclaimed author of several historical biographies, among them *Mary, Queen of Scots*, *Cromwell*, and *Royal Charles*. *Your Royal Hostage* is the seventh mystery featuring Jemima Shore Investigator; the earlier ones include the full-length *Oxford Blood*, *Cool Repentance*, *A Splash of Red*, *Quiet as a Nun*, and *The Wild Island*, and a collection of short stories, *Jemima Shore's First Case*. A television series based on the Jemima Shore mysteries was aired nationwide in 1983. In 1986 Antonia Fraser was chairman of the Crime Writers' Association.

She lives in London with her husband, the dramatist Harold Pinter.

BANTAM
SHOP-AT-HOME
C·A·T·A·L·O·G

Special Offer
Buy a Bantam Book
for only 50¢.

Now you can have Bantam's catalog filled with hundreds of titles plus take advantage of our unique and exciting bonus book offer. A special offer which gives you the opportunity to purchase a Bantam book for only 50¢. Here's how!

By ordering any five books at the regular price per order, you can also choose any other single book listed (up to a $5.95 value) for just 50¢. Some restrictions do apply, but for further details why not send for Bantam's catalog of titles today!

Just send us your name and address and we will send you a catalog!